I0544835

EVERNIGHT PUBLISHING ®

www.evernightpublishing.com

Copyright© 2019

Kory Steed

Editor: Karyn White

Cover Art: Jay Aheer

ISBN: 978-0-3695-0037-3

WHEN LIGHTNING STRIKES TWICE

DEDICATION

For Mark, who loved me first.

WHEN LIGHTNING STRIKES TWICE

WHEN LIGHTNING STRIKES TWICE

The Lightning Series, 3

Kory Steed

Copyright © 2018

Section One
Picking Up the Pieces

Chapter One
Home

Monday, January 4, 2010, 12:30 PM

When Big Daddy cleared the ridge, and Jason and Aaron's home came into view, Rod, the owner of Pacific North Air Transport, eased the lumbering, cargo chopper towards the helipad. Jason and Aaron barely recognized the place. The large, open, three-acre lawn contained within the fortified stockade had shrunk in size by nearly half, and the free-rolling grounds that Jason had so carefully designed were now nothing more than a muddied memory. A second helipad had been installed next to the original one to accommodate the increase in air traffic their home would see as supplies, materials, and personnel were flown in during the coming days and weeks.

In reality, the place looked more like a military compound than their home. Almost immediately, Jason swallowed any misgivings that rose up in his mind. All it took was for him to remember the spray of gunfire that could have easily taken Aaron's life, threatened his billy goat, Jasper's, and nearly took his own.

No sooner had the wheels touched down than Aaron was up and doting over Jason to ensure he was okay to climb down from Big Daddy's hold.

"Braden, be careful with him!" Aaron's voice cracked with angst. "I don't want him stressed in any way."

Braden smiled, tight-lipped. "I've got him, Aaron. Don't worry."

"I'm sorry I'm being a mother hen right now, but I won't feel that he's safe until we're inside the protection of the stockade's walls."

"I understand, Aaron. I promised you that I would take good care of him, and I meant it. I'm going to take real good care of the both of you."

Jason patted Braden's arm as he looked deeply into Aaron's eyes. "It's okay, Braden. I'm fine, really, I am. I think Aaron's been more traumatized by this whole ordeal than I have."

As the rotors slowed to a stop, Aaron stepped out and began to scan the clearing around the stockade and the tree line beyond as he paced back and forth. The whine of a vehicle's gasoline engine reached everyone's ears. Jack, Rod's righthand man, could be seen through Big Daddy's cargo hold door, sitting behind the wheel of a decked out, six-seat ATV, as he came up the old path that had been expanded and paved with stone during Jason and Aaron's absence.

The vehicle had barely come to a stop before Jack was out of the driver's seat and running toward them. As Aaron cleared the rotors, Jack raced right up into the hold and grabbed hold of Jason in a gentle, but firm, bear hug.

"It's good to see you, boy, so good to see you. God, I want to give you a real hug, but I'm afraid I'd crush you or break something. Is this okay?"

Jason returned the hug. "Sure, Jack. It's much appreciated, and it's good to see you, too."

Jack released his hug and grabbed Jason by the arms, just below his shoulders, gently squeezing them as he spoke. "I can't tell you how worried I've been about the two of you. I just can't. Oh, you're gonna be so surprised by everything we've gotten done. You're hardly gonna recognize the place, but it's exactly like you said you wanted it. Just you wait. Just you wait and see."

Rod got out of the pilot's seat. "Jack, that's enough." His normally gruff voice slightly softened. "Leave him be. There'll be plenty of time to get reacquainted."

"Oh, Jason," Jack went on. "Wait 'til you see the kitchen, and the cottages, and the living room, and the—"

"Jack," Rod said more firmly.

"Oh, right. Sorry." Jack turned around and hopped down to the ground, just beyond the doors. "Hello, Aaron, my boy," he said, spreading his arms wide for a hug as he walked towards him, but Aaron's eyes were focused on the tree line. "Aaron, my boy," Jack said, play-punching Aaron's arm. "Aaron. It's me, Jack."

Aaron recoiled, but after a moment, his expression softened, and he smiled. Jack jumped into his arms. "Good to see you, lad. Good to see you." Jack kissed Aaron's cheek. "The place is fixed up real nice for you. Real nice."

"Sorry, Jack. I was scanning for intruders."

"Oh, there's no need for that, my boy. Nobody's gonna get anywhere near this place now. Wait 'til you see the armory!"

"Jack," Jason called from the doorway. "Aaron's got to do what he's got to do. If you'd just give me your hand for a minute, I can climb down."

Jack released Aaron and dropped down to the ground. "Oh sure, sure. Sorry, sorry. I don't seem to know what to do with myself right now. It's like I'm jumping out of my skin or somethin'."

As Jack scurried back, Rod, raised his hand and opened his mouth to speak, but Jason shushed him with a wave before stepping down with Jack and Braden's help, being careful not to bump himself. He was still sore along his left ribs where the chest tube had been placed.

Jason kept his right hand on Jack's left shoulder and squeezed it. "Jack, I'd like you to meet Braden. He's a nurse, and he's going to be staying with us for the time being. Braden, this is Jack, one of my oldest and dearest friends. He's an all-around good guy, but he's also a joker so watch out for his pranks."

"How you doin' there, young fella?" Jack pumped Braden's hand. "How you doin'? Good to have you here."

Braden winced at the strength of Jack's grip. "It's good to meet you, sir."

"Oh, none of that sir stuff. I'm Jack to just about everybody, and you're family now. Welcome! Welcome! Now we're gonna take it real slow gettin' Jason down the path here." Jack looked towards Jason. "I ordered this baby with a special suspension so you should barely feel a bump."

As a man in his mid-fifties stepped down, Jason continued the introductions. "And this is my dear, oldest friend, Dr. Conrad Tolbert, whom I've spoken of often. He's agreed to stay with us for a while until we get back on our feet."

"Hello there, doc," Jack said taking his hand into both of his own. "It's a pleasure. A real pleasure."

****

While Jason rode in the ATV with Aaron holding tightly around his back, he noted the changes to the stockade fence. "I see they've installed the surveillance cameras and security lights. I think I hear the generator running. How come?"

Rod turned around from the front passenger seat. "That's because your solar system can't power all the new stuff right now. All of the new solar panels haven't been hooked up yet, but that should be completed within a day or two. It's the overnight cold that's been slowing down the work outdoors in the early mornings hours. We're also running the furnace for supplemental heat in the main cabin, but we're still keeping the wood stoves going. You'll see it all, Jason. Don't worry about a thing. Once you're up to it, we'll go over everything with you and Aaron."

When they reached the stockade's gate, Jack hopped out and punched in the security code. The door opened automatically, but instead of swinging outward on hinges, like it had in the past, it traveled along the stockade's wall on a motorized, supportive rail system. After Rod drove through, a large, military-looking man in a uniform closed the gate with a switch on the panel inside the walls.

"Hello, Mr. Ackerman, Mr. Jaeger," he said, extending his hand to each of them. "I'm Thaddeus Steinecker, your Chief of Security. My staff and I are pleased to be at your service. We're at your disposal and ready to answer any questions you may have. Whenever it's convenient for you, I'll review all the changes and upgrades we've instituted."

Aaron smiled tightly. "Thank you, Chief. We look forward to it.

Chapter Two
Miss Charity

Once they came to a stop by the front porch, Aaron hopped out and reached back in for Jason.

Jason waved him away and began to climb out of the ATV. "Aaron, you or Braden or whomever can walk behind me, but I can manage the stairs. I need to do this by myself. Please let me."

Aaron hovered in front of him. "Okay, Jason. Whatever you say."

Conrad placed his hand on Aaron's forearm. "Let's let him try the stairs on his own."

Aaron nodded.

Jason paused as he placed his foot on the porch's first step. "Rod, before I go inside, how's Jasper?"

"He's doing good, Jason. The vet said she's never met such a gentle billy goat, but I think that's more because he was shot. She's was real happy with his progress, and she's signed off on him. Since I flew him back up here, after his week in the hospital, he seems to have settled back into his old cantankerous self. His horn looks a little funky though with that chunk missing, but it sure hasn't affected his appetite any."

"Good. Good. I'll go see him later today or tomorrow, depending on how I feel." As Jason climbed the steps, he noticed the rocking chair that previously shattered under Rod 's weight during the attack had been replaced. "New rocker?"

"Yes, Jason. We've taken care of it," Jack interrupted, as he lightly punched Rod in the arm. "I ordered a new, fortified one. I don't think that even all of Rod's two-hundred and fifty pounds could make a dent in this one."

Rod rolled his eyes.

"Good afternoon, sirs." Everyone turned their attention toward the faint, island-accented voice that originated from the front door. A tall, heavyset, middle-aged, African-American woman stood, holding it open. "I'm Charity Hopewell, your new Chief of Household Operations and cook."

"Pleased to meet you, Miss," Jason said as he walked toward her, extending his hand. "I've heard a lot about you from Rod and Jack. How would you like me to address you?"

"Oh, no, sir. You two have been through so much," she answered as she softly pulled Jason into her big bosomed chest and rocked him gently. "I think a hug is in order, and Charity or Miss Charity is just fine."

"And we're Jason and Aaron, if you will."

Charity released him and waved her arm. "Please, everyone come inside against the cold before we make any more introductions."

"Hello there, Miss Charity," Aaron said once the front door had been closed. "I'm Aaron. Thank you for agreeing to do this for us."

"It's my pleasure, Mr. Aaron. Now where's my hug?"

Aaron leaned down into her arms.

After she let go, Charity rubbed her hands together. "I've prepared a little something to warm you up. Then we can do the introductions proper. Now let me help you off with your coats."

Charity directed everyone to the new, sixteen-foot dining room table that occupied a section of what had once been the cabin's common area while she hung their coats on several of the twenty, large brass and porcelain hooks that now ran half the length of the cabin's front wall. Then she disappeared back into the kitchen.

A man whom Jason didn't know rose from the

table. "Hello there. I'm Lars, Rod's brother-in-law."

A huge smile spread across Jason's face. He shook the offered hand and then pulled Lars into a firm, extended hug. "Finally, a face to go with the voice. Thank you for all the updates you gave me over the phone while Aaron and I were in the hospital. I would have lost my mind with worry without them."

"Of course, Jason."

"You dropped everything to come up here and help me, a complete stranger. I can never thank you enough for taking care of my animals. I don't know what I would have done without you."

"It's been a pleasure. They've been no problem at all. Is it okay that I still call you Jason, now that we've met?"

"Oh, goodness, yes, yes, of course. Of course, it is. Lars, this is my partner, Aaron."

"Hello there, Lars." They shook hands.

"I'm a big fan of yours, Aaron. A big, big fan. Damn shame about your injuries keeping you from returning to the team. I followed your college career, and I was really looking forward to seeing you advance the Bighorns to the playoffs."

It was the first time someone had mentioned what in truth was Aaron's expulsion from the team in almost two weeks. A faraway look spread across Aaron's face, and he was silent for a moment before returning his attention to Lars. "That's very kind of you, Lars, but there's more to the story."

"There always is, Aaron."

Jason brow furrowed. "So, how are my babies?"

"They're some of the best-behaved livestock, um … sorry, Jason. I forgot for a moment that they're more than that to you. They're some of the best-behaved animals I've cared for in years. It's obvious how well they've been treated, but I had a little trouble with the nanny goat, Heather, getting her to let me milk her. It wasn't until Jack told me about the oats that things smoothed out."

Jason smiled. "Sorry, that's my fault. I've spoiled her. And Jasper? How's Jasper doing?"

"He's still a little weak, but the vet said he didn't lose as much blood from the gunshot as you thought. Though he lost a fair amount, she thinks his reaction has been compounded by the emotional shock from the intruder's attack, but he's doing well. Still, I've been giving him extra rations of whatever he wants to eat to help build him up. I don't know whether he's just normally well behaved like all the other animals or whether it's from the trauma, but he's very gentle, especially with me, a stranger. That's not very common for a billy goat."

Jason smiled, and his face softened. "It's probably a combination of the two. He's always been very good with me, but then I've had him since he was a kid. The only time I've ever had to worry was when he got too affectionate. He's knocked me over a few times with those horns of his. I got him the same time I got Heather, but he was really still a baby. They came from the same breeder, but I was sure to require that their blood lines were different for when I decide to breed them."

"Well, regardless," Lars said, "he's very gentle. His horn is healing nicely, but it's going to be a while until the callus turns into bone-hard horn again."

Jason rested his hand on Lars's shoulder. "If you have the time, and when I'm up to it, I'd like to sit down and talk with you about livestock. We're going to want to expand our numbers at least a little bit in the near future, so we can remain self-sufficient, and I could sure use your advice."

"I'd be happy to."

Chapter Three
Coming Up to Speed

Charity returned, pushing a two-tiered wooden service cart loaded with two platters that were stacked with sandwiches cut on the bias, a large, steaming tureen filled with vegetable soup, and bowls and soup spoons.

While she ladled out the soup, Jason made the introductions. "Miss Charity, this is a dear old friend of mine, my oldest friend, Dr. Conrad Tolbert, who I worked with in a hospital ER more years ago than I care to remember."

"Delighted, sir."

Conrad nodded. "Likewise."

"Next to Dr. Tolbert is Braden Darby. Braden is the nurse who took care of Aaron this past fall and then both of us these past two weeks."

Braden waved. "Hello."

Charity smiled broadly. "A pleasure I'm sure,"

"They're going to stay with us for a while to help Aaron and me get back on our feet."

"When will we meet the security staff?" Aaron asked.

Charity placed a filled soup bowl down in front of him. "As far as I know, Mr. Aaron, they'll be here at dinnertime. I can call over there if you want to meet with them now."

"No, that won't be necessary. Dinner will be fine."

"I see what you were saying about the partitions, Rod." Jason pointed to the structures that now separated the kitchen from where they now sat in the new dining room and also separated the dining room in front of what used to be his and Aaron's bedroom area.

Rod nodded. "I thought it might be a good idea. I

called the architect who designed the place. With a little financial incentive, he came up with a new floorplan in less than a day. The common area was huge so we had no problem dividing it up into three large rooms, separating off the kitchen. This partition separates the dining room from the kitchen," he said, pointing to it. "It'll provide Miss Charity with some privacy while she's working in there and us when we're meeting in here as we get things started with Nathan's Promise, at least temporarily.

"If you decide you want to have the initial meetings in one of the new structures, we can easily put all the partitions away and return the common area to its previous layout. They literally fold up into themselves in just a few minutes. Right now, the second partition provides for a large living room between the dining room and where your new master bedroom begins. The old bathroom has been enlarged into a master bath that connects directly into the master bedroom. We've also installed a two-person whirlpool tub in there.

Ding-dong-dong-ding.

Jason's head swung around as he looked for the source of the soft-sounding chimes.

Dong-ding-ding-dong.

There was a pause, then, *dong.*

"My grandfather clock! It's one o'clock! The chimes!"

"Oh, yes, Mr. Jason," Charity said. "I fell in love with it the moment I saw it. The family my mama worked for had one similar to it. I noticed someone had disconnected the chimes' weights, and a real grandfather clock's chimes are so beautiful. I just reached in, hooked up the weights and raised them on their chains. They came back to life immediately."

Jason smiled. "Miss Charity, Aaron and I had talked about that, but I never got the chance to call a repairman in to fix it."

"Mr. Jason, there was no fixin' needed. It was a simple thing to turn them back on."

"How did you know how to do it?"

"It became my job to take care of that old grandfather clock when I was still a girl. There's really nothing to it."

"Well thank you for that."

"My pleasure, and if they're too loud you just let me know. I know how to adjust that, too."

"I will. Now … darn, I forget where we were." Jason scratched his head.

"I had just told you about the master bath," Rod said.

"Right, anything special about that?"

"Nothing, other than I think you'll love what we've done for you in there."

"So, what's next?"

Rod handed out papers with typed up notes and small, yellow-lined pads. "Here's my list. The pads are for notes. I took it upon myself to also purchase two oversized, overstuffed sofas with several ottomans and four, matching, overstuffed, reclining chairs for the living room. The sofas pull out into king-size beds so they'll provide extra sleeping space if we ever need it. The chairs recline all the way and can be used as single beds for sleeping as well. They're quite ingenious.

"Also, these temporary partitions can be replaced with permanent walls if you decide that's the way you want to go. They're on recessed wheels so we can slide them back and forth if we ever need extra space in here or in the living room. I hope you like what we came up with."

"It looks great so far, Rod. Thanks. We'll take the big tour before dinnertime, but after this, I'm going to need to go lie down for a while. Even though it's only early afternoon, it's been a long day."

Aaron raised his hand. "How is everyone getting in and out of the cabin to the new structures, Rod?"

"I'm glad you asked. I made an executive decision early on that I didn't consult either of you about. You were both still in the ICU at the time, and I had to make the decision that day. It will be easier if you let me go through everything in order."

Aaron put his arm around Jason. "You're right about that. Jason had a rough time in the ICU. Neither of us would have been able to focus on anything at the time."

Rod nodded. "As I thought about it, I realized there would probably be more people here at different times than we first estimated. For now, I've ordered each of the cottages as single bedroom units, with two double beds, except for the security office. It's not too late if you prefer that some have a king or queen size bed in them, and they can also be laid out as two, smaller bedroom units with a double bed in each. Either way, they'll have decent sized closets, dressers, and night tables."

"I think time will tell, Rod," Jason answered, "but I don't know of any couples who will staying up here. at least in the near future, so we'll just go with what you've chosen."

Rod continued. "Each cottage unit has a good-sized bathroom and the kitchens have apartment sized appliances with adequate counter space. There's also a living room and a washer and dryer in each unit. They're all completely furnished, too, and they've got great soundproofing so the occupants will have privacy and won't be terribly disturbed by any activity that's going on outside. I had them designed that way because after you're finished with them they could be sold as completely ready to live in cottages, or, depending on how soon housing will be needed for future staff at Nathan's Promise, they can be moved anywhere and be ready for immediate occupancy, once the utilities have been hooked up."

"Good thought," Jason said.

"As far as the dryers are concerned, on the chance that they all might be turned on at the same time, I switched off their power and posted a sign-up sheet for times to use the laundry room dryer, so as not to overwhelm the generator. The solar-battery systems in each cottage won't be able to handle the drain from their own dryers until they're fully charged, and anyway, I didn't see the need for so many at this point in time. Once things settle down, we can decide who will be staying where permanently. I'll turn the dryers back on in those cottages, if needed. There's also drying racks for laundry in each unit to encourage folks to use them as an alternative. I see now that I was right to order the extra cottages because you're going to need a lot of help recovering after your and Aaron's hospitalizations."

"You're right." Jason smiled a tight smile. "That's why I asked Conrad and Braden to accompany us. I'm already feeling the effects of moving around so much."

"Do you need to lie down, Jason?" Braden asked.

"No, I'm fine right now, just a little stiff. Thanks, Braden. It will pass." Jason turned back to Rod. "Please, Rod, continue."

"Sure, Jason, but I can continue this later."

"No, I want to hear this."

"We both do," Aaron added.

"Certainly." Rod looked down at his notes. "Dr. Tolbert and Braden can each have their own quarters, and Jack and I have been bunking together whenever we've been up here. Miss Charity also has her own quarters. Since she is your new Chief of Household Operations, we thought it best to create a small office for her in it. It will be away from the cabin so she has a quiet place to do any paperwork, ordering of supplies, or whatever she might need to do."

"And I can't thank you enough for that, Mr. Jason and Mr. Aaron," Charity added. "My little cottage is spectacular. I've never had such luxurious accommodations in any place I've ever worked."

Aaron nodded. "Our pleasure, Miss Charity."

"If I may?" Conrad raised his hand.

Rod turned to look at him. "Yes, Doctor?"

"I didn't think of this until just now. I'd like to have a place set up so that if the need arises, I have somewhere to examine and treat anyone who might become ill or injured. Would that be possible?"

"I hadn't thought of that, Doctor."

"Neither did I, Rod," Jason added. "I'm sure we can set aside a cottage for something like that, at least temporarily."

Conrad continued. "I've brought some emergency equipment with me, but I think some kind of permanent *clinic*, if you will, should be set up, and soon. You never know what might happen. It doesn't need to be done immediately, but we're up here on our own. There should be something in place, just in case."

Rod jotted on his notepad. "We'll get right on that, Doctor. If you can put together a list of what you'll need, I'll meet with you to go over it as soon as we're finished here. Now, where was I? Oh, yes, the security folks have one unit. We turned the living room into an office, electronics room, and the armory, and there are two bedrooms with bunks, one for the women, and one for the men. It does have two separate bathrooms with showers in each, but we had to sacrifice the kitchen in order to do that, but we did put in a microwave. It's a rather no-frills setup, and it's rather tight, but the chief said he preferred it that way. All the walls have extra soundproofing because of the mixed personnel sleeping there.

"That leaves five more units. Right now, Lars is in one. He'll stay until you're ready to take over caring for the animals."

"And there's no hurry, Jason," Lars added. "I'll stay on as long as you need me."

"Thank you, Lars. That means a lot."

Rod continued. "One of the units will become a meeting room, one will be your office, and the one that Lars has been staying in can be used by other folks who come up here like Claudia and Winston, the architect, the construction foreman, or whoever. Presently, two units are not assigned for anyone's use. Whenever there's a unit unoccupied, we're going to make it available to the security folks so they have a place to go during their down time when they're not sleeping or working."

"It's not too late to order more units, is it?" Jason asked.

"No. Why?" Rod asked.

"Good, then order six more. I want two for immediate guest quarters, and plan on making one into an R&R facility for the security staff. I'll talk to the chief about that when we meet with him. One will become Conrad's clinic, and that will leave two extras.

"Make sure that the R&R facility is as big as security will need it to be, okay? Be sure to have it decked out with whatever kind of exercise equipment, entertainment systems, books and magazines, or whatever they want, and make sure it has its own bathrooms with whirlpool tubs in each or a larger room with a multi-person hot tub of some kind.

"If it will have a hot tub room, make sure there are two, double shower rooms, too, one for the men and one for the women. The security staff should never have to share or be put out by other visitors."

Rod whistled. "You've assigned four of the units. What are the other two for? Do you really want that many, fifteen units, plus your and Aaron's office and the meeting room?"

Jason nodded. "Let's make it an even sixteen. Something tells me we're going to need more housing than either you or Aaron and I have considered. Just do it. Though I can't think of any other specific need right now, I'd feel more comfortable if we have a couple of extras, just in case. I'd hate to come up short all of a sudden."

"I'll take care of that right after lunch," Rod answered, "but I have a thought on that. Right now, the two unused units and the unit that was going to be your office haven't had the internal walls put up or been fitted with their bathroom fixtures, appliances, plumbing, and the like. That's supposed to happen tomorrow or the next day. For the most part, they're still empty shells. If we're going to do this, why don't we see if one of them will work for Security's R&R facility and have it fitted however the chief likes? I'll talk to him when we're done here to see what he wants."

Jason nodded. "That's a good idea, but order one of those larger models we saw back in the hospital for the R&R center, Conrad's clinic, too. I don't believe that what we currently have will fit what either of them will need. I'm sure the guards will want exercise equipment, and they should have an entertainment center for movies and video games with couches and chairs, and a library, and make sure it has its own kitchen. Come to think of it, the female guards shouldn't have to bunk with the men. Convert one of those extra units into quarters for them. Also, if we have injuries or illnesses, patients may need to stay and sleep in the clinic while they're being monitored, if only temporarily. Order a couple hospital beds for it. Conrad, will you take care of that?"

"Absolutely, Jason, you've given me a few ideas." Conrad began to jot down on his pad.

"Thanks, Rod for all of this," Jason said.

"There's one more thing," Rod continued. "I had the three empty rooms at the back of the cabin turned into two bedrooms. They each have two double beds. The middle room has been divided and turned it into two bathrooms. We knocked out doorways that connect directly to the two new bedrooms. They're really very nice."

"Now you've really thought of everything," Aaron said, "but what about my *special equipment gift* to Jason that was put up in the room on the left?"

"Don't worry about that, Aaron. It's been installed in in a new room that connects right into your new, master bedroom. On the other side is a large walk-in closet that also opens into the bedroom, and we put two over-stuffed recliners in there."

"Thanks. That's a relief."

Jason looked at his notes. "I can see from your handout that you've built in redundancies for every conceivable mishap we could face, but if you don't mind, I'd like to hold off for the time being discussing this any further. I need to save my strength right now."

"Sure, Jason, we can go over this any time."

"Thanks, Rod. I knew you were the right man for the job. Miss Charity, how are the construction crews being fed? It seems like you're going to have your hands full enough with feeding all of us."

"They've been taking care of that themselves, Mr. Jason. Mr. Rod said they're using the same kind of semi-trailer kind of quarters that the crews used who first built your cabin."

"Oh, that's what those trailers were that I saw as we came in to land."

"Yes. They keep to themselves for the most part, but so far, I've sent over a big pot of stew or hearty soup, a few roast chickens and a pot roast with all the fixin's, and some casseroles, something different every night. There's twelve of them plus the foreman. I'm sure they work up some mighty big appetites come dinner time."

"That's real nice of you, Miss Charity. Rod, are their units self-contained?"

"No, we've plumbed them into the house septic and water with temporary underground hookups. We dug a trench, laid flex-pipes, filled it with stone, and then covered the stone with dirt. That way we can pull the pipes out from their end after they're all packed up and gone. You'll never know anything was there once we reseed and the grass and wildflowers grow back. They do supply their own electricity and heat with their own diesel generator, and they heat their water with their own propane heater."

Jason pushed away from the table. "Thank you, everyone. I think that's all. Now if you don't mind, I'm going to go lie down for a while. I'm pooped. Aaron, if you want to keep talking you go right ahead. Braden can help me get settled. I'll just need someone to show me the way."

Aaron stood up. "Where you go, I go, Jason."

"Thanks, Aaron, that would be a big help."

Rod got up from the table. "I'll show you back to your room."

"Why don't you let me check you over, Jason?"

Conrad said. "Just to be on the safe side. You've had quite a morning already. Braden can give me a hand."

"Certainly, Conrad."

Chapter Four
Setting Ground Rules

"Well, my boy, your lungs sound good," Conrad said as he put away his stethoscope, "but you do look a little peaked. Remember, you lost nearly three units of blood between your hemothorax, your surgery, and post-op drainage. I'm going to ask Miss Charity to provide you with a lot of red meat with all of your meals, and I'm keeping you on iron supplements until your hemoglobin levels return to normal. Please don't push yourself too hard. From what I've seen, you've surrounded yourself with some really efficient and knowledgeable people. Let them carry the ball for a while."

"I will, Conrad, but there's certain things that only Aaron and I can do. We'll make the big decisions and leave the how to's to everyone else, just like we've been doing for the past two weeks."

"If it were up to me, I'd have you stay in bed for the remainder of the day. That meeting drained you. Why don't you start fresh tomorrow with your new staff?"

Aaron sat down on the edge of the bed next to Jason and rubbed his back with his hand. "That might not be a bad idea."

"I'll think about it, but right now, all I know is I need to rest."

Conrad placed his hand on Jason's shoulder. "How are you feeling otherwise?"

"Otherwise?"

"Emotionally? Psychologically? Spiritually? Any nightmares?"

"No, not really, not since the one I had my first night in the ICU."

Aaron pulled Jason in close. "Well, he can't get to you anymore."

"I know. I just feel so guilty about you and Jasper and how put out everyone else has been. They're all completely innocent. It was me that Garrison was after, not any of you, but you've all paid for it."

Conrad gently squeezed Jason's shoulder. "It wasn't your fault, Jason."

"I know. I know, but he brought a gun up here. He shot up the barn and nearly killed Aaron in the process. He blew out Jasper's horn and nearly caused him to bleed to death. And now he's dead."

Aaron crouched down on the floor in front of Jason and placed his hand on his knee. "And he tried to rape you and probably would have killed you, regardless of what he said. He deserved to die."

"If only I could have talked him down, none of this would have happened."

"No, Jason," Conrad said. "Look at me." Jason lifted his head. His eyes welled with tears. "He was crazy with hatred that he allowed to fester for nearly two decades. There's no way to talk someone like that down."

"He could have been helped. The VA could have helped him."

"I don't believe that, Jason. He wouldn't accept their help. He blamed the army and you for something he himself caused. In all my years as a physician, I've come across a lot of bitter, angry people who are consumed with hatred, and they're all the same. There's nothing that anyone could have done for him. He was the only one who had the power to change himself, and he didn't want that."

"I don't want to talk about this anymore, Conrad."

"I understand."

"I'll help you into your pajamas, Jason," Braden

offered. "Do you want to help me, Aaron, so you'll know how to work around his surgical sites?"

"Um, Braden, we usually sleep in the nude," Aaron answered.

"Oh," Braden answered.

"Both of you, please sit down for a minute." Jason directed Conrad and Braden to two new recliners against the wall, opposite their bed. "There's something I need you both to be clear on. Look, guys, it's easier to just say this outright so that I'm sure we're all on the same page."

"Go ahead," Conrad said.

"Yes?" Braden added.

"You know that Aaron and I are gay. I want you to understand that, in our own home, we are going to live as a couple, just like any other couple does, and couples are affectionate with each other and they have sex. Our sex life is a very important part of us, and I want to be sure that you both are all right with that. I don't need you to understand it or agree with it, but I do need you to respect it. If you don't think you can stay here because you're uncomfortable about it in any way, you can leave with no questions asked and no hard feelings. I truly mean that. There really will be no hard feelings."

Conrad smiled and nodded. "Jason, thank you for bringing it up, but I knew in my heart you were gay from early on in our friendship. Because you never mentioned it, I didn't feel like I had the right to bring it up, but you never lost my respect or my admiration. I'm old enough to know that life only brings you so many opportunities for happiness. I couldn't be happier to know that you've found someone who loves you as much as you deserve to be loved."

"Braden?" Jason turned his focus to him. "You look like you're about ready to jump out of your skin.

What's wrong?"

"I … I'm not sure what to say."

"Conrad, would you give us some time to talk to Braden, alone?" Jason asked.

"Sure. I assume my luggage has made it up here by now. I'll just go and get myself settled into my room, and then I'll meet with Rod to go over my," he made air quotes, "*clinic*."

****

"What is it, Braden?" Jason asked after Conrad left.

"I don't know what to say, because I don't know about myself. I just don't know … what I am."

"Braden," Aaron said, "this is a safe place. You can speak openly and freely. You can tell us anything."

"Aaron, Jason, I don't know who I'm supposed to be, regarding sex, I mean. I've been thinking about this a lot since your last night in the hospital, last night. When Aaron got … well you know, when I gave him his massage, and he…"

"When I got aroused?" Aaron asked softly.

"Yes, when that happened … I just don't know."

"Have you been with anyone, a woman or a man, sexually?" Aaron asked.

"I don't think so. I mean I've never … I mean, you just started talking about gay sex. I've never let myself even consider … for me, I mean. Oh, my God! This is so inappropriate for me to be saying this to you. I'm so, so sorry."

"Not at all, Braden, take your time." Jason grunted and winced as he eased himself back on the bed and rested his eyes.

Braden went on. "I just can't stop thinking about it sometimes. Sometimes it's all I think about, I mean what it would be like."

"How old are you, Braden," Aaron asked, "if you don't mind my asking?"

"I'm twenty-five."

Jason opened his eyes and looked at them. "Guys, I'm sorry, but I'm fading fast. I really need to sleep now. Aaron, why don't you take some time to talk to Braden in private?" Jason yawned and closed his eyes.

"Are you sure you'll be okay?"

"Yes, I'll be fine. Could you help me get undressed first?"

"Sure, Jason. Braden, why don't you go on and have a seat out in the living room? I can manage. I'll be out in a few minutes."

"I'm sorry, Jason. I'm sorry, Aaron. I shouldn't have said anything. You've hired me to take care of you. This is so unprofessional of me."

"Listen, Braden," Jason said, "we hired you because we like you and trust you and because we like you, we would want to help you with anything … anything at all. I just feel bad that I'm so tired right now. Just go sit down in the living room. Aaron will be out to talk to you in a few minutes. Don't worry. Everything is all right."

After Braden left, Aaron helped Jason to get out of his clothes. Then he put him to bed and kissed him before going out to talk to Braden.

****

Aaron sat down in a chair, opposite Braden. "Listen, Braden, I don't need to know everything that's gone on in your life, and I don't want to cross any boundaries you may have, but from what you've said, you seem to be confused about your sexuality. The only way you're going to find out who you are is if you're honest with yourself. Once you've done that, you can decide what you want. If you do realize that you're gay, please know, it's a lot easier now for gay men than it used to be, but we still have to be careful. Right now, you're in as safe a place as you could ever be."

"Aaron, I've been afraid of taking the first step. I'm still a virgin. I've never really been with anyone. There was this one guy once, but all we did was … well we didn't have sex, real sex, I mean."

"How did you feel when you were with him?"

"Like I was on fire. Like I wanted more, but I was afraid, and so was he. We just, well we just used our hands on each other."

"You mean you masturbated each other?"

"Yes, having him touch me like that and being allowed to touch him, I can't tell you how it made me feel to have another guy want to do that with me."

"Did it feel right to you, like it was how sex should be for you?"

"Yes, but it also felt so wrong. I was raised to believe that homosexuality was a sin."

"You're not alone there, believe me. Listen, I'm very sorry, but I have to get back to Jason. Will you give a minute? I'll be right back."

****

Aaron returned a few minutes later. "Braden, I've talked to someone who I think can help to answer some of your questions, but only if you want to. I know that Jason would be very comfortable talking with you about this, and so would I, but circumstances just won't allow for that right now. Do you think you'd be comfortable talking to someone else?"

"Do you trust them?"

"Yes, I do."

"Then sure, I have so many questions. When can I meet them?'

"Right now, if you want."

"Right now? Who?"

Aaron got up and walked around the partition. "Come in, Rod."

****

When Aaron returned to their bed, Jason had fallen asleep, so he got undressed and slipped under the covers without making a sound. When Jason rolled into him, Aaron cradled him in his large, muscular arms and fell asleep alongside him.

Chapter Five
Evening Nibbles

9:20 PM

Jason woke with a start. "Aaron! Aaron, what time is it?"

"Huh? What?" Aaron lifted his head and looked around. The only illumination in the room came from dim lights at the bases of their night table lamps and a nightlight plugged in by the door. "They're new." Aaron pointed to them. "I have no idea, baby. The microwave's not in here. Wait, there's a clock here, too. It's, oh wow, we overslept. It's 9:20."

"At night? Is it tomorrow?"

"I don't know."

"Help me get up." There was frustration in his voice. "I've got to get dressed. Everyone's waiting on us to eat dinner."

"Just hold on, baby. I'll go out and see what's happening."

Aaron put on a robe and walked barefooted out of the bedroom and through the living room. He returned two minutes later. "Seems they didn't wait for us after all. There was a note from Conrad. He told them that you needed to rest so they went ahead without us when we didn't come out.

"Miss Charity also left a note saying there are two platters in the refrigerator for us if we're hungry and that we can call her if we need her. It says she'll be up 'til eleven, but that we can still call her at any hour."

There was a knock at the door. "Excuse me, gentlemen." Thaddeus Steinecker called from out of view. "Just checking to see that everything's all right."

"Yes, we're fine. Come in, please," Jason answered.

"Did something happen?" Aaron asked.

"No, Mr. Aaron, sir."

"Then what made you come in to check on us?" Jason asked, confused.

"Motion sensors, sir, and video surveillance. They've been installed throughout the cabin except for here in your master bedroom, your master bath, the walk-in closet and the *other* room that connects into here. The other room has a numeric code lock on the door, sir. I've been instructed that it's off limits to security personnel.

"There are sound sensors everywhere, but they're programmed to only activate for certain kinds of sounds. The sensors are turned on after everyone leaves the main cabin, when you're alone in here. That's our protocol right now. It's one of the things that was on my agenda to discuss with you, but it can wait until the morning.'

"Do you know if everyone has gone to bed?" Jason asked.

"Not as far as I know, sir. They've all gone to their quarters, but there's lights still on in every unit."

"Is there a way to contact everyone and ask if they can meet us in the dining room, informally? I don't want anyone to have to get dressed again, and if they're ready to turn in, please tell them not to bother."

"Absolutely. I'll take care of that right now. Unit one to base," he whispered into his wrist, "contact all parties and have them assemble in the main cabin dining room for an informal meeting. Specify only if they are able to attend."

He nodded his head as if he was listening to someone. "Everyone's being contacted, sir. If you don't need me, I'll see to it that everyone gets settled."

"Yes, thank you. We'll be right out," Aaron said, "but a question. What was all that?" Aaron pointed to his wrist.

"Transmitter, Mr. Aaron, sir. Receiver's in my ear. All security staff are outfitted the same."

"Before you go, Chief, did Rod speak with you about an R&R facility for you and your staff?" Jason asked.

"Yes, he did, Mr. Jason. That was extremely generous of you, sir, but I don't think it's necessary. We've never been offered anything like that before. What you've provided for us here is palatial compared to what we're accustomed to, and the meals have been incredible. Usually it's more of a barebones kind of deal."

"Well, shame on whoever you worked for before." Jason shook his head. "You're working for us now. We treat everyone like they're family."

"So I've noticed, sir."

"From what I've heard, you're rather barebones in there anyway, compared to the other units. I'm very serious about an R&R facility for your staff, Chief. It's cold up here, except for the summer months, and even summer nights drop into the fifties. There isn't much you can do after the sun goes down.

"At some point, I was planning to talk with you about patrolling into the forest beyond the confines of the stockade fence, so there's going to be even more work for your staff. If you need to bring up more personnel, let us know so we can ensure they're properly accommodated.

"I can't think of a better way to wind down after a strenuous workday than to be able to relax your tired and sore muscles in a hot tub. All the other residential units have two-person whirlpool baths. Your staff will have no different. If they require a workout room with weights or exercise equipment, I want those things to be available to them, and they should also have some sort of entertainment available to them during their down time, whether it be a library, or TV, or movies, or video games, or whatever."

"To be honest, sir, I was trying to think of a way for them to keep themselves in shape. There isn't an inch of space left in the security quarters with the two bunk rooms, two bathrooms, my office, the electronics room, and the armory."

"Well, it's already been settled. You're getting an R&R facility, but we may want to think a little more about additional sleeping quarters, particularly if you end up bring up more officers. How many of you are there right now?"

"There's seven of us, Mr. Jason, five men and two women."

"That's an awful lot, and the women shouldn't have to bunk in the same quarters with the men. I've already talked to Rod about providing separate accommodations for them. Tell you what. You and Rod and Aaron and I will meet again after you've had time to talk it over with your staff. Try to come up with a list of all of your needs."

"Very good, Mr. Jason, sir. Mr. Rod briefed me earlier, but it would be good to sit down to go over everything with you and Mr. Aaron. I'll go now to make sure everyone gets settled into the dining room."

****

After Chief Steinecker left, Jason started to get dressed. "What happened with Braden?"

"I talked to him for a few minutes, but I wanted to get back to you so I asked Rod to talk to him."

"Rod? Really? Rod?"

"Yes, I knew he's been gay the longest, and he's had a lifetime of experiences. I thought he would be the best person to help. I did ask him to be gentle with

Braden, and he promised that he would."

****

By the time Aaron had helped Jason get dressed and he'd dressed himself, everyone had gathered in the dining room. The security staff stood at attention against the partitions. Charity pushed in the serving cart loaded with several platters of cookies, brownies, finger sandwiches, and two kinds of fruit juice in pitchers as Jason and Aaron arrived and took their seats at the dining room table.

"Everyone except security staff who are currently on duty are present, Mr. Jason, Mr. Aaron," Chief Steinecker announced. "Please allow me to begin by introducing the members of my staff who are present. From left to right are Ryan, Dustin, Natasha, and Shane. Patrick and Alexandra are on patrol right now. I'll see to it that you meet them tomorrow."

"Thank you, Chief. Hello, everyone." Jason noticed that the officers all wore sidearms. He also noticed how Shane kept glancing at Braden. It made him wonder, but he decided to let it go and address the group. "Thank you, everyone for coming back. I apologize for oversleeping, but I'm glad we can have a few minutes to talk."

Charity spread her arms to encompass the entire group. "Now, Mr. Jason, we all know you and Mr. Aaron have been through a terrible ordeal. We're here to help you get better, and with all the changes that have been made in your absence, we're all going to help you get settled in. We're at your service, not the other way around."

"Thank you for that kindness, Miss Charity. I'm sure I'll be back to snuff in just a few days."

"You're welcome, Mr. Jason. Now I need to get back into the kitchen and check on the milk I have warming."

Jason spread his hands out across the table in front of himself. "Let me start out by asking, how does everyone find their quarters? Are they satisfactory? Are they comfortable? Is there anything you need or want?"

Conrad propped his elbows in front of himself. "Jason, have you seen them? They're like hotel suites. I can't speak for anybody else, but I couldn't be more comfortable."

"Jason," Jack added. "We made sure that they're stocked with all sorts of goodies. They've got minibars, too, and microwave ovens."

At the mention of the whirlpool tubs, Jason noticed that Shane twitched momentarily. *Shane glanced at Braden again,* he thought. *Was that longing I saw on his face?* Aloud he said, "Well, I'll have to take a look at them. Maybe tomorrow when it's light outside."

Charity returned, carrying pots of chamomile tea and hot cocoa. As she walked around the table and poured cups for everyone, Aaron asked, "Chief, how do we contact security or anybody else? Is there some sort of communication system that was used to call this meeting?"

"There are portable phones assigned to each unit, as well as several in the main cabin. Everyone can keep the one assigned to their quarters with them if they like. You also have one inside each of your night tables right now. I've kept them turned off because I didn't want you to be disturbed by mistake. I'll show how to work them before you retire for the evening. There are also panic buttons hidden in all the units, and there are several here in the main cabin."

"Thank you, Chief." Jason then addressed the group. "I've heard people refer to the cottages we ordered as units, suites, quarters, and cottages. Other than the security unit or office, whichever it's going to be, and Aaron's and my office, and the conference room, I think we should come up with one term for them. What do you all think?"

"If I may, Mr. Jason," Charity offered, "I think cottage is the word we're looking for. They're really small homes, plain and simple. Yes, they're grandly appointed, but they're really our homes, for the time being. Nothing else really fits."

"I agree," Conrad added.

"Me, too," Braden said.

"Any objections?" Jason asked. Everyone shook their heads no. "Then it's settled, they're now cottages. There's one last thing for the group. When can we get together tomorrow? I'd like to meet so we can begin to draft our provisional plans for Nathan's Promise."

"Whenever it's convenient for you, sir," Miss Charity answered.

"Very good, let's meet at ten. Thank you all for coming back. Now I don't know about Aaron, but I've heard there's a dinner plate with my name on it in the kitchen. I'm famished. If anyone wants to stay, feel free. Otherwise we'll see you tomorrow. "Oh, I forgot. Miss Charity, how are we doing meals around here?"

"That was on my list of things to review with you, Mr. Jason. What are your thoughts?"

"Well, there's certainly room enough around this table for everyone. I'd sure enjoy eating with all of you. That way we could get to know each other better. How do you all feel about it?"

Everyone seated at the table agreed. Except for Shane, the security staff looked to the Chief to answer. Shane looked only at Braden.

Okay that's definitely longing I'm seeing on Shane's face right now. Is that a bulge in his crotch? Oh shit. He's adjusting himself, Jason realized. Then he said, "Chief Steinecker, what about your staff?"

"I hadn't thought about that. We've been keeping to ourselves for the most part so as to not interfere with the running of your home. There are usually three officers on duty each shift, two patrolling the grounds, and I'm usually the one in the office who's monitoring the surveillance cameras from morning to evening, so two would be missing at any one time. They're on ten-hour, rotating shifts so that everyone eventually patrols at night. Because of this meeting, right now one officer is patrolling and the other is monitoring the cameras."

"Well, I'm extending an open invitation to all of you to join us whenever and however you like. You're also welcome to attend the meeting, Chief, your staff, too, if they're interested and if you have the time. I'd be interested in your thoughts where security is involved."

"Thank you, Mr. Jason. I'll meet with my staff separately and get back to you on meals, and I'll be sure to make the time to attend your meeting."

If Shane doesn't stop adjusting himself, someone else is going to notice, Jason thought, but he said aloud, "Very good. That's all I have for the moment."

As the security staff began to leave, Aaron stopped them. "Please don't go. Join us for a few minutes, and please, by all means, sit down and make yourselves comfortable."

Now Braden is looking Shane up and down. I think there's some chemistry there, Jason thought.

"Thank you, Mr. Aaron," the chief answered. The officers followed his lead and moved to joined in at the table where small talk ensued.

While Aaron and Jason ate their dinner, the rest of them made a dent in the platters Miss Charity had laid out. When Miss Charity continued to fuss over everyone while they snacked, Aaron asked her to sit down as well. Reluctantly, she acquiesced. The security officers were the first to leave.

"How did you whip up all those sandwiches so quickly, Miss Charity?"

"I always have nibbles ready to go, Mr. Aaron. Some were left over from lunch, and the rest I just threw together. There's nothing to it, if you know what you're doing."

"Then I'd say you're an expert."

Charity giggled. "Now aren't you just the sweetest man."

Chapter Six
Braden's Coming Out

Once Jason finished his dinner, Miss Charity took his plate into the kitchen. Jason excused himself from the table and said good night to the rest of them. He wanted to relax in the living room, but he asked Braden to accompany him for a moment. Aaron went with them.

"Braden, how are you doing?"

"I'm better now, Jason. Thanks for asking. I talked with Rod for a while, and he explained a lot of things to me, and I mean … a lot. Boy oh boy, I had no idea, but I am feeling better about myself."

"I'm glad. If you ever want to talk or have any questions at all, even about the practical aspects of being gay, I want you to know you can talk to Aaron and me about anything."

"Practical aspects?"

"Yes. Sorry to be direct, and I'm trying to be sensitive here, I mean questions about man-to-man sex. It can be scary your first time."

"It really can be, Barden," Aaron added.

"I don't know if I'm allowed to ask this, guys, or how to ask it."

"You can ask us anything," Aaron said.

"I mean nothing bad or disrespectful by this, but do you think you could help me with my first time? I'd trust you both completely."

"No, Braden. That will never happen!" Aaron nearly shouted.

Braden jumped.

Jason put his hand on Aaron's arm. "I'm sorry, Braden. What Aaron meant was, we're flattered, but I'm sorry, no, that could never happen. We're dedicated to each other. You may well find a lot of young gay men who are into that, and that's fine, but we're not. I do urge you to be careful your first time though. Be sure that it's with only one man, and one who you've come to know and really trust, for safety's sake."

Braden lowered his head. "I'm sorry, both of you. I'm really sorry. I meant no disrespect, and I'd never want to come between you. It's just that I don't know how this all works. You hear things and read things, and you see things, on videos I mean."

"You could never come between us, Braden," Aaron answered in a measured tone, "but Jason is right. Your first time should be with someone you trust."

"The things you see on videos aren't necessarily accurate," Jason said. "We'll always be here to answer any questions you may have or offer whatever guidance you ask for. Like Aaron said earlier, you're in a safe place right now, and again, you can come to us about anything."

"I'll keep that in mind."

"Braden, I was very lucky my first time," Jason continued. "He was a medic in Iraq, and he very kind and extremely gentle, and he went very slow. He spent hours preparing me emotionally and physically before he entered me. I hope you *will* be careful when you choose your first. It can be very traumatic for you if his focus isn't entirely on your wellbeing."

"Where would I ever find such a man?"

"I don't have an answer for that. It could be someone you've known for a while, who agrees to be your first, or it could turn out to be someone you recently met. Is there anyone you can think of who could be that person for you? I don't want to know who it is. I'm just asking so that you think about it."

"I don't know, Jason. I really don't."

"It's not something you need to rush into either,"

Aaron added. "There's plenty you can do all by yourself. There's all kinds of things that can provide you with tremendous sexual pleasure while at the same time, helping you to adjust to having a penis inside you."

"I've never used anything like that, Aaron. It's all I can do to just masturbate, with my upbringing and all. It's put a real damper on my sex life."

"Aaron," Jason said, "go show Braden our toy collection."

****

When Braden returned, he was carrying a small box. "Jason, I had no idea. When Aaron showed me how many different kinds of *toys*, as he called them, there are, and how they work, it blew my mind. He explained everything to me. Are you sure it's okay for me to take these?"

"Goodness yes, Braden. They're yours."

"I'll pay you for them."

"You'll do no such thing. There's more in there than the two of us could ever use. Go ahead, try them out."

"Thanks, both of you. Really, thanks. Again, I'm sorry for asking you guys to be my first. I think I'll turn in now."

"Come here, Braden," Aaron pulled him in for a hug. "No hard feelings. I mean that."

"Thanks, Aaron. I really appreciate it. Good night then."

After Braden had gone, Jason leaned over to Aaron and whispered, "Did you notice the security guard, Shane?"

"Why are we whispering?" Aaron whispered back.

"I don't know what kind of surveillance is in here right now."

"So what about Shane? I remember one of them was a Shane, but I can't remember which one he was. Why?"

"He was the one on the far right. Did you notice how he was looking at Braden?"

"No. Do we need to be worried about him? Do you think he'll hurt him? I didn't notice Braden acting effeminate, did you?"

"Oh, no, nothing like that. That's not what I meant. He kept glancing at Braden. There was definitely longing on his face, and before he sat down, Braden was checking him out top to bottom, and I mean *bottom*. Then Braden kept glancing over at him while we were all sitting at the table. I was certain their eyes were going to meet, but I didn't see it happen. There would have been fireworks, I'm sure."

"Do you think there's something there?"

"No, not yet anyway, it's way too early. Braden just got here, but there's potential for something to develop. I've just got this feeling. We'll just have to be sure about him. Shane's a big, muscular guy, and he's packing, and I don't mean just his sidearm. I wouldn't want Braden to be hurt, as in traumatized sexually, or physically roughed up, or even emotionally damaged."

"When you say you noticed he was packing you mean you were looking at his junk?" Aaron tone sounded hurt.

"Oh, no, Aaron, I didn't look at him like *that*, but I noticed that every time he glanced at Braden, he had to adjust himself. He concealed it pretty well with his hands folded strategically in front of his crotch, but I know I saw a bulge behind his fly that got bigger, as in, he was sporting a semi."

"You mean he had a hard-on?"

"He was getting there. From the size of that bulge

in his pants, he's definitely hung. Didn't you notice him walking out a little stiff-legged after he got up to leave?"

"No, but I'll keep my eye on him, Jason. Don't worry about that."

"We both will, but let's not say anything to anyone. If I'm wrong, I wouldn't want to embarrass either of them, or get Shane in any trouble."

"Agreed. I'm just glad you weren't looking at another guy like that, that's all."

"Aaron, baby, you have nothing to worry about. Didn't we just have this conversation with Braden? I'm committed to you, and to us. You're the only man I've ever truly loved, and you always will be."

"Sorry, Jason, I should know better. I guess I'm still on edge after the shooting. I find I'm questioning just about everything right now, like nothing's safe anymore, and I hate it. It's not me."

"I understand, Aaron. Really, I do. Now to change the subject, I'd like to try to take a shower before I go back to bed, but I might need your help, if you wouldn't mind."

"Why would you ever think you need to ask? I'm here for you."

"Thanks. First though, I'd like to try out one of those new recliners in the bedroom Rod ordered for us. I'm too awake to try to force myself to go back to sleep right now. I think it's from all the chocolate on Miss Charity's platters. I'm going to read for a while, see if that makes me sleepy. Care to join me?"

"That's a good idea. Hey, I'll pick up where I left off with *One for the Gods*. While I was in the hospital back in October, I kept wondering what ever happened to Charlie and Peter. When I was transferred to rehab, I looked for the book, but it wasn't in their library, and I was afraid to ask. It could have raised questions."

"It's probably out of print now. I wonder where the copy you were reading ever got to?"

"If I can't find it, I'll ask Rod in the morning."

"Yeah, I'll have to ask him where all my books are now, and my video library. We still haven't seen the place beyond our bedroom."

"We'll take the grand tour tomorrow."

Chapter Seven
Security Briefing

As Aaron was helping Jason ease back in the recliner, Chief Steinecker knocked on the door.

"Come in," Aaron called out.

"I'm sorry if I'm disturbing you, gentlemen, but I promised I'd show you how to use the phone system. I've had it turned on in here."

Jason struggled to get back up. "Yes. Thanks."

"Please don't get up, Mr. Jason. I'll just bring one of the phones over to you." He walked to the right side of the bed and opened the night table drawer. "Oh, there's a book in here, too, *One for the Gods*," he said lifting it up and then putting it back. "I'm not familiar with it. There's some other things in here, too."

"I was wondering where that got to," Aaron said.

The chief walked back from the night table. "So, the phone looks like any regular portable home phone. In-house numbers are two digits. There's a directory on the back of each phone. Be sure to precede the extensions one through nine, with a zero. For an outside number, dial star-eight, then wait for the dial tone, and then dial the number like you would normally. That's all. Any questions?"

"Yes, we now have a regular phone line?" Jason asked.

"Yes, Mr. Jason. Rod Livingston had the system hooked up on my request. With all that happened to you, you've hired us to protect you. We can't do that efficiently without being able to contact the outside world. It's not a wired system, it's an independent, dedicated, secure, encoded satellite system. It's more dependable than using your internet connection. We also have a radio system in the security office. Should we lose power and there's an emergency, we can contact any of the emergency services with it. Any other questions?"

Yes," Aaron said, "You mentioned earlier about panic buttons."

"Yes, I was going to go over them next. There's one just under the lip of each night table on the side between the table and the bed. They're recessed, which helps to conceal them, and it makes it very difficult to activate them accidentally. As you can see, there are sconces on the walls. They were installed at my direction. They're normal lighting fixtures, but the one on the right side of each wall, as you face it, is a panic alarm. Press the base, just like you would a panic button. There's another one in the shower. It's the tile with the billy goat painted on it. To activate it, press against it. The sconce on the right side of the bathroom mirror works just like the ones here in the bedroom. Would you like me to show you the others that are located throughout the cabin?"

"I think we can do that tomorrow, Chief," Jason said. "Thanks so much."

"Would you like to test them while I'm here? I can call the security office to let them know."

"That won't be necessary. Aaron and I are going to read for a while and then we're going to turn in. We can go over everything in the morning."

"I have a few questions, Chief."

"Yes, Mr. Aaron."

"If I want to get up in the middle of the night and get something from the kitchen, or if I want to go anywhere outside of the bedroom, I don't want a security officer to come charging in here. What do I do to prevent that?"

"That's a real good question, Mr. Aaron. You could call the office to let us know, but if you forget to do that, or if you simply don't want to, we'd see you on the surveillance cameras. They're equipped with infrared so we can see at night."

"You mentioned that there are motion sensors. Can you also hear us in the house?"

"The system is designed to detect sharp or very loud sounds, like something crashing or a gunshot. The system is programmed to recognize the sounds associated with a break-in or an attack. Otherwise, we don't hear a thing. They're programmed to automatically turn on to pick up all sound if you hit a panic button, or if we activate the infiltrator protocol. If that were to happen, all the lights in the entire cabin will automatically turn on and an alarm and recording will sound. The cottages are setup similarly."

"You're sure about that, Chief, I mean about hearing us in the cabin?"

"Yes, Mr. Aaron."

"I have your word on that?"

"Yes, sir."

"What are you getting at, Aaron?" Jason asked.

"I'm talking about privacy, Jason, when we want privacy."

"Mr. Aaron, Mr. Jason, may I speak frankly?"

Jason nodded. "Yes, Chief, please do,"

"All of my staff know you're gay. None of them cares one iota about that. They've all been thoroughly vetted and had psychological testing to determine any bias on their part, and I don't employ anyone who has a bias against any group in general. I can tell you that some of my staff, and I employee about fifty in this state, would be empathetic to your concerns. As far as I'm concerned, their personal lives are theirs to live however they choose. We're here to protect you, not spy on you.

"Personally, my big, I mean my older, brother is

gay. He helped to raise me, and he protected me when I was a kid. He's the most decent man I've ever known, and I'm the godfather to his and his partner's two kids. So please know, you have nothing to fear from us."

"Thank you for being so clear, Chief. Now I feel stupid for bringing it up." Aaron offered his hand.

"You're welcome, Mr. Aaron." The chief shook it. "But you shouldn't feel that way. You have every right to voice any concerns you might have, and I encourage it. It would make me uncomfortable to learn that a client doesn't trust us completely. Is there anything else?"

"Yes, Chief, Aaron and I look forward to your briefing tomorrow on the new security measures you've instituted. Thank you for showing us the phones and explaining everything else to us, and thank you for being so upfront about our concerns."

"You're welcome, Mr. Jason, Mr. Aaron. I'll say goodnight then."

"Good night, Chief," they said together.

Chapter Eight
You're Making Me Hard

11:00 PM

When they'd finished reading, Aaron went into the bathroom and turned on the propane water heater and turned up the thermostat. He helped Jason get undressed and then washed his entire body as he stood with him under the gentle, warm rain setting of the showerheads. At the same time, Jason tried to lather the parts of Aaron's body he could reach, but he was forced to stop often when Aaron lingered over his chest, or belly, or cock and balls, or when Aaron embraced him, kissed him, hugged him, or simply caressed him for love's sake.

"Oh, Aaron, the way you're touching me. You're making me hard."

"That was my intention, baby."

"I don't think I have enough left for sex. It's not that I'm sleepy, it's just that I don't have much energy right now, but what you're doing, it feels so damn good."

"Then I'll just keep doing it, baby. Let me show you how much I love you and don't worry about coming. Just enjoy it.

"I love you, Aaron."

"I love you, too, baby."

****

After another ten minutes Jason said he needed to lie down so Aaron dried him with new, soft, plush towels and led him back to their bed. Curious about what the chief had said earlier, Aaron opened the drawer to his night table. Seeing what was also in there, he raised his eyebrows and smiled and then took out a bottle of water-soluble lube.

As they lay together, Aaron reached his hand to Jason's groin and began to caress his cock and balls. He drew his hand to his face and inhaled deeply of Jason's musk mixed with the mild, masculine scented soap, then returned his hand and caressed him some more.

"My love," Aaron whispered. "I know what the doctor said about not overexerting yourself, but I'd like to suck you a little. Would that be okay?"

"Oh, Aaron, baby, that would be wonderful, but I feel bad. I don't think I can reciprocate just yet. I know we were able to make love last night in the hospital, but right now, I feel like I'm running on reserve power."

"That's okay, baby. You've been through a lot today, emotionally and physically. I want to do this for you as much as for me. I've missed the taste of you."

"Then I'm all yours. Just go slow. I don't know how much stimulation I'll be able to handle."

Aaron slid his head under the covers and began to run his tongue over and around Jason's nipples, gently sucking them and raising them to engorgement. He moved on down the ridges of Jason's six-pack abdomen, lingering in his navel, and then followed his treasure trail until he reached his treasure trove.

When Jason spread his legs apart, Aaron gently nibbled the tender skin between his thighs and groin, avoiding the hanging globes within his love sack, hoping to ignite the flame of Jason's passion.

"Oh! Oh, baby. Oh … oh … oh, Aaron."

Aaron ran his tongue across the mound of short, trimmed hair above the base of his cock and then down and up the front of the shaft, avoiding the glans. Jason's cock thickened and grew. It jumped up and continued to grow until it stood firmly at attention. Jason threw off the covers.

"I'm yours, baby. Do with me what you will."

"No, baby. I'm already where I want to be."

Aaron licked his cock like a lollipop. When the

first bead of pre-cum surfaced, he was there with his tongue and ran it across the slit in an abrupt strike. Jason's body shuddered, and Aaron's cock began to engorge.

"Oh, my God, Aaron!"

Aaron lifted Jason's sack and buried his nose in it. Then he inhaled sharply.

Jason began to pant. "Baby. Suck me. Please suck me."

But Aaron ignored Jason's pleas. He nibbled along the underside of the shaft moving up and down its length, stopping just below the throbbing head. Then he massaged its length with his tongue and lips and sucked against it as if he was trying to pull marrow from a bone.

Jason began to squirm. "Aaron, suck the head. Suck the head!"

Aaron sucked in both of Jason's balls and began to work them with his tongue, gently pressing them against the roof of his mouth.

"Please, baby, please."

Aaron rolled Jason's balls around with his tongue.

"Please, Aaron, suck me."

Aaron opened his mouth and slurped Jason's sack between his tongue and the roof of his mouth.

"Oh, God! Please!"

Aaron released Jason's balls, buried his face below his sack, and kneaded his P-spot with his tongue. Then he drew Jason's legs forward just enough to bury his tongue into his anus where he began to drill and suck against the external sphincter.

"I can't take it, baby. I can't take it. Make me come."

Aaron lifted his mouth. "You're almost ready, baby."

"Please, make me come."

Aaron ran his tongue across Jason's quivering hole.

"Please, Aaron!"

When Aaron's tongue finally penetrated the last barrier, he smeared some lube over a finger and slipped it in. He remembered what Jason had done to him their first night together back in the cabin and began to massage both sphincters to relax them and once they'd relented, he slipped in another finger.

"Aaron, I'm not kidding. I can't take much more."

Aaron slid around to Jason's side and grabbed his cock with his other hand and drank in the stream of honey-nectar that had dripped down the shaft and slurped again at the puddle that had formed its base.

Finally, he slid his lips just over the head and gently sucked while he massaged the corona with his fingertips, searching for Jason's prostate with the fingers of his other hand, buried deep inside him. When he found the swelling, walnut-shaped gland, it was nearly hard, so he began to press against it and stroke it while he withdrew and advanced his fingers past Jason's ever widening sphincters.

"Oh, God," Jason gurgled. He could barely speak. Then he lost his speech altogether and just grunted and moaned as he tossed his head from side to side and bunched the sheet into his balled fists.

Aaron advanced the shaft deeper into his throat, then drew back, then deeper again and back again, until his lips became planted against Jason's pelvis. He slid back and picked up the pace as he tightened his hand around the shaft extending the sensation of his mouth with his hand while he pumped its length up and down.

Sharp, rumbling groans began to rise from deep

within Jason's chest as he gasped for air and pounded the bed with his fists. Slowly, Aaron withdrew his fingers and turned Jason onto his side. He squeezed a liberal amount of lube into his hand and then slathered it over his burgeoning erection. He pulled Jason against him and in one, gentle motion, entered him, advancing slowly until he was firmly planted deep inside the recesses of Jason's core.

Reaching over Jason's side, Aaron grasped his cock with his still slick hand and began to slowly pump it in time with the motion of his hips as he advanced and withdrew his cock, drawing the head past Jason's prostate and his shaft through his spasming sphincters.

"Oh, baby. Oh, baby." Aaron moaned as waves of pleasure spread from his core and out through his body. "Oh, my Jason. Oh, my love."

With each pass, Jason's prostate tightened, and he moaned and moaned. When he began to shudder, Aaron knew there were but a few seconds remaining. He quickened the pace of his hips, driving the head of his cock past Jason's orb while he tightened his grip against Jason's shaft. Jason's abdominal muscles tensed and tensed until they could tense no more.

Aaron felt the fluids begin to shift deep inside himself as his orgasm approached its crescendo.

"Oh my God!" Jason groaned.

"Jason, I love you. I love you," Aaron whimpered.

Jason's balls pulled up tightly against his shaft and unleashed stream after stream of thick white cum so forcefully that it passed Aaron's hand, and reached the edge of the bed. Aaron scooped up as much as he could and sucked it from his hand, as he himself reached the point of no return. He groaned and drove his cock so forcefully into him that Jason was shoved to the edge of the bed.

Aaron pulled Jason tight against his loins and grasped his cock again as his own prostate began to contract, emptying his seed into Jason's depths. Grunting sounds like those of a buck in rut erupted from Aaron's throat.

Jason's prostate continued to contract as his cum flew past Aaron's hand, and splashed onto the bedroom floor, forming a puddle. Drenched in sweat, their bodies took over as they wriggled and spasmed in mindless abandon until finally, depleted, they fell still.

Jason's body went limp. His head fell to the side. His only sign of life was his slow, deep breathing and the trickle of tears that ran from his eyes. As if it had a mind of its own, his cock continued to jump while his prostate spasmed and his vas deferens contracted, but there was no more of his seed left to expel.

Aaron withdrew and began to shower Jason with kisses. Each touch of his mouth caused spasms to run through Jason's body. After he'd covered every part of Jason that he could reach, Aaron's animal lust drained away. He returned his attention to Jason and pulled the covers over him.

He slid off the bed and wiped up the puddle on the floor with a towel. After depositing it in the hamper in the bathroom, Aaron returned to bed, cradled Jason in his arms, and fell asleep.

Chapter Nine
Shane

Tuesday, January 5, 2010, 6:30 AM

There was a bounce in Jason's step when he got out of bed. After the previous night's lovemaking, he was invigorated and ready to begin the day. His newfound energy allowed him to shower, trim his beard, and get dressed by himself. After noticing the cum stains on the sheets, he took out a new set, with pillowcases, from the linen closet and set them on his recliner. He'd change the bed the moment Aaron woke up.

****

Aaron found Jason in the kitchen, hand grinding fresh roasted beans and putting them into the European, porcelain-cone filter. "That's new," Aaron said pointing to a restaurant-grade gas range.

"Rod must have ordered it." Jason paused briefly. He had a faraway look on his face. Then he finished filling the cone and began to pour boiling water over the grounds.

Aaron walked to him and began to rub his back. "How are you feeling about all these changes to your home, Jason? Has it been difficult for you?"

"It's *our* home now, Aaron, but I have to admit that I've experienced a few, brief pangs of regret. No, not regret so much as remorse. Then I immediately remember seeing you in the dirt in the barn, and they disappear. My focus now is on the future, on *our* future, on looking forward to the life we're going to build together and what we're going to build up here. There's nothing more important than you and the animals, and Nathan's Promise."

Aaron leaned down and kissed him on the cheek. "I'm glad for the both of us. We're going to make a difference in so many lives."

"I know." Jason's voice was soft.

"Hey, now just look at this kitchen." Aaron waved his arm to take in all the new things. "It's as modern as they come. That's a positive change, isn't it?"

"I guess it makes sense, considering Miss Charity is here now. I can't expect her to cook for so many people with my old, cast-iron, wood stove, but I'm glad Rod didn't have it removed. There's just something about cooking and baking bread with wood heat. The smoke adds a flavor that can't be duplicated, except for cakes and pies that is. You definitely don't want that flavor in them."

"You're right about that, Mr. Jason." Charity walked into the kitchen all preened and polished. "My mama taught me to cook on a wood stove. The same one her mother taught her to cook on. The thing is, with me cooking so much in here for the security staff and Mr. Lars, and Misters Rod and Jack, it was getting a bit hot with both the gas stove and keeping the wood stove going.

"I knew it would get even hotter after you and all the other folks started to arrive, so I've only kept embers going in it for the past week. I've restricted the damper on the flue so it will burn slowly. That way if I want the smoky flavor in something, I can simply stoke it up and it'll be ready to go. And you're right about feeding all these folks. It's so much quicker and more efficient with gas."

"Well, thank you for putting up with my old wood stove. I'd miss it terribly. It makes the best bread, and I'd hate to lose the proofing box."

"When you feel up to it, Mr. Jason, I'd sure appreciate it if you showed me how you bake your bread. There's always something new to learn from another cook that you can add to your own ways. Now why don't you two have a seat in the dining room, and I'll whip you up some breakfast. What would you like?"

"I can make our breakfast, Miss Charity," Jason said.

Charity placed her hands on her hips. "No, sir, I'll not be having that. You just got out of the hospital yesterday. Please allow me to dazzle you with my talents."

Aaron pulled Jason by the arm to lead him out of the kitchen. "Then we'll leave it to you, Miss Charity. Why don't you surprise us?"

"Are the chicken's eggs still being gathered?" Jason asked. "I've missed them."

"Yes, Mr. Jason. That fine Mr. Lars has been bringing them in every day, and goat's milk, too. I haven't had that since I was a girl. It's been a real treat. Oh, and that reminds me. Would you mind teaching me how to use your butter churn, too? It's a remarkable little machine."

"I'd be happy to."

"Wonderful. Now go have a sit down in the dining room. I'll make something for you from both your eggs and butter. How does that sound?"

"That would be wonderful," Aaron answered. "We'll be in the dining room."

As they left, Jason whispered to Aaron, "I have to go change the bed. I don't want Miss Charity to see the mess we made last night."

"I've already taken care of it, love. I saw the sheets you set out, and I found the washing machine. I stripped the bed and remade it, and put the sheets and pillowcases in the washer and started it."

A few minutes later, Charity carried in two plates of steaming omelets packed with diced peppers, onions, ham, and oozing with cheese. "See how you like these. There's just a little bit of a kick in them, but if you don't like them, I'll whip you up something else."

Aaron took a bite. He sat up straight and inhaled through his nose as a smile spread across his face. "What is that I'm tasting? Jason, do you taste it?"

"I think it's hot sauce. Am I right, Miss Charity?"

"Right you are, Mr. Jason. I used just a little bit since I don't know your tastes yet. As time goes on, you can let me know how hot you like things or if you like spicy things at all. We'll get it all figured out."

"Delicious," Aaron proclaimed.

"Aaron's right. This is wonderful. Thank you, Miss Charity."

"You're welcome. Now I better get started on breakfast for the troops. They'll be here in just a little while."

****

Twenty-five minutes later the security staff arrived and helped themselves to juices, goat and cow's milk, coffee from a big percolator, and a pot of tea from the side table. Then they took their seats. When Chief Steinecker came in he signaled to two of the security staff.

"Mr. Jason, Mr. Aaron, may I introduce Alexandra and Patrick? They were on patrol when we met last evening."

Aaron and Jason stood up and shook their hands.

"Nice to meet you," Aaron said.

"Welcome, I'm Jason."

"Ryan and Dustin are on duty right now. Natasha and Shane will go on this evening."

"Very good, Chief. Have you been able to speak with your staff about what we talked about last night?" Jason asked.

"Yes, I did, briefly, at shift change and before the others turned in. It made a big impression on them. They're going to let me know what they'd like by the end of this morning. I'll review that with you when we meet later today."

"That will be fine, but why can't I talk to them now? Most of them are here."

"If that's what you prefer, certainly."

While everyone ate, Jason and Aaron asked questions and listened to the officers as they discussed the R&R facility. After Charity pushed in the service cart, she began to dole out pancakes, scrambled eggs, scrapple, sausages, and toast to all the officers. When the others arrived, they also took seats, and Charity served them, too.

"It's a good thing you ordered such a big table, Rod," Jason said. "It looks like it holds this group just fine, and then some."

"You're right. You can't see it right now because of the tablecloth, but it's really two tables, side by side. Each one by itself seats ten to twelve with the leaves folded out. They'd hold twenty-two to twenty-four if you put them end to end, but the room isn't long enough for that the way it's presently set up."

"Well, I'm glad you took the initiative. I'd have never thought we'd need this many place settings. Oh, another thing, we spoke with the chief last evening and he's in agreement. We're going to proceed with the two, living-quarters cottages for the officers in addition to their R&R center."

"Very good. I'll get right on that with the construction foreman."

"I've also decided that I want to expand the patrols outside of the stockade into the surrounding forest. That will require more security staff. After the renovations and the new cottages are made ready, the current security unit will hold the chief's office, the electronics and surveillance center, the armory, and his personal quarters. I'm not second guessing anyone. I'm sure you were only trying to keep costs down for us, but we've got the money, and we've got the space so we're just going to do it."

Chief Steinecker put down his coffee cup. "That's real generous of you, Mr. Jason."

"Not at all, Chief, it's a necessity."

"As I think about it now, expanding the patrol perimeter to well outside of the stockade will also provide for more exercise for my officers. I was concerned that patrolling inside the stockade would not only not be enough for them, but it could become too familiar and things could be easily overlooked."

"Then it works out to the benefit of everyone, Chief." Jason turned to Lars. "Lars, again I want you to how much I appreciate your coming up here on such short notice to take care of my animals. Even though you offered to stay, I'm sure you'll be wanting to get back home."

"Really, Jason, I can stay as long as you need me."

"Well, why don't we see how I'm feeling after I go see them today? I've been itching to get some work done in the barn, and that'll give me an idea of how much of strength I've gotten back."

"That sounds like a plan, Jason."

Conrad cleared his throat. "Jason, I'd like to give you a once over before you take on any such activity. Why don't you give me a few minutes after breakfast?"

"Sure, Conrad, sure. Oh, goodness, Lars, what did you do about Christmas? Rod had told me that he was going to spend the day with your family. You didn't have stay up here, did you? I'd feel guilty if you missed Christmas with them?"

"No, Rod and I went home for the day and came back the next morning. Jack took care of the animals while I was gone. He took to it real well."

"Really, Jack? That was very generous of you. I'd have never suspected you'd have any interest in that."

There was a twinkle in Jack's eyes. "Truth is, I've never given farm animals a second thought, but I knew yours, and I knew how well behaved they've always been, so it was no burden at all. Though I'm sure Heather appreciated it when Lars got back. My milking skills are a bit awkward, but she put up with me for a day."

"I think the animals know you're back, Jason," Lars said with a smile. "I suspect they've caught your scent. They were a little rambunctious this morning, and Nellie and Sarah kept sniffing the air."

"I'll go and see them after breakfast. Will you come out there with me? If they get too excited, especially Sarah, I could get knocked over. I'll need someone who knows how to handle them, just in case."

"I'd be happy to."

For the next half hour or so, Jason and Aaron made small talk with everyone, but particularly the security staff. It helped to get a sense of them as people. Once Aaron figured out who Shane was, he made a point of engaging him in conversation. "I only noticed it just now that your name tag reads *Steinecker*. Are you related to the chief?"

"Guilty as charged. I'm his son."

The chief sat up straight and listened in. Jason perked up at this news and eventually joined the conversation.

"If you don't mind my asking, Shane," Aaron continued, "how old are you?"

"I'll be twenty-eight in April."

"Any brothers or sisters?"

"Two, sir, I'm the oldest. Then there's my sister, and the youngest is my brother."

"I'll bet you look out for them, too, don't you?" Aaron added.

"Yes, sir, I do. I always have. That's how I was raised. I take after my father in a lot of ways."

"Sounds like you were brought up right," Jason said. "Are either of your other children in the security field, Chief?"

"My son, Tyler, is nineteen. He enlisted in the Marines last year. He's currently on his first tour in Iraq. Marylou is twenty-four. She did one tour in the army. She's now a cop in Hinnen Valley. Shane was also in the Marines, and he did three tours in Iraq and finished up in O-eight.

"Then you have something in common to talk about with Jason, Shane," Aaron said. "He was in the army and did two tours in Iraq back when it all started."

"I'd heard that, Mr. Aaron. Mr. Jason, sir, I'd sure like to hear about it some time, if you wouldn't mind."

"I wouldn't mind at all, but I was in the army as a medic. I'm sure I didn't see nearly as much action as you did."

"Did you go out on missions?" Shane asked politely.

"Yes, quite a few, but again, I took care of the guys more than I ever fired a weapon."

"No disrespect, sir, but I'd say you probably saw a lot more action than I did, especially if you were over there at the beginning. What we saw were mostly skirmishes."

"I never thought of it that way. Anyway, just let me know when you'd like to talk. I'll be available just about anytime."

"Thank you, sir. It would be an honor. I could stop by before I go on duty this afternoon. Would that be good for you?"

"That would be fine. Just find me wherever I am, and I'll make the time."

After the conversation, Jason thought, *Braden listened to everything that the chief and Shane said, but with Shane, he hung on every word. No doubt about it. He's more than a little interested. I wonder if they'll get together somehow?*

"Mr. Jason," Charity said, "I'll be sure I have something available for everyone to nibble on while they're sitting down at the meeting."

"I don't think that'll be necessary, Miss Charity. That's only in a couple of hours from now, and it'll be lunchtime by the time we're done."

"I'll still have a few things ready, just in case. You never know when someone's going to have a hankering for a nibble."

"Thank you, Miss Charity. I guess we're done here. Conrad, you said you wanted a minute?"

"Yes, I did. Why don't we go to your room?"

Chapter Ten
Forgive Me, Babies

No sooner had Jason sat down on the edge of his bed than Conrad started in on him. "Jason, I'm only going to say this once. It's not going to happen, not today and not this week. You had a thoracotomy only twelve days ago and pneumonia on top of that. I'll not have you lifting bales and toting barges the day after you got your sutures out. Not if I'm going to be responsible for your health. Not if you want me to stay."

"Thank you, Conrad," Aaron said. "He won't listen to me."

"Really, Conrad? Nothing? Nothing at all?" Jason asked.

"Nothing! Absolutely nothing! You've been very lucky. Don't forget that."

"But what about what you said about sex? You said I could do that as long as I listened to my body."

"Yes, I did, and now I'm thinking better of it. You're one of those guys who always pushes the limit, all the time, and it's never been a problem for you before because you were healthy. You said you'd take it easy with sex, and I was struggling between being so happy that you'd cheated death twice and feeling sorry for you. That's why I gave you my blessing, and I appreciate you seeking out my advice, but it wasn't my place to do so. I wasn't even a part of your treatment team."

"Well, I didn't feel comfortable asking Dr. Baum about it."

"I understand, really I do, and I said yes because I believed that Aaron wouldn't do anything to put you in jeopardy. I can't say the same for your animals. Besides, there's manure everywhere out there. I went and checked for myself. Yes, it's a damned clean barn, but you've got chickens flying around in there. That stirs everything up. And don't forget, doing chores in the barn requires a tremendous amount of core strength. You don't have that right now. Not after just having your chest opened in two places.

"Let me be clear about this. You are not to do anything but pet them. Understand? No milking, no lifting feed buckets, no mucking out stalls, no reaching over your head to take down hay, no carrying anything, *nothing*, nothing at all. And take a good, long shower when you get back. I don't want you picking up some airborne pathogen in one of your wounds."

"Very well."

Aaron laughed. "Ooh, if he does, can I give him the penicillin shot in his ass? I owe him back from before. Twice!"

Jason smiled. "Prick."

"Exactly." Aaron smiled back, then kissed him on the cheek.

"I remember reading that in your chart while you were in the hospital, Aaron. I promise you, if he needs it, you'll be the one to give it to him. Just remind me to dull the needle before you do."

"Gee, thanks, Doc."

"One last thing." Jason and Aaron looked at him. "Lay off the sex until you hear otherwise from me. Not until I see some color return to your face."

"But…" Aaron raised his hand. Jason reached out and pulled it down into his lap, then shook his head, "*No*."

****

8:45 AM

The sound of brays and bleats pierced the crisp morning air. "I told you they knew you were back," Lars said as they approached the barn.

"They probably heard my voice just now," Jason answered.

"True, but they already knew you were back,"

"Do you really think so?" Aaron asked.

"No doubt about it."

Jason stopped outside the barn door. "It makes sense, Aaron." He turned to Lars. "They're my babies. They know me. Nellie's known me since the day she was born, same with Sarah. I raised Nellie from a foal after her mother was killed nine years ago by large cougar when she tried to protect her daughter, but that cougar never got anywhere near her baby. I saw to that. Since then, she's been like my daughter. All the animals are like my kids. We're family."

Lars stood still, wide-eyed. "What do you mean, you saw to that?"

"I shot him dead where he stood with his mouth crushing her throat." A tear spilled down Jason's cheek. "If I'd only gotten there thirty seconds sooner, she'd still be alive."

As Lars opened the barn door, they found Nellie prancing around her stall, swishing her tail, throwing her head up and down, and braying her little heart out. Sarah paced and brayed, too, and Heather and Jasper's bleating became louder as they stood up on their hind legs, reaching over the stall's rail with their necks. Big John crowed, and the hens clucked up a storm as they circled around Jason's feet. Both Nellie and Sarah rushed forward and threw their heads over the railing, as they reached out for him.

"Hello, girls, I've missed you." Between the two of them, pressing in to nibble Jason's chest so forcefully, they pushed him backwards. "Now, now, it's all right. Everything's all right. I'm here now. I'm here."

Nellie lifted her head over Jason's shoulder and

caressed his back with her lips, and Sarah nibbled the hair on his head and then slobbered her tongue across his face. "Oh my, you poor girls, you're shivering. It's okay. It's okay, girls. I'm not going anywhere." Jason began to cry. "I've miss … missed you both so much."

Lars placed his hand on Aaron's shoulder and whispered, "I've never seen such devotion from donkeys before."

Aaron walked to Jason's side. "Hello there, Nellie. Hello, Sarah." Nellie reached for Aaron's ear with her lips, and Sarah placed hers over his nose and mouth before they both returned to Jason.

Jason threw his arms around their necks and held them as he wept. "I'm sorry, girls. I'm so sorry."

Lars's voice broke with emotion. "They really love you, Jason. It's amazing to witness."

When Nellie let Jason go, she gently nuzzled her nose into the center of his chest and then stepped back and looked at him with one eye. Sarah stepped back and snorted in his face. "Message received, girls. I'll never leave you again. Now let's go see the other two kids."

Heather and Jasper jumped up and down on their hind legs and reached their necks over the top of the gate bobbing their heads and flailing their tongues as they tried to nibble Jason's shirt. Their bodies trembled as their little tails went a mile a minute.

"Oh, Jasper," Jason's voice caught as he ran his fingers over the hole in his horn. "Look at what that bastard did to you. I'm so sorry, boy. I'm so sorry he hurt you."

Lars put his hand on Jason's back and spoke softly. "The vet says she'll come back in another couple of weeks, after his horn is completely healed to fill in the hole with an epoxy resin. She said she can make it look just like his horn, that once she's done there'll be no evidence that a bullet ever touched it."

"That'll be great, Lars, thanks." Jason wiped at his tears. "Now let's get you milked, Heather."

"Oh, sorry, Jason, I took care of that earlier. I didn't realize you'd want to do it yet. You're still recovering from surgery."

"You're right, but no, I won't be doing any kind of work with any of them, not for a while, Conrad's orders. And anyway, I was going to ask you to do it. I had wanted to do some straightening up out here, but that's out for now, too. So, if your offer's still good, I'd like you to stay on for a little while longer. I'll have Rod fly you back as soon as I'm able to manage on my own."

"Jason, I'll be happy to stay for as long as you need me."

"What about your wife and kids? Don't you need to see them?"

"I do, but let's take it one day at a time."

"Thank you, Lars. Thank you. I promise I'll make sure you get time to spend with them."

"Like I said, Jason, one day at a time."

"Thanks. Thanks so much."

Aaron's voice became quiet. "I'd offer to learn how to do it all, but for right now I can't. Doctor Chandler's instructions were no bending over where I'd be straining 'cause of what it would do to the pressure in my brain. Not for at least a month she said."

"What happened, Aaron?" Lars asked softly.

Aaron pointed down below the latch to a spot along the edge of the gate post of Heather and Jasper's stall. Then he grabbed the post and squeezed so tight, his hand turned white. "I got a second concussion, right here, against this post. See where there's a chunk missing from it? Jason pulled it out of my head. I crashed into it when I tackled the motherfucker who attacked him. Sorry, I don't usually curse, but it's too raw for me right now not to.

"I knocked myself out in the process, but Jason tells me Jasper went right over top of me, even as that bastard blew out his horn with the rifle, hit him so hard he broke his ribs and drove him airborne, right into the hooves of Nellie and Sarah. They finished him off. Big John helped, too. He got to him first. Ripped his face and hands to shreds."

"It's okay, Aaron, you don't have to talk about it."

"Yes, I do, Lars, I need to say this at least once, at least to one person."

Jason choked. "Oh, Aaron."

Lars put his hand on Aaron's shoulder. "Then go ahead."

"Jasper timed it just right, 'cause I had a hold of his legs just long enough. When Jasper broke through the gate to attack the son-of-a-bitch, he rammed into him so hard that he broke the bastard's ribs. Then I hit the post and was out cold. I must have let go just at the right moment because Jasper's momentum carried through and sent him right to Nellie and Sarah. Sarah broke his collarbone, and Nellie whipped around and delivered the fatal blow. Crushed his skull with her back hoof.

"We worked him over like a boxer. Big John's jab-jab, jab-jab, and Jasper's and my, and Sarah and Nellie's one-two, one-two punches, and he was down for the count. Permanently. I'm glad that motherfucker is dead, 'cause if he hadn't died, I would have killed him."

Lars put his hand on Aaron's shoulder and gently rocked him. Jason leaned down with his head resting on the back of his hands as they gripped the gate. Tears spilled from his eyes.

Lars patted Jason on the back. "Then it's settled,

both of you. I'm here for as long as you need me. I'll just call home to let them know and to give my foreman some instructions."

Section Two
Building a Foundation

Chapter Eleven
Getting Down to Business

10:00 AM

"Thank you, all of you, for wanting to do this," Jason said as he opened the meeting. "It means the world to Aaron and me that we have this kind of support. Before I forget to say it, please feel free to take notes on the pads in front of you so we don't miss any important ideas you come up with. Aaron, would you like to say a few words?"

Aaron stood up. "Yes, thank you, Jason. You've all heard to some degree or another that Jason and I want to open a rehab center called Nathan's Promise. Do you all know the story behind who Nathan Taggart was to me and why the center will be named in his memory?"

When several people shook their heads no, Aaron recounted the story of the plane accident that killed his former life-partner and trainer, Nathan, and their history together on the Nevada Bighorns football team. Murmurs of sympathy were expressed by everyone when he finished. Then he went on.

"Thank you, one and all. When I first thought of honoring Nathan's memory, I didn't really know what I wanted to do, but I knew I needed to do something. Then I came up with the idea of a rehabilitation center. Rod and Jack have heard most of this, but I think it's important for everyone to understand a little bit about it."

After explaining about who the center would serve and answering a few questions, Aaron continued. "Now you may be asking yourself why another center, and why one that focuses on the multicolored gay community. It's simple. There's a lot of discrimination based on sexual orientation in many parts of the country, all over the world in fact, and it's rampant in the field of sports. I know this from personal experience as the team's quarterback. Because the center will not discriminate against anyone, we're using the acronym, LGBTQS. We wanted to be sure to include the S for straight athletes. In addition, it will also be open to members of the armed forces, law enforcement, and high-school athletes.

"Jason and I realized we can't do this alone, and that's why we want your help to get us pointed in the right direction. Here's the list of what's been discussed so far." Aaron passed out copies of what they'd drawn up with Jack and Rod. "That's everything that I have."

Jason stood up. "Rod and Jack have agreed to handle the transportation of people and materials. We've asked all of you here to act as our spearhead committee because we either know you and want your input, or because you've come recommended to us.

"This is going to be a multimillion dollar project. It's going to employ dozens of people right from the start, and I'm telling you all right now that there's a position in it for each of you, if you want one. We need to ensure that we involve the right people even before we break ground, even before plans are drawn up, and we want your thoughts and ideas.

"Because of the life we've chosen to lead and where we've chosen to live, we've decided to conduct as much of the business as possible from our home. That's one of the reasons why we're installing all the cottages, and brought in Miss Charity and Steinecker Security Systems.

"Because we've been fortunate with the weather recently, we're hopeful that the housing, security, and meeting facilities will be finished by the weekend. Once that's completed, we'll be completely operational. Once it's finished, if the weather becomes an issue, we'll be able to easily hunker down up here until spring.

"I'd like to now open up the floor to anyone. First, please tell us anything you'd like us to know about yourselves."

After a long moment no one had spoken, so Jason broke the silence. "Miss Charity, would you mind if I begin with you?"

"Not at all, Mr. Jason."

"Rod has told me a little about how he came to learn about you, but would you mind telling us about your work experience and anything about your life that you'd like to share?"

"I was born in Louisiana, but I don't remember anything about it because we moved to South Carolina along with my maternal grandmother when I was two. My parents found work with a wealthy family who kept a summer home on St. Croix. We moved back and forth with the family, living in a separate cottage on both properties, until I was in my late teens. That's where my accent comes from.

"My mother was their cook, and my father was their handyman. They allowed my grandmother to come with us because my parents wouldn't take the positions without her. My grandmother brought her cast-iron wood stove with her to their South Carolina home, and that's what I learned to cook on.

"When my father died, the family hired a new handyman whose wife also cooked. He wouldn't take the job unless his wife was also hired, so my mother lost her job. We were homeless for a time, and as a result, my grandmother lost her wood stove because we had no home for it. Eventually, we found employment with an agency, as temporary domestic workers.

"After a year, I took a job in the kitchen of a privately owned Victorian hotel in South Carolina where I worked my way up to chef over five years. I was there for thirty-three years. The hotel had been in the same family's possession for five generations, but the last owners were an elderly couple. When the Missus died three years ago, her husband gave up on life and died within a few months of her.

"The couple had wanted their three children to continue the business, but they had all moved away years before and established roots and started families in other states. None of the children were interested in the hotel, so within a year, they sold it to a developer who had it declared structurally unsound so he could demolish it and build a modern resort on the property.

"I was most recently employed as the food service manager in a state-run nursing home, a position I held for two years until I heard from Mr. Rod about coming here to work for you."

"May I ask why you left your job at the nursing home?" Aaron asked.

"At the nursing home, there was very little in the way of a creative outlet for me. I was required to follow their recipes and use their prepackaged food supplies. It was as dismal for the residents as much as it was for me.

"I put feelers out for a new job within a few months of my being hired there, but nothing ever panned out. Two weeks ago, I heard from an employment agency who put me in touch with Mr. Rod, and here I am."

"And we couldn't be happier. Thank you, Miss Charity," Aaron said.

Jason turned to the chief. "Chief Steinecker, what would you like us to know about your company?"

"Thank you for the opportunity to attend this

meeting, Mr. Jason, Mr. Aaron. I find it heartening to learn about the mission of Nathan's Promise and the history behind it.

"I started Steinecker Security Systems ten years ago after working in private security for five years. Before that I was a Marine for twenty-five years. We're contracted throughout the state and provide security for private citizens, large corporations, and small businesses. All of our employees have either a military or law enforcement background, and as I've already told you, each of them has gone through vigorous vetting.

"Though on a smaller scale, the services we're providing for you are in line with the highest level of security we provide to any of our largest clients. If you'd like to know whether we could handle the security for Nathan's Promise, we're more than qualified."

"Thank you, Chief," Jason said. "I think everyone has gotten to know Dr. Conrad Tolbert and Nurse Braden Darby over the past twenty-four hours, but I'd like to tell you why they're here. I worked with Dr. Tolbert in a suburban ER after I was discharged from the army. He is also ex-military, having served as an army physician for over twenty-five years.

"Braden was Aaron's nurse during his recovery from the injuries he sustained in the plane accident, and he was the private-duty nurse for both of us during our hospitalization the past two weeks. We also recently learned that Braden is a licensed massage therapist. I trust both of these men completely, and they bring a diverse wealth of healthcare knowledge and experience with them.

"On Thursday, my attorney, Claudia Duncan, and my financial advisor, Winston Tanner, will arrive to add their expertise towards bringing Nathan's Promise to life. This morning's meeting is intended as a brainstorming session. I'd like everyone to put their heads together to ensure we cover every conceivable aspect that will impact the development and implementation of Nathan's Promise. The floor is yours."

While the meeting continued, Miss Charity brought in lunch, consisting of steaming bowls of beef stew and fresh, homemade buttermilk biscuits. After she cleared the table she brought in a chocolate and carrot cake from the supplies Aaron had brought with him when he returned from the hospital the first time and served them with coffee, tea, and milk.

Chapter Twelve
Agony and Arousal

1:45 PM

After the meeting and lunch ended, Jason thanked everyone for attending before they returned to their cottages, excitedly talking amongst themselves about their participation in Nathan's Promise.

"Braden," Jason said, "would you mind working on my shoulder? It's more than a little tight. I didn't realize just how much effort it is to just move around. Conrad was right when he told me I shouldn't take care of the animals yet." He turned to look at the doctor. "And no, Conrad, I promise, I didn't do a thing this morning but pet them."

"Sure, Jason," Braden answered. "With the damage done by the bullet and because they had go through and move your pectoralis muscle groups when they explored the wound, they're going to be stiff for weeks. I'll go and get my massage table. Where would you like me to set it up?"

"How about in the bedroom? There's plenty of room in there."

"Sure thing. I'll meet you in a few minutes."

****

2:15 PM

There was a knock at the bedroom door.

"Come in," Aaron called.

"Oh, sorry, sir." Shane blushed and stopped short as he limped into the room. "I didn't realize you were, um, … ah, busy. I was told you were in here."

"How can I help you, Shane?" Jason said from the massage table as he turned his head to look towards him.

"You said I could stop by to talk about Iraq, but

I'll come back another time."

"Oh, yeah, sure, don't be silly. Come on in."

"But, sir, you're—well, you're … you're not dressed, sir."

"That's okay, Shane. I've been through too, too much recently to worry about that. I don't mind if you don't, but if it makes you uncomfortable, I understand."

"No, sir, it isn't that. In any other situation it wouldn't bother me. It's just that, well, sir, I work for you."

"I'll never go parading around naked in front of you, Shane, but this is who I am. Come on in and have a seat."

Braden continued to massage Jason's back while Aaron watched from the side. "So, you see, Aaron, you work the rhomboid muscles in this direction, like this. You always go with the direction of the inside edge of the scapula, that's the shoulder blade. The muscles run in the same direction. We'll need to be careful for the first few weeks, because his body is still rebuilding them. You don't want to press too hard and open up what the surgeon repaired."

Aaron nodded while Braden spoke.

Jason scrunched his face. "Shane, why are you limping on your left leg?"

"It's nothing, sir. I tripped over what turned out to be a large, buried bolder while I was patrolling the stockade two nights ago. It was concealed by uneven ground with only the top sticking out, but it was hidden just enough for me to not see it in the shadows with my flashlight. I think I pulled my groin muscle. It wasn't so bad yesterday, but after patrolling again last night, today it's gotten a little worse. I'm sure it'll work itself out though."

"I wouldn't say it's nothing. You're favoring

your leg and wincing when you move, and I just heard you grunt when you sat down. Is that why I didn't see you at lunch? Your father said you were skipping it."

"That's what I told him, sir."

"So he doesn't know that you've been hurt?"

"I'm not hurt, sir. I just pulled a groin muscle."

Braden pulled the sheet over Jason's back. "Okay, Jason, you can roll over now."

After Jason had turned over, Braden raised his head and torso to twenty degrees and then pulled the sheet down to reveal his right shoulder and chest. "So, Aaron, with the pectoralis muscles, particularly in the clavicular region, we'll need to be just as cautious with the amount of force that's applied for the same reasons. Under the scar there's a lot of repair work that's still going on. I'm not going to do anything directly over the scar today, because as you can see, it's still red because it's young, but I'll work on the muscles in the region."

"I see," Aaron said, nodding his head.

"Are you okay, Shane?" Jason asked. "You're turning red."

"It's just a cough I was trying to suppress, sir."

"You know what, Shane. You should let Braden take a look at you. He's a licensed massage therapist. He might be able to work out any stiffness you have there."

"I'd be happy to take a look at you," Braden said, enthusiastically.

"Nah, that's okay." Shane blushed again. "I wouldn't want to be any bother. I've had this before. I'll just let it take care of itself."

"Braden, could you work on my thighs now?" Jason asked. "They've been cramping up off and on ever since I was tied down to that table. He had them really stretched apart at a wide angle before he tried to rape me. Since earlier today, with walking out to the barn and being with the animals, they've become more than a little sore. I must be more out of shape than I thought."

"Sure, Jason, but believe me, you're not out of shape, not in the least. You were shot, had a thoracotomy and chest tube insertion, were on a ventilator, developed pneumonia, and you lost three units of blood. That's why you're fatiguing so easily. It doesn't matter how well-developed your musculature is or physically fit and active you've been. You must allow yourself to rest or you won't heal properly."

"Guilty as charged." Jason smirked. "Message received."

Aaron noticed that Shane watched as Braden reached under the sheet with a small towel and then pulled the sheet up to Jason's abdomen. The towel was strategically placed to just cover Jason's package, outlining his ample endowment. Shane blushed.

Braden began to massage the insides and fronts of Jason's thighs in long, lingering strokes. Then he shifted to a deep, kneading stroke beginning at the inside of the left thigh just under where the bottom corner of the towel covered him.

Shane blushed again when Jason's balls and the head of his cock were exposed, dangling beneath the towel, each time Braden's hands moved to the top of his thighs.

"Oh, that's it," Jason groaned and closed his eyes. "You've got great hands, Braden."

"You see, Aaron," Braden instructed, "it's like you want to grab a hold of the muscle inside of your hands, palm side down and then pull it up while at the same time pushing it out of your hands between your fingers and palms."

Shane shifted his position in the chair several times and adjusted his pants as his groin began to swell, but Aaron concentrated on Braden giving Jason his massage.

"The longer you wait," Braden stressed to Shane, but with his eyes focused on Jason's thigh, "the stiffer it will get, and that's going to make your groin more painful. It will require longer and more intense work for me to give you some relief from it. It might even take a few sessions before your stiffness is completely gone."

"Shane," Aaron said encouragingly as he and Braden turned to look at him, "accept the offer. Let Braden help you. I can attest to the benefits of massage after my football practice sessions, and I can personally attest to Braden's skills. He's as good as any masseur I've ever used."

Shane's face was beet red. He squirmed. "Okay, I put myself at your disposal, Braden," he said as he stood, stiffly. "When would be a good time for you?"

"How about this evening, after dinner?"

"Shane, your face is flushed," Jason said. "Go see Dr. Tolbert to see if he can give you something for that cough."

"I'll do that, sir. Thanks. I'll come back some other time to talk to you about your tours in Iraq. Thanks again."

Chapter Thirteen
Here, Let Me Help You

2:50 PM

"Mr. Jason, Mr. Aaron, sirs, I don't quite know how to ask this."

"What is it, Chief?" Jason slid forward in his recliner.

"I'm terribly sorry, sir, but there's a problem at another one of my contracts. I can't really go into it, but I need to ask if I can leave."

"Certainly, Chief. I'll put Rod and Big Daddy at your disposal."

"I'll be back sometime tomorrow. In the meantime, I've taken Shane off duty to rest. He informed me only just now that he injured himself while he was on patrol two nights ago. He said he didn't see a boulder in the dark and stumbled over it.

"I've put him on the desk to watch the monitors when he can move around a little better, but for now, he's off duty. He's obviously hurting because he was red in the face when he told me just a few minutes ago and then he went straight to the bunk room and crawled into bed."

"Thanks for telling us, Chief," Aaron said.

"That young nurse, Braden, has offered to take a look at him. I'm really glad there's someone up here who can take care of my boy. I went right to his cottage and told him so right before I came over here to talk to you."

"That's true, Chief. I can attest to his skills. Today he worked on my legs and the shoulder I was shot in. He gave me a tremendous amount of relief. If he needs further care, Dr. Tolbert is also here. You can tell Shane to go see him if Braden can't help him."

"Thank you, Mr. Jason. If I may, I feel it only

proper to tell you before I leave that I've never had a contract with such generous people as you and Mr. Aaron. My staff all feel the same way."

"We appreciate that, Chief," Aaron said, "and take all the time you need. We mean that. Don't rush back if it's going to take longer to take care of whatever you need to take care of. Your staff seems very capable. You've trained them well."

"Very good, Mr. Aaron, Mr. Jason. I apologize that I won't be able to meet with you today to finish up our discussion about security protocols and to discuss your offer for the new R&R center and more living quarters. If you have any questions in the interim, talk to Shane first, but any of my staff can advise you. I'll be leaving then within the half hour."

****

"What do you think, Jason?" Aaron said after the chief left.

"It's completely up to them, Aaron. Completely up to them."

****

6:45 PM

"Come in," Braden called from inside his cottage as Shane knocked at the door.

"Hello, Braden, I come bearing gifts." Shane grimaced as he stepped over the threshold and handed Braden a bottle of whiskey.

"What's this for?"

"For being nice enough to help me out. Sorry, but I've already started in on it. I thought a few swigs would help me to relax a little. You know, take the edge off."

"You didn't have to do that, Shane, but no more alcohol." Braden took the offered bottle. "You've had more than a few swigs. A third of the bottle is gone."

Shane struggled to take a few more steps into the

living room.

"Oh, your limp has gotten even worse. Here, let me help you." Braden put his arm around Shane's waist. "Lean on me."

Braden began to guide Shane down the hallway, depositing the bottle on the kitchen counter as they passed it.

"I feel like such a fool being here." Shane grimaced each time he moved his left leg forward. "This isn't your responsibility, and anyway, you really work for Mr. Jason and Mr. Aaron."

"If there's one thing you'll learn about them, it's that they're the kindest, most giving people you'll ever meet. Now, let's see whether I can give you some relief."

"Thanks so much, Braden." As the whiskey began to take effect, Shane stopped and placed his meaty hand on Braden's chest. He leaned his face in close. "I won't forget this."

"There's a lot of different kinds of massage techniques. Have you ever had a therapeutic massage before?"

"No, not really." He grimaced and forced himself to take another step.

"The philosophy I follow is that the needs of the client determine the technique or techniques that I use. I won't know what you'll require until I'm able to get my hands on the afflicted areas to feel what muscles and other structures might need attention. Often there are multiple muscle groups and nearby structures involved wherever an injury occurs because they all work together to produce movement.

"When something's out of sorts, the nearby muscles try to step in and cover for the injured ones by supporting the skeletal structures in the area of the injury, and that puts additional stress on them because they then have to move in ways they weren't designed to move. As a result, they can also become affected. It's never simply *a pulled muscle*. You've probably injured the adductor muscle groups, the muscles that pull your leg inward where they attach to the floor of your abdomen at the groin, and maybe some tendons and ligaments, too."

"I've heard from my father, who was told by Mr. Jason, that you're very good at what you do, and from what I witnessed this afternoon, and what Mr. Jason said, he's right. You do seem to have the magic touch. I place my body in your able and experienced hands, and I trust you completely to do with it whatever it is you think it needs."

"The only thing I want you to know, and I'm sorry because this might be uncomfortable or embarrassing for you, particularly since you've never had a therapeutic massage before, is that because of where your groin is, I may have to expose you a little to gain access to the areas that need attention."

Shane felt the warm sensation from the whiskey as it coursed through his body and loosened his tongue. "Braden, I give you complete liberty to explore my body however, wherever, and as much and intensely as you need *or want to*. I'll cooperate with whatever you ask of me. I'm in such dire need of *release* … uh, sorry, sorry, the whiskey must be affecting me. I meant relief right now that I'm willing to have you do anything to me. Just show me where to go, and let me know how much I should take off."

"We're headed back to my bedroom. I've set up my massage table in there. I thought it would give you more privacy in case someone knocks. It could be a bit awkward and embarrassing for you if you're lying on the massage table, right inside my front door, with that region of your body exposed."

"That makes sense. Privacy would be a good thing at a time like this." He grunted and hobbled forward again.

"May I make a suggestion?"

"Sure, Braden, anything."

"You appear to be even worse off now than you were this afternoon. You can barely take a step with your left leg. As tight and stiff as you are, a massage will be painful if not impossible for you to tolerate, even with as much whiskey as you've got in you right now. Since it's been forty-eight hours since your injury, I think it would be easier on you if you soak in my whirlpool tub for at least a half hour before we get started. The heat will help to relax and loosen up all the structures down there, making them much more pliable and receptive to being explored with what I'll need to do to bring you some relief."

"That would be wonderful, Braden, but are you sure? I wouldn't want to put you out. These are *your* private quarters. You sure you want another man in your bathtub?"

"Of course, I'm sure."

Shane suddenly realized how he was acting and the feelings he was allowing to surface. He tried to fight them. "Okay, if you say so. I trust you, but really, it only hurts when I try to swing my left leg forward. Otherwise I'm great. Maybe we should just skip the tub."

"It would be best if you didn't. I wasn't expecting you to be this stiff before we got started. The more relaxed I can make you, the easier it will be for both of us. I'll have to heat up the water before I fill the tub, but it shouldn't take more than a few minutes."

Shane was losing the battle going on in his mind. He decided to just give in and let happen whatever was going to happen. Actually, he was hoping for it. "Okay,

Braden, if you say so. Lead the way."

After a few more steps they arrived at the bathroom door. "Here we are. Once I get you in there, I'll go and get a chair."

"If you don't mind, I'd rather stand. Having to sit down and get back up will only hurt more."

After Shane was past the door, Braden started the propane heater. "It only takes about sixty seconds before it begins to get hot."

Chapter Fourteen
The Smell of Musk

"This is very kind of you, Braden. You don't even really know me, and you're letting me get into your bathtub." Shane began to pull off his sweatshirt. "I wore boat shoes. I can slide them off with a little effort, but I could use your help to get the pants off once I have them down around my ankles, particularly with my left leg."

After Braden started the water, he turned around to face Shane. "Oh my."

"What's wrong, Braden?"

"I'm sorry, it's just that you're so—so … um, I'm sorry."

"What is it?"

"Nothing, Shane. Sorry."

"Please tell me. What's making you so uncomfortable?"

"I'm not uncomfortable, I'm stunned. You're so … muscular. You've got a body I've only ever dreamed of having. I've worked out and worked out, but I can't put on the kind of muscle mass you've got."

"It's genetics, purely genetics. There are no steroids in this body, that's for sure. You've got more of a swimmer's body from what I can tell. There's nothing wrong with it, your body, I mean."

"If you say so, oh, sorry, here, let me help you with your shoes." As Shane braced himself against the wall, Braden bent over and lifted his feet, one at a time, out of his shoes. "There, they're off. That wasn't too difficult, now your sweatpants."

Shane looked towards the ceiling as he slid his thumbs under the waistband and began to slide it down. It caught in the front momentarily when it met the ample bulge of his crotch. Braden's face was just inches away from Shane's goods. When they popped out from under the waistband, the jockstrap he was wearing barely restrained its contents. It was nearly stretched to its limit.

"Oh!" Braden fell backward onto his butt.

"Did you trip?" Shane looked down when his pants dropped to the floor.

"I must have. Here, lift your right leg. Good, now your left."

Shane flinched and sucked in his breath.

"I'm here to help you, Shane." Braden moved closer and leaned down. "Put your weight on your right foot. I'll lift your left out of the pants."

Braden lifted his head after he'd freed Shane's foot. The fabric of Shane's jockstrap bulged to the point where small openings formed between the stretched, knitted weave of the pouch's elastic fabric, exposing the skin and engorging veins of his penis's shaft, the redness of his swollen glans, and the hair that covered his enormous balls. Body heat, vented through the openings in the fabric. Moment by moment, the jock's pouch moved further and further forward, pulling away from where it had nested against Shane's groin only moments before. Braden licked his lips, leaned in closer, and inhaled Shane's musk. Shane watched silently. He didn't dare utter a word.

Braden shook his head. "Are you okay for me to let go? I need to test the water temperature."

A slow smile spread across Shane's face. "Yes, I'm fine."

****

Braden turned on the tap and ran his hand under the water. "It feels perfect to me. I'll help you get in."

Without asking, Shane slid his thumbs under the jockstrap's waistband and pushed it down. His thick, pendulous penis was not flaccid by any means. It still hung downward, but barely so. Now free of its restraints, it jutted out in front of his ample ball sack. The veins on the shaft continued to engorge, and the shaft moved forward and upward ever so slowly as it filled more and more with blood from each of Shane's thunderous heartbeats.

Braden's mouth began to water as he eyes locked on the ample, mushroomed head at the end of Shane's thickening, growing shaft. *I've seen larger penises in the hospital,* he thought, *but this one is worthy of any man's praise, and good God, he trims his pubic hair. That looks like a professional job. And the carpet matches the drapes, light brown with some blond mixed in.*

"Is this okay, Braden, that I'm taking off my jock? I don't want to get it wet. I can't go back to the barracks with a soaking wet jock. The guys would wonder what I'd been up to. Braden? Braden?"

When Braden looked up, Shane was staring at the ceiling. "Um, it's fine, Shane." *Keep it together, Braden. Keep it together.*

"Would you mind helping me slide it all the way down? My leg … it's tough to move."

"Oh, sure."

As Braden kneeled down at Shane's feet again, he reached for the jock's elastic strap, now stretched between the middle of Shane's muscular, hairy thighs, his penis, inches from Braden's face, only inches above his hands. The glisten of a bead of pre-cum begin to emerge at the slit. Braden froze in place.

Shane looked down and watched Braden closely. Braden jumped when the bead quickly enlarged as Shane flexed his shaft. The bead lingered at the very tip, and then Shane flexed again. Slowly, more of the glistening fluid emerged, causing the bead to slip downward until it could cling no more. From an ethereal tendril, the bead hung, momentarily suspended. Then it floated downward, closer and closer to Braden's arm.

With great control, Shane flexed once more, sending a stream of pre-cum from his slit. It quickly followed the bead, overtook it, and then landed with a splash on Braden's forearm.

"Oh! Sorry about that, Braden. That happens sometimes when I haven't … when I haven't, you know. I'm sorry … when I haven't … taken care of myself in a while. It builds up and then it just spills out. I've been laid up with my leg for two days. That's a long time for me."

Braden took a deep breath, slid the jockstrap down and lifted Shane's legs, one at a time, until it was off. "Here, I'll help you into the tub." He stood up and wrapped his arm around Shane's waist, and led the way.

"If I'm going to have to lift my leg, Braden, I think I'm going to need you in front to steady me. My groin is more painful than I admitted. Wow, sorry, I can't believe I said that just now. I'm not used to people seeing me vulnerable. In the Marines you had to suck it up. You never admitted your pain."

"You're not in the Marines anymore, Shane. If you're going to need me in front of you, I'm going to have to take my shoes and pants off before I get in the tub. Hold on."

Braden threw his clothes in the corner on top of Shane's and then came to his left side and wrapped his arms around Shane's waist to brace him. After Shane lifted his right leg over the edge, Braden stepped into the tub and squatted down a little so he could wrap his left arm around Shane's torso. Shane's shaft continued to swell until it began to press against Braden's belly, oozing pre-cum down the front of him. "I'm going to brace you now and help you lift your left leg in."

"Thanks, Braden. Really, thanks."

Braden wrapped his right hand around the back of Shane's thigh and began to lift against his torso, steadying himself with his left arm. As Shane's leg cleared the tub's edge, his body began to move forward. His cock pressed firmly against Braden's groin, grinding every ridge and vein along its length against the sheer, white fabric of Braden's underwear. When Braden let go, Shane's cock had grown even more and was now protruding forward and upward at an angle of forty-five degrees to his abdomen.

Shane blushed as he pointed to his growing cock. "I have to apologize for him. He seems to have a mind of his own sometimes. He's been that way ever since I hit puberty."

"It's fine, Shane. I've seen a lot, even during my short nursing career."

"How long have you been a nurse, Braden?"

"Two years, but I've been a massage therapist for almost five. I'll help you down into the water. I'll turn on the jets once the tub is full enough."

Chapter Fifteen
You're Very Handsome

As Braden wrapped both of his arms around Shane's torso, their faces were inches apart. "Have you ever had guy patients come on to you?"

Braden nearly dropped Shane as he lowered him into the water. "That's a strange question to ask."

"I ask it because I could understand how easily it could happen. You said you've seen a lot. I thought that might mean you also experienced a lot." Shane held onto Braden's back and leaned his face closer still. "You're very handsome."

Braden blushed and lost his grip around Shane, causing him to fall against his body as his knees landed in the tub. Trying to catch himself, Braden's right hand was suddenly on Shane's swollen erection and then it closed around it, grasping it tight. As Shane's legs hit the water, they splashed onto the fabric of Braden's nylon briefs, turning them transparent.

"I'm sorry if I made you uncomfortable, Braden. I was just speaking the truth. Um … you can let go of me now." Shane directed his gaze to Braden's hand, wrapped around his fully erect cock.

Braden's neck and face flushed as he let go. "I think I should leave you alone while you soak, Shane. Call me when you're ready for your massage." Braden turned his head away and reached for the button to turn on the whirlpool jets.

"Whoa, Braden, I'm sorry if I upset you."

"I normally wouldn't admit this, Shane, but you did. Why does everyone assume all male nurses are gay?"

"I never said you were gay, Braden."

"You inferred it by saying guys would come on to

me."

"Um, Braden, I never said you were gay, but I'm wondering what *that* means." Shane pointed to Braden's underwear. The head of his erect cock was sticking out over the top of the elastic, and his shaft and balls were visible through the sheer fabric. There was a bead of pre-cum glistening at the slit.

"Oh, my God! Shane, I didn't know. I'm sorry. Oh, my God, I'm sorry!"

"Braden, it's no big deal. Look at me." Shane lifted his hips above the water with his right leg. His erect cock was massive. Eight inches in length and seven inches around, it glistened and bounced as he used his right leg to thrust his hips up and down.

"Braden, even straight guys get hard-ons around me. I seem to have that effect on men of all persuasions. Often, it's admiration. Back in the Marines, when we'd get back from a patrol, just about every guy had a hard-on in the shower. There's something about combat that fuels testosterone and male aggression, and it stimulates the release of male musk."

"It's not that, Shane. I'm not feeling aggressive towards you."

"Then do you know what it is, Braden?"

"I can't."

"Try."

"No, I can't."

"Let me make it easy for you, Braden, and please don't be offended by what I'm about to say. If I'm wrong, I apologize. I find you extremely attractive, Braden, and I'm terribly aroused right now. My heart feels like it's beating out of my chest, and my head is swimming. I can't think of anything I'd like to do more than to suck your cock, and not that I'd expect you to want to, but I'd love it if you wanted to suck mine, too, but there's no strings attached, really. Please, Braden, let me suck your cock."

"This must be the alcohol talking, Shane."

"I didn't have that much, just a couple swigs."

"Yes, you did. You've had a good third of the bottle."

"This is *not* the alcohol talking, Braden. It's me talking. Shane."

"But, you were a Marine, and you came here for a massage, not this, or was that just a ploy?"

"Braden, there are gay Marines. There have always been gay Marines, and there will always be gay Marines, and no, this isn't a ploy. I really did pull my groin muscle."

Braden began to shake. He sat down on the edge of the tub. Shane lifted his hand out of the water and rubbed Braden's back. "It's okay, Braden. You're okay."

"Shane. Shane, I'm a virgin. I've never been with anyone before. How do I know what I want? How do I know for sure if I'm gay?"

"Braden, even if you're not gay, it doesn't mean you can't get aroused by another man. It happens all the time. Tell me, what are you feeling right now?"

"I'm feeling … I'm feeling like I want to…"

"Go on, you can say it."

"I'm feeling like I want to touch your body."

"Good. Touch away." Shane nodded his head. "Go on, touch me."

"And that you'd not only let me, you'd want me to. Oh, God. What have I just said?"

"If that means what I think it means, Braden, please do me the honor of allowing me to be your first."

"Really, Shane. You'd let me touch your body? Anywhere?"

"Yes, anywhere. Anywhere, and any *way* you'd

like. It's yours to do with what you want. Heck, you were going to touch it anyway. I really did come here for a massage, but now I think I want more, and I think you do, too."

"No. No, this is wrong. I'm sorry, Shane. You came here for my help. You better go before something happens that we'll both regret."

"Braden, the only thing I'd regret is if nothing happened between us tonight. I want you to touch me, and I want you to let me touch you, and caress you, and kiss you, and suck you, and even fuck you, if that's what you want."

"But—but, you're so big. Your cock, I mean your penis, it's so big. I can't imagine anything like that inside me. I don't know what I want."

"Who says it has to go inside you? There are many different things we could do. If you're willing, I'd love it if we could combine the massage you planned to give me with whatever might happen between us. That is if you want to try."

"Shane, I've never done anything except once I engaged in mutual masturbation."

"Then you're practically a blank page. Please let me be the one to introduce you to the wondrous pleasures that a man can offer to another man. I've never been given that opportunity, that gift, and it would mean so much to me to be your first."

"I don't want to be hurt, Shane."

"I'd never hurt you, Braden, never. Come into the tub with me. Let me show you just how wonderful it can feel to be touched by another man."

Braden swallowed. He pulled off his shirt and underwear and threw them onto the pile of clothes. Then he slid in.

"I should tell you right now, Shane, and I give

you my word on this, my HIV status is negative. I was tested six months ago after a needle stick, then again a month later, and then again, two months after that. It's hospital protocol. I've never been with anyone, so it's impossible for me to have contracted it through sex. Will you tell me yours?"

"I'm negative also, Braden. I have the paper in the pocket of my sweatpants if you want to see it."

"I trust you, Shane, but why would it be in your pants?"

"Do you want the truth?

"Of course."

"Because … well … because I found you attractive the first time I laid eyes on you. Then when you were massaging Mr. Jason's legs, it was all I could do to hold myself together. It was very arousing, watching you work on him. Then all of you were telling me to let you give me a massage, and I put it all together in my mind.

"I sort of hoped the opportunity would present itself, and look, now it did. Besides, I always have the most recent results with me. You never know when and where an opportunity might present itself. You should also know that I haven't had unprotected sex since the last test was drawn three weeks ago. The truth is, I haven't had *any* sex since then, that is, except for some self-pleasuring, and I've never, ever had unprotected anal sex. I still get checked regularly, at least every six months, because anal sex isn't the only way you can contract it."

"I'm glad you told me, Shane, and I'm glad my first time, whatever this turns out to be, is going to be with you."

"Good, now lie down on your back, against me."

Chapter Sixteen
In the Closet

Shane wrapped his arms around Braden's torso in a gentle hug, then moved his hands to his hips and pressed him downward against his unyielding erection.

"Oh, God. It's so big, Shane. I can't."

"I'm not going to hurt you, Braden." Shane began to run his fingers across Braden's nipples. He squeezed the water from a sponge over Braden's chest and pulled his ears one after the other into his mouth and sucked on the lobes.

Braden began to shudder. "That feels … that feels so, so good."

Shane easily lifted Braden's body upward and began to slide him up and down across his own, making sure his rigid cock slid between Braden's butt cheeks. With each pass, it slid deeper and deeper between Braden's crack. When his cock was where he wanted it, he lowered Braden against him and reached for his cock. It jumped at his touch, so he encased it in his thick, muscular hand and began to slowly slide up and down the shaft.

Braden sucked in his breath. "My God."

He groaned, then groaned again. "My God."

Shane pressed the head of his cock against Braden's twitching hole. Braden cried out. "Shane, I'm going to orgasm if you don't stop!"

Shane let go of Braden's cock and lifted him up into the air, turning him over and pulling him in. He slid Braden's seven-inch cock into his mouth and began to gently suck as he held him around the hips, lifting and lowering him, forcing his cockhead to slide to just inside his lips and then drive it to the back of his throat. Braden's cock strained against the blood coursing through it.

"Braden, your pre-cum is wonderful," Shane said as he momentarily disengaged from his cock.

"Shane, I'm going to…"

Shane watched Braden's ball sack tighten up against his shaft.

"Shane! Shane! Shane!"

Shane wrapped his arms around the back of Braden's thighs and forced his cock to the back of his throat, receiving his gift. The gift of his first true time with a man. Shane swallowed greedily of Braden's spunk as he pumped his head back and forth and pressed with his tongue along the underside, hurrying the musky cream along to its final destination.

Braden's body swung wildly from side to side, but Shane held on. Braden reached his hands behind Shane's head, pressing his groin against his face, as he forced his cock past the back of Shane's throat. Shane resisted, but he was unable to break Braden's hold. Braden held tight until the last stream spewed from his loins. When it ended, Shane continued to suck, pulling every last drop from deep within Braden's core.

Braden began to sob. Shane lowered him and held him in a soft but firm embrace as he slid them both deeper into the water. "You were wonderful, Braden, wonderful. It was perfect. So beautiful. So beautiful."

"Kiss me," Braden pleaded.

"Taste your cum." Shane drew Braden's mouth to his own and sucked in his tongue. Then he drove his tongue deep into Braden's mouth and then drew Braden's tongue back into his. Braden responded and sucked back, pulling the remnants of his own spunk into his mouth, and swallowed it.

"Thank you, Braden. Thank you for giving that to me," Shane whispered. "I'll never forget it. Never. Oh,

Braden, you're a beautiful, beautiful man."

They lay like that for what seemed an eternity as the warm, soothing water swirled around them.

****

7:55 PM

Braden ran his fingertips across Shane's muscular, hairy chest. "Is it okay that I touch you like this?"

"Braden, you can touch me anywhere and any way you like."

"Did I orgasm too quick? Did I disappoint you? I don't know what's normal."

"For your first time, and as far as we went, no, not at all. And no, you didn't disappoint me in the least. I could tell you were really turned on. It can happen quickly when you're that aroused. As time goes on, you'll learn to how much foreplay you want, how to control your response to it, how long you want it, and all the different things you can do to prolong it."

"That's good to know." Braden moved his hand down across Shane's belly ending at the base of his thick, but now flaccid, penis. He lifted Shane's balls in his palm and felt their heft. They were nearly the size of limes. "I've never touched a man like this. Your testicles are so big, and your penis is so thick. To touch you, it's wonderful. It feels so right."

"It is right, Braden. It's right for you, and it's right for me, too. And we call them balls and a cock."

Braden blushed. Shane smiled, then laughed out loud.

"It's okay, Braden. You'll get used to it."

"I'd have never thought you were gay, Shane, but I was attracted to you too, the first time I saw you, I mean. Does that make me gay?"

"I felt the same way, Braden. Last night when we

were called back to the cabin, I couldn't stop looking at you. You're so damned handsome. Does it make you gay? Only you can know that for sure."

Braden blushed, again.

"No, really, have you looked at yourself in the mirror? Do you see what the rest of the world sees? You really are a looker, Braden, and you have a great body. No, you're not bulky with muscle, but you're very muscular."

"I can't believe a man is saying these things to me. It just seems so strange."

"Well, get used to it. You're going to be turning heads and breaking a lot of hearts for many, many years to come. Believe me."

Braden sighed. "So where do we go from here?"

"I was hoping you were still going to give me a massage."

"You mean here?" Braden asked as he squeezed Shane's cock.

"There, too, but I'd like to get back to work A-SAP. I really do need some help with my groin."

"Then let me take care of you, but I was serious when I asked where do we go from here? You know, how do we act around everyone else after tonight?"

"I see what you're getting at. It's too early to tell. We've only just met, and the guys and gals I work with don't know about me. Not that I think they would be repulsed by the idea, but I'm the owner's son. There's certain things that are expected of me."

"Does your father know?"

"No, he doesn't. My sister and my brother know, but I haven't told Dad yet. I'm sure he'll have difficulty with it at first, just like any parent does when they don't suspect, but I'm not afraid of him learning the truth. My uncle, his older brother, is gay, and Dad loves him and is completely supportive of him and his family. I want to be able to tell him when I'm ready, and when I think he's ready to know."

"I can respect that. So, we'll just act like acquaintances?"

"No, we can be new friends. Like I said, Dad knows I came here tonight for your help, and that's all he needs to know."

"Then that's what we'll be, Shane, and though I understand that we really just met, I can't believe that we won't grow to become good friends and stay that way for a very long time. So how about that massage?"

"I'm ready if you are. How should we do this?"

"We'll begin like any other massage I've ever given. You'll lie on the massage table either on your back or on your front, whichever side you want me to begin on, and we'll go from there."

Chapter Seventeen
Loosened Up

8:15 PM

Braden returned to the bathroom. "I've turned up the heat in my bedroom a little for you. With you lying still, and with your skin exposed to the air, I don't want you to get a chill. That'll make you tense up or shiver or both, and that's bad for a massage. You need to be able to relax, completely."

"Thanks. You were right by the way, the whirlpool really helped loosen me up. I think I can make it by myself. And remember, I'm hoping you're going to use *all* your talents on me."

"I've never done anything except mutual masturbation, but I'll try, Shane."

"Good, then I'll start out lying on my belly, and you can finish up with me on my back."

As they made their way to the bedroom, Braden followed closely behind Shane with his hands on his hips, to ensure that if he stumbled, he'd be able to catch him.

"Your hands feel so good on me, Braden. Remember, I'm giving you free rein to do anything you want to me."

"That'll give me a pretty big canvas to work on. I know a lot more techniques than I've ever been able to use on anyone. You'll be my first for the unconventional ones."

"I'm all yours, Braden. Oh, by the way, I cleaned myself out and washed my ass three times before I came here, on the off chance you might want to fuck me."

"That's good to know. Now let's get you lying on your belly."

****

"This table feels real comfortable, Braden."

Braden covered Shane's back and butt with one sheet folded in half and then overlapped another sheet over his butt that also covered his legs.

"That's because it was made for massages."

"Is there a cut out for your cock and balls?"

"No. They're used by happy endings massage parlors, and there's always a girl or guy under the table sucking or playing with the client's genitals. And besides, they'd get real cold hanging in the air. To confirm, you're giving me free rein, right?"

"Absolutely. I can't wait for whatever surprises you have in store for me."

"I have an idea then. Position your junk so that your penis and scrotum are pulled down, between your legs."

"This sounds interesting." Shane adjusted himself as instructed.

"Do you want a full body massage or should I concentrate on *the goods*? I only ask because it's been about an hour and a half since you got here. How long before your absence will raise suspicions?"

"I'm not worried about that at all. Hell, I could stay here all night and just say we got drunk, and I passed out on your sofa or the extra bed."

Braden pulled the sheet down from Shane's neck, uncovering his back, until it exposed the top of his butt crack. Then he poured oil from the small of his back to the base of his neck. "That feels so warm."

"Right out of the bottle warmer. It spreads better that way." Braden gripped Shane's shoulders and lifted and squeezed the muscles. Then he ran his hands down along his sides, across the top edge of his buttocks to the top of his crack and up his spine, repeating the movements again and again. Then he changed to alternating between circular motions and kneading each muscle group, pressing firmly as his hands glided and squeezed, glided and squeezed. When Braden used his elbow, Shane let out a deep groan that ended with a sigh.

As Braden finished and pulled the sheet over Shane's back, he was snoring softly. Braden was sure he was asleep when Shane didn't answer to his name being whispered. He uncovered Shane's right leg and repeated the same techniques he used on his back, but he added repetitive pulling movements, using his palms, from the inside of the leg over the top and down the outside.

When the right leg was completed, Braden pulled it out to the edge of the table, flexing the knee a little, and then covered it and repeated the same strokes on his left leg. Shane remained fast asleep the entire time. His breaths were heavy, and sighs and gentle moans escaped his mouth.

After positioning his left leg in the same way, Braden covered it and then lifted the bottom edge of the sheet to reveal Shane's buttocks. With his legs spread apart in a slight frog-like position, Braden had unrestricted access to Shane's cock, balls, and anus.

He poured warm oil over Shane's hairy, muscular gluteal mounds and drizzled it down his butt crack until it emerged to cover his scrotum and then overflowed onto his cock shaft, eventually bleeding into the sheet. He climbed onto the table and kneeled between Shane's thighs. Then he grasped each cheek firmly and began to push them up and out, exposing his anus. He began to knead the cheeks and pull them apart as he barely grazed his thumbs across the opening of Shane's hole. Shane's breathing changed from a steady rhythm to intermittent short gasps whenever Braden's thumbs found their mark.

When he focused his fingers in circular motions around the outer sphincter, Shane gasped, lifted his head, and then fell back to sleep. Ever so gently, Braden began to make the circles smaller and smaller until the outer sphincter relaxed and opened on its own. He rubbed the pad of his middle fingertip up and down the opening and slowly worked it in. He drizzled more oil over his finger and watched it slide into the opening as he advanced ever so slightly, repeating the circular motion until he met the resistance of the internal sphincter, but soon, it, too, opened and invited Braden to explore the depths of Shane's erogenous zone.

Shane began to moan softly in his sleep as Braden advanced deeper and deeper until he found the spongy, twin-mounds of his prostate. He reached down with his other hand and rubbed his thumb in a circular motion just beneath the back of Shane's glans, along the frenum and then traced his thumb up under his sack to the base of the shaft. Shane's cock began to swell and grow as it crept along the sheet like a turtle extending its head from its shell.

Braden reached under the shaft and lifted it from the sheet as he began to massage the head between his fingertips and his thumb, and then advanced his other finger deeper until it again pressed against Shane's growing prostate.

When Shane's moans deepened, Braden slid his fingers along the cock shaft to the base and back up to the tip, repeating the motion and intensifying the pressure. He was rewarded by the appearance of a bead of clear nectar, which he leaned down and licked with his tongue.

Shane opened his eyes. "Braden, oh, my, God. What are you doing to me? It's so good. It's so good. Don't stop. Whatever you're doing, please don't stop."

"Is this really good for you, Shane?"

"Yes. Yes, it's wonderful. It's amazing. It's like

nothing I've ever felt before."

"There's so much more I can do for you, if you want me to, or do you want to come now?"

"God, how can you make me choose? I could go on like this forever, but I want to come so badly. It's so wonderful. So wonderful. My asshole is vibrating. It's beautiful. Beautiful. I never knew I could experience such pleasure. There's such a warmth deep inside my groin, and it's spreading out all through my body and there's a tingling that's starting inside my cock. It's inside my prostate and my balls, too. You're a devil. You're a devil, Braden."

Braden leaned down again and sucked the glans of Shane's cock into his mouth as he began to rub his prostate in circular motions. A stream of sweet and musky nectar was expelled from the slit, followed by a steady trickle. Shane curled his toes and lifted his head, shaking it from side to side.

"So good. It's so good, Braden. God, you're incredible. I want to come so bad. I need to come. I need to come!"

"But, do you want to come … now? That's all I need to know, Shane. We've only grazed the surface of what I can do for you, but if you really want to come now, I'll give it to you."

"Devil! You devil! I want to come, but I don't. I want more. I want more. I can't believe there can be more than this. It's impossible. You're a liar. You're a liar, Braden. There can't be more than this. There can't be. It would kill me. You'd kill me."

"Do you want to experience something more intense than this, Shane? Do you?"

"Yes! Yes! Please, yes!"

"Very well."

Braden returned his mouth to Shane's cock and

began to suck. He pressed deeper with his finger against his prostate. Then he added a second finger, spreading Shane's anus apart even further. He began sliding his fingers in and out past the sphincters as he sucked harder and harder against Shane's straining shaft. When his fingers were buried to their hilt, he tapped Shane's prostate three times. Then he added a third finger, stretching Shane to the limits of his tolerance. Then he stopped.

"What are you doing? Why'd you stop? Don't stop!"

"To give you a break, Shane. I want this to build and build. I sensed you could come at any second, but I want to make this last for you, Shane."

"Oh, my, God. I can't take it!"

"But you want to take it. You want to. Trust me. You said you trust me, right, Shane?"

"Yes, but why are you torturing me?"

"I'm not torturing you, Shane, I'm preparing you."

Braden began again, slowly sliding his three fingers in and out of Shane's anus as he lowered his mouth to his glans and sucked it into his mouth. When his fingers were buried to the hilt, he made slow circular motions against the turgid gland, buried deep inside, causing it to shudder and spasm. He was rewarded with a fresh trickle of pre-cum.

"Oh … oh … oh, Braden, Braden!"

"I'm here, Shane. I'm here for you."

"Braden … oh, Braden, torture me … torture me!"

Braden stopped again, resting his fingers just inside the internal sphincter as he removed his mouth from his glans. He lifted Shane's shaft into his closed hand and squeezed it firmly, then released it, then squeezed it again. He slid his fingers round and round his anus, massaging the circular muscles between his thumb and fingertips until they lost all their tone.

Again, he began, advancing his three fingers in to their hilt, stroking Shane's hardening double-lobed orb, side to side and up and down, side to side and up and down. He took Shane's cock into his mouth again and sucked it to the back of his throat. Then he grazed over Shane's prostate in circular motions. It spasmed and hardened, and his trickle of pre-cum became a stream.

"Please, Braden … I'm ready … I'm ready to come."

"Soon, Shane … soon."

"Please make me come … Please! I can't … I can't take it anymore."

"Yes, Shane. It's been nearly forty-five minutes now. I think you're ready."

Braden pressed firmly against Shane's prostate pushing it over the edge from firm to rock hard while he slid Shane's cock head into his mouth and sucked it like he was drawing the cream out of the center of a donut.

Shane's cock began to spasm.

"I'm coming, Braden … I'm coming."

"Give it to me, Shane."

"Oh, God … I'm coming!"

Braden lifted the shaft further off the sheet and pressed it up against his P-spot between his balls and hole, effectively closing off the urethra, as he rammed his fingers in and out, pounding Shane's love nut while sucking his cockhead even more strongly. Shane's prostate quaked and quaked some more until it began to in spasm. Braden pulled his mouth away and watched the shaft and glans swell and darken with each attempted ejaculation as his vas deferens contracted and contracted, but they weren't strong enough to overcome the pressure he exerted against it. He went back down on the shaft and sucked it with all his might.

Shane's body began to shudder and bounce, and his legs pounded the table as he threw his head back trying to scream, but his throat clamped down tight. Nothing but a brief high-pitched rush of air escaped his mouth. His face turned a dark blue-purple color. He couldn't breathe at all.

After nineteen contractions, Shane's prostate went limp. His body collapsed, and his skin glistened with sweat that dripped down into the sheet. His breathing became deep and heavy as air began to rush back into his lungs, and his color began to lighten.

Chapter Eighteen
That's What the Books Say

Braden released Shane's still swollen, rock-hard cock and withdrew his fingers, but his anus gaped open after being ravaged by his unrelenting pounding. He gently kneaded the flaccid globes of Shane's buttocks and pulled the sheet to the floor. Then he closed Shane's legs and lay down on top of his body.

The head of Braden's semi-erect cock barely touched the opening of Shane's anus. He reached his arms around to Shane's chest and hugged him tightly. Tiny quivers rose from Shane's back. Braden hugged him even tighter. His shaft began to engorge and lengthen until its head pressed just into Shane's still gaping hole. His cock continued to grow as it entered the hole and began to snake its way into Shane's depths. Braden began to nibble the back of Shane's neck.

"No man … no man has ever done that to me," Shane whispered. "I can't even begin to describe it. I—I went somewhere. It's like … it's like I was someplace else. Where did you send me, Braden? Where was I?"

"I don't know, Shane, but I'm so happy it was good for you."

"Good? Braden, good doesn't even come close. There are no words strong enough, powerful enough to describe what it was. There just aren't any. It was the most unique and intense orgasm of my life."

"Oh, God, Shane, I'm inside you," Braden whimpered. "I didn't mean to. I'm sorry. I didn't mean to do it. Oh, God, my penis … I mean my cock is inside you!"

"Fuck me, Braden. Please, fuck me. Fill me with your seed."

"May I, Shane?" May I please?"

Braden's hips began to thrust against the muscular mounds of Shane's buttocks. "Oh, God! What's happening to me, Shane? I can't control it. I can't control myself. I'm fucking you, Shane. I'm fucking you. I don't think I can stop. I can't stop!"

"Yes, Braden, fuck me. Come inside me. Come inside me now!"

"God … Oh, God … Shane! Shane, I'm going to come."

"Give it to me, Braden."

"Shane, I'm coming!"

"Oh, Braden!"

"I'm coming inside you! I'm coming inside you, now!"

Braden hips drove against Shane's ass, impaling his cock deep within the recesses of Shane's rectum as he unloaded another wave of thick, hot cum. His thrusting became violent, striking and reddening Shane's buttocks as his balls made thwacking sounds as they slapped against him. As he continued his assault, Braden's spunk oozed out and was rammed back into Shane's depths.

Braden collapsed.

****

9:20 PM

"Shane, there's so much more for me to give to you, if you'll let me. I didn't get past the first stage."

"I can't believe it, Braden. It's not possible."

"I promise you there is. At least that's what the books say."

"You mean you really have never done that before … to anyone?"

"No, I really haven't, nothing. I've never done any of it. And you're the first man I ever made love to. I didn't fuck you, Shane. I made love to you. That's what it felt like to me. You're my first, and I'm glad it was you. We were the first for each other in different ways tonight."

"Can you climb off me, please, Braden? There's something I need to do."

"Sure." Braden struggled to lift his body up and then step to the floor. "Sorry, my legs are a little weak right now. What do you need to do?"

"This." Shane sat up. He reached out and pulled Braden to him and looked deep into his eyes. Then he took Braden's face into his hands and kissed him gently on the lips, keeping his eyes opened so he could see Braden's face. "Braden, I think I love you. No, I'm sure of it. I've never said that to anyone before, but I love you. I love you, Braden. I know I do. I'm in love with you.

"That place you took me. It was there where I realized I'd found the man I've been looking for my whole life. You've given me something I'll never find with another man. I'm in love with you, Braden."

"Shane, you can't mean that. It's touching that you said it, but it's the orgasm talking right now. It's just not possible. We only met yesterday."

"But, Braden, didn't you just say you made love to me?"

"Really, Shane. Don't say it again. You'll only regret it. You'll realize that tomorrow, after your head has cleared."

"Okay, I'll stop, but I know I'm right."

"Shane, please don't."

"I'm sorry. I'll stop."

"Thank you. Now I still have to work on your pulled groin muscle. Just give me a few minutes to regain my strength. Lie back down on the table please."

"Really, you want to do more? I can barely feel my groin."

"You'll feel it tomorrow, I promise you. Your body is coursing with endorphins right now. They're natural narcotics produced by your brain. If you don't let me work on it tonight, you're going to be even more stiff tomorrow than you were when you came here."

"I'll do anything you tell me to, Braden. I trust you."

"I'm going to get some orange juice. Do you want some?"

"Yeah, that would be great."

Chapter Nineteen
Release Again, Then Relief

9:35 PM

After Shane lay back on the table, Braden covered him and exposed his left groin and thigh. "I can feel the injury, Shane. The muscles and ligaments are inflamed. Close your eyes and try to let yourself drift off. You may be tender here, but I'm going to use some techniques that could stimulate an erection again. It's normal if it happens."

"It's impossible, Braden. There's no way I could get hard again. Not after what you just put me through. I'm done. It wouldn't surprise me if I couldn't get hard for another month."

"If you say so. If you do get an erection, do you want me to ignore it?"

"It won't happen, Braden. I'm telling you."

"Okay, whatever you say."

Braden began with very focused fingertip pressure directed gently into Shane's left groin. Shane winced and sucked in his breath, but he didn't complain, so Braden continued. Then he began to vibrate the area by rapidly shaking his fingertips as he pressed downward, deeper. Shane relaxed some more.

When Braden moved his fingers in circular motions up into the rock-hard muscles of Shane's lower abdomen, Shane began to take slower, deeper breaths. He moved his fingers in circles across Shane's pubic bone, just above the base of his shaft and then down between it and the crease between his thigh and scrotum as he pulled and pushed with steady force until the muscles moved freely under his fingers. With each pull and push against the muscles, his fingers brushed against Shane's scrotum. With each pass, it contracted and pulled up towards the base of the shaft.

Braden moved down to the top of the inside of Shane's thigh, repeating the same circular motions, causing his fingers to pass beneath Shane's scrotum. Shane's cock began to thicken and move on its own.

Braden climbed onto the table and straddled his body so that his back was to Shane's face. He placed his palms and fingers between Shane's thighs and against his perineum and his thumbs over the manicured pubic mound. He leaned down and began to firmly and slowly knead the area like bread dough, increasing blood flow to the muscles in the region, but the left thigh muscles and groin were not the only parts of Shane's body to benefit from his touch. Each time Braden squeezed and lifted, surges of blood were forced into Shane's shaft, and it grew rapidly, making the glans swell until it purpled.

"Braden," Shane whispered. "I didn't believe you, but you were right. I think I feel my cock getting hard again."

"Shane, you're rock hard and your scrotum just went limp. Your balls are resting on the sheet. God, your cock is huge from this angle, and it's dripping pre-cum at an amazing rate. Do you still trust me, Shane?"

"Yes, Braden. I'd trust you with my life." Shane began to take deep, slow breaths.

"May I go down on you? I really want to do this. I've never experienced it before, and I want yours to be the first cum I taste. May I?"

"Yes, Braden. Yes."

"Then prepare yourself. You might have an orgasm even stronger than the first one because you didn't ejaculate at all. All that cum is still packed in your ducts, and your body's shifted even more semen and pre-cum into the area because it thinks you already came."

"Yes, Braden. Dominate me. I'm your servant.

Do whatever you want to me."

Braden climbed down and moved to the foot of the table. He reached underneath and removed the two stirrup leg supports and hooked them into their slots. "Shane, slide your butt down towards me to the edge of the table. I'm going to lift your legs into stirrups so I can use my mouth on your anus without you having to lift your legs."

"Oh, yes, Braden. Yes!"

Once Shane was in position, Braden placed his hands in a circle around Shane's fully erect cock and balls and with his thumbs pressed firmly against his P-spot. He began to knead and lift the underlying muscles again with his powerful grip as he leaned his face in and began to lick Shane's anus. Shane's cockhead swelled with each contraction of Braden's hands and fresh pre-cum began to bead at the slit.

"Oh, oh, oh, Braden," Shane moaned.

Shane's anus had finally closed. Braden shaped his tongue into a wedge and pressed and wiggled it inward, causing Shane's external sphincter to relent against the assault. Braden slowed the pace of his massage, but applied greater pressure causing the muscles to turn to putty under his hands. As he squeezed, Shane's rock-hard cock bounced and filled some more. Braden pulled his tongue out and rose to move his mouth over the nectar beading at Shane's cock slit. When he lowered his mouth and began to suck on the head, he was rewarded with a stream of pre-cum- mixed with the some of the semen that had made its way into the urethra.

"Suck me. Oh, suck me … oh, Braden, Braden!" Shane began to pant. He tossed his head from side to side and squeezed his nipples, causing them to swell and redden.

Braden released Shane's cock and returned to his

ass, driving his tongue in deeper as he sucked the sensitive skin into his mouth. Shane's body convulsed with violent tremors, nearly throwing him off the table, but he grabbed the edges and held on. When Braden's tongue pierced through the last barrier he slid it into the depths of Shane's rectum and plied the opening apart with his fingertips, tasting the remnants of his cum, as he began to devour the tender flesh.

Shane began to slide his body up and down the table, driving his ass into Braden's face. "Fuck me, Braden. Please, fuck me!"

"Shane, this is going to be different. If you really want to come again, it's going to take a lot more stimulation than what I think I could give you with my cock."

"Don't question it, Braden. You're a sex master, a sex master."

"There's something else I can use that will drive you wild."

"Then do it! Do it, Braden!"

Braden let go and reached under his bed. He pulled out the box that Jason and Aaron gave him. He took out a package and broke open its seal, then removed a black, oddly U-shaped prostate massager with a thick, bulbous head on the end. After inserting the battery and lubing it up, he brushed just the tip of the bulb against Shane's hole. Teasingly he moved it up and down as Shane's hips thrust back and forth over the edge of the table.

"Braden, what is it?"

Braden eased the tip of the head into Shane's hole and pulled it back out, then eased it in further and pulled it out again.

"Oh, oh … Oh, my God! Yes, yes, Braden … Braden! Ram it in me!"

"Trust me, Shane." Braden eased it in again until the full size of the bulb stretched both of Shane's sphincters open and held it in place.

"It's big, whatever it is," Shane said.

"It's a little bigger than you are, Shane. It's eight inches around. How does it feel?"

"It's amazing. Is there more?"

"There's a lot more, Shane."

He pushed it in further until the bulb was sucked in, disappearing into Shane's depths, leaving the thinner shaft pressing against the sphincter muscles and the handle pressing against his P-spot.

"Oh, I feel it inside me, Braden. It's filling me up. It's pressing on my prostate."

"That's the idea. If you contract your anus, you'll feel it move and press even more."

Shane squeezed tight and immediately lurched upward. He groaned. "Oh, God! That's amazing!"

"Contract whenever you want to feel that, Shane. I'm going to suck your cock now."

Braden leaned over and wrapped his lips around Shane's glans and began to suck it. Then he lifted his ball sack and began to massage each ball with a hand as he slid his mouth down the shaft until it hit the back of his throat. Braden's cock began to grow, too.

Shane contracted his anus muscles. "I can't—I can't take it. I can't … take it, Braden. Braden … Braden. It's too intense. It's so intense."

Braden released Shane's balls and wrapped his right hand around his cock, stretching the skin downward as he slid his mouth up and down the shaft. He made a ring with his left thumb and fingers and gently tugged against the nectar-filled balls, stretching the sack away from the base of his cock. Shane sat up and reached between his legs to grab hold of Braden's head. He began to push it down.

Braden pulled away. "No, Shane, you've got to let me do this."

"But I need to come, Braden. I need to come. Make me come, please!"

"I will. I promise I will. Keep squeezing your ass to press the head of the massager against your prostate. You'll be rewarded, trust me."

Braden's cock had filled and was now pressing against the edge of the table. He returned his mouth to Shane's shaft, but slowed his pace so he could linger over the glans. He drove the tip of his tongue into the slit to open it and then focused his mouth over it to suck out the pre-cum that filled his urethra. As he drew it over his tongue, he rolled it around his mouth, savoring the freshness of the musky, viscous liquid.

Shane threw his head from side to side and began to thrusts his pelvis into Braden's face, forcing the pre-cum and old cum to be expelled from the head. Braden swallowed every drop. He pumped Shane's shaft faster, then slowed, then sped up again as he gripped Shane's cock even tighter.

"Make … make me … me come. Make me … make me come. Braden … Braden! Make me come!"

Braden made a ring with his thumb and fingers and quickly pummeled the ridges of Shane's cockhead, using the oozing cum as lubricant. Then he reached down and pressed the button on the massager, bringing the vibrating bullet encased within the it to life. As it began to create continuous, glancing blows across Shane's spasming prostate, Shane began to whimper.

"Please, Braden … please. I'm begging you."

Braden's prostate tightened.

"Shane, please don't whimper. Please don't make that sound. It makes me … it makes me—I'm going to

… I'm going to—"

Braden lunged forward, ramming his cock between Shane's cheeks against the massager. His buttock, thigh, and back muscles spasmed, locking him in place. His fist tightened around Shane's shaft, pummeling it as Shane thrust his hips up and down. They exploded together.

Braden lowered his mouth and greedily swallowed Shane's spunk. It was a massive load. Thick ribbons of white, glistening, musky nectar rushed into his mouth. He pressed his face against Shane's pelvis, forcing his massive, rigid cock past the back of his throat. He felt each surge as Shane's urethra swelled and pressed against his tongue until the load was forced into his esophagus, creating a warm sensation as each wave of Shane's spunk slid towards his stomach.

Braden's cum spewed against his chin and across his face until it dripped down onto Shane's belly. As Braden lifted his head, it continued to fly and landed on Shane's chest and face, covering the front of him.

When it was over, Braden fell to the side half landing on his bed, half on the floor where he gasped for breath.

Shane's arms fell out to the sides over the edge of the table. His anus couldn't relax. The massage was still pounding his prostate, forcing it to contract in spasms. Braden reached for the power button, but was too weak to stand. Shane's body lurched up and down, uncontrollably.

When he recovered, Braden lifted himself from the floor and sat on the bed. Shane's body flailed as he tried to remove his legs from the stirrups, but he didn't have any strength left in them. When Braden finally reached up and turned off the massager, Shane collapsed.

When he finally stopped gasping for air, he

spoke. "Braden, you were right. You were right. I didn't believe you, but you were right. It was huge! I haven't come twice in the same day in such a short span of time since I was twenty. You're amazing."

Braden smiled. "I'll help you up, but I need a minute myself."

After Braden eased the massager out of Shane's ravaged hole, he helped him to sit up. Shane nearly fell off the table, but Braden caught him and steadied him until he was able to hold himself up. Finally, he was able to speak. "Braden, I can't make it back to the barracks. There's just no way."

"I'm not surprised. Sorry about what just happened. I had no idea it could cause such violent reactions. I probably shouldn't have pushed you like that."

"Are you kidding? No! It was fantastic! It's just that I'm wiped out."

"You can sleep here, but we're going to have to get your clothes back on you, just in case someone comes looking for you."

"You're right. Thanks. We should probably tap that bottle and take a few shots so that we'll smell like alcohol in the morning. Otherwise my story won't hold water."

"I'll go get it," Braden said.

Chapter Twenty
Discovered

10:55 PM

Braden returned with the whiskey and two glasses and poured about three shots into each of them. They drank it down and then Braden poured a good amount into the toilet and flushed it to make it look like they'd drunk a good three-quarters of the bottle. Then he set it on the night table. He helped Shane into his jock and then his clothes, and guided him to one of the two double beds. After folding up his massage table and putting it in the closet he returned.

Shane lifted his arm towards Braden so Braden crawled onto the bed next to him. He pulled Braden in tight and kissed him on the lips.

As he drifted off to sleep, Shane whispered, "I love you, Braden. I really love you."

Once Braden was sure Shane was asleep, he crawled into his own bed and was asleep almost as soon as his head hit the pillow.

****

Wednesday, January 6, 2010, 12:05 AM

When no one answered the door, Ryan, the security guard, silently slipped into Braden's cottage. Not finding anyone in the living room, he made his way down the hallway to the bedroom with his flashlight pointed to the floor. Braden woke up. "Who's there?"

"It's me, Braden. Officer Ryan. I've been looking for Shane. I can't find him anywhere. He hasn't come back to the barracks."

"He's here." Braden pointed to the other bed as Ryan came through the door. "He was in quite a bit of pain and polished off more than half the bottle of whiskey he brought, but I had some, too." Braden pointed to the bottle on the night table next to Shane. "There was no way I could get him back to his quarters, and I didn't think it was a good idea for anyone to see him like that, so I helped him to the other bed to sleep it off. I hope that was okay?"

"Sure, Braden, sure." Ryan wrinkled his nose.

What's that smell? Ryan thought to himself. *That's not just booze. Oh, wow, it's … that's cum! Wow! Shane and Braden? They went at it?*

"Sorry to bother you," Ryan said aloud, "but we had to be sure nothing happened to him."

"A bottle of whiskey is what happened to him, that's all. I tried to stop him, but what could I do against someone as big as he is? I'm sure he's going to pay for it in the morning."

"You're probably right there. Were you able to help him? I know he was in a lot of pain when he headed over here."

"Yes, I think we made some progress and worked out some of his stiffness, but he did a real number on himself. It may take a good week and a few more sessions before he's back to normal. We had a great talk afterwards. He's a really nice guy."

"Very good, glad to hear it, and you're right. He is. I'll let myself out then. Good night, Braden."

"Good night, Ryan."

No mistaking that smell, Ryan thought to himself as he closed the door behind him. *No mistaking that smell at all, but that's Shane's business. Braden "worked out some of his stiffness", huh? I'll bet. Just what kind of talents does this Braden have? I wonder.*

I've had my own stiffness to deal with, and it ain't easy to take care of in such tight quarters, bunking with a bunch of other guys, buy hey, I'm open-minded. I wonder if Braden would consider? Nah, not even going to go there. Too risky, but how long are they going to be able to keep it a secret from the chief? He's not going to hear it from me, nope, that's for sure. No, nobody's going to hear it from me.

****

8:15 AM

"Braden, Braden wake up. Braden wake up." Shane gently shook Braden's shoulder.

"Huh? What?"

"Braden, wake up. It's after eight. Everybody else has been up for hours. They're gonna wonder where I got to."

"Shane?"

"Yeah, it's me, remember?"

"Remember? What are you doing in my cottage?"

"Braden, last night. Remember last night?"

"Oh, wow, yeah, I think so. Oh, yeah, last night, sorry, I was really out of it. I don't drink alcohol that often. It knocks me for a loop. What do you remember?"

"I remember the most incredible night of my life, Braden. That's what I remember. You've ruined me. I can never be with another man, not after you. Not after what you did to me last night."

"So, I didn't dream it. It really happened?"

"Braden, it really happened. It's the next day, and you were wrong."

"What? What was I wrong about?"

"It wasn't the orgasms talking. It wasn't the whiskey talking. It's not only possible, it's real!"

"Shane, what are you talking about?"

"I'm going to say this slowly and clearly, so there's no way you can misunderstand me. I know we only met two days ago. Yes, my head is very clear. No, I don't regret a thing, and I'm going to say it again, and again, and again. I love you, Braden. I'm in love with you.

"Maybe you don't love me back. Maybe you can't right now. I know this is a lot to take in, but I know it at the depth of my soul to be true. If I have to spend the rest of my life convincing you of how I feel, I'll do it, and if I have to spend the rest of my life making you fall in love with me, I'll do that, too. I love you, Braden Darby. I love you."

"Oh, Shane!" Braden jumped out of his bed and into Shane's arms, wrapping his legs around his waist in the process. He hugged Shane as he kissed his face, his eyes, his nose and cheeks, and his mouth. "Oh, Shane, yes, yes, I love you, too. Oh, shit! Your groin! I forgot. I'm sorry."

"Braden, I'm fine, as long as I don't try to walk, but you should probably get down. We shouldn't push it."

"How does it feel?"

"It's tight, but it's so much better than it was last night. I feel a little tugging, but nothing like the pain I had yesterday."

"You're right, Shane. We shouldn't push it. You could reinjure it in a heartbeat. Your groin is at a vulnerable point right now, and you'll probably feel pain off and on, the more you use it."

"It's not the only thing that's vulnerable right now, Braden. My heart is, too. I don't know what to do. I want to shout to the world that I'm in love, but that's childish."

"It's not childish to want to do that, Shane, not at all, not if it's how you really feel, but you should probably take some time to think it out. Like you said, you'll have to tell your father at some point, and you'll have to think about how it'll affect your career."

"I'm not ashamed of it, Braden. Are you?"

"No, not at all, but this is all so new to me. Just as new as it is to you, I'm sure. We should give it some time and let it all settle in."

"Are you afraid, Braden?"

"A little, but I'm not going to let that affect how I feel about you. We just have to be mindful of how we act."

"Why? Look at Mr. Jason and Mr. Aaron. They're not afraid. They're living their lives right out in the open."

"Yeah, but they're rich. They have that luxury. We don't, and we work for them."

"I think I understand what you're saying, but remember, Mr. Jason said there's jobs for both of us with Nathan's Promise, if we want them."

"Shane, would you want to leave your father's company? It's something you'll really need to think about. Look, we could talk about this 'til the cows come home, but right now we have to think about the next hour, the next day, the next week. It's like you just said, people are going to wonder where you are, and if I don't show my face soon, they're going to wonder where I am, too."

"You're right."

"I need some coffee before I do anything. You want some?"

"Yeah, I already put the pot on before I woke you up. It should be done by now. I'll head back to my quarters after I have a cup."

"You better brush your teeth before you have that coffee, Shane. I can still smell cum on your breath, even through the remnants of the whiskey. The toothpaste will remove the smell and the coffee will wash away the mint from the toothpaste."

"Good idea."

****

Braden walked out onto the porch in a robe and slippers, sipping from a steaming mug. He breathed in the fresh, crisp air as he blew across the top of the mug to cool it. Officer Ryan waved from the window of the security office and then stuck his head out the front door. "How's Shane this morning?"

"He's still asleep. He tied a good one on last night, but I'll wake him up in a minute. I just needed some coffee before I start my day."

"Very good, Braden, I'll see you later."

****

"Oh, wow."

"What is it, Braden?"

"The smell."

"What smell?"

"The smell of sweat, and musk, and cum. Stale cum. The whole place reeks of it. It smells like a locker room mixed with sex in here. It's not just your breath." Braden smelled himself, then smelled Shane. "Shane, we're both covered in it. It wasn't until I came back inside that it hit me. We're covered in sex."

Shane smelled his sweatshirt. "I can't go back to my quarters smelling like this. What am I going to do?"

"Get in my shower. I'll think of something."

****

As Braden approached the security office, Ryan came out to meet him. "Hey, Braden, what's up?"

"Ryan, I'm really sorry to put you in this position, but can you keep a secret?"

"Is something wrong?"

"Well, not really. I need a change of clothes for Shane."

"Why? What happened?"

"He stinks like booze, and his clothes do, too. He

says he can't let the rest of the security staff smell him like that because he's the boss's son. Can you get me a pair of his sweats from his locker?"

"Everyone's either on patrol or over in the main cabin having breakfast. He can sneak back over. I won't say a word. Cross my heart."

"That's great, but he's already in my shower. Can you get me a pair for him anyway?"

"Sure, sure, I'll be right back."

****

"Here you go, but I have to tell you something, Braden."

"What's that?"

A sheepish expression creeped over Ryan's face. "I think that whatever is on Shane is on you, too. You're rather ripe. You might want to take a shower before you go to breakfast."

Braden staggered for a moment.

"Are you okay? The color just drained out of your face."

"I'm sorry. I'm sorry to involve you in this, Ryan."

"Braden, I smelled it last night when I came into your cottage. I smelled everything last night, but don't worry. Your secret is safe with me. Both your and Shane's secret is safe with me."

"What?"

"I mean it. I've been thinking about this since I left your cottage, about how I feel about it. It doesn't bother me, not in the least. This morning I realized that I'm happy for Shane, really for both of you. He's been lonely for a long time. I sensed it when I first met him, and that hasn't changed for as long as I've known him. Just promise me something."

"Promise you?"

Ryan put his hand on Braden's shoulder. "Yeah, please don't hurt him, Braden. He doesn't look it, not a big guy like him, but he's a real sensitive soul, and he's a good guy. Please, don't hurt him. That's all I ask."

As Braden walked away, Ryan thought, *I was out of line even thinking that last night. There's no way I'm going to jeopardize Shane's happiness by approaching Braden to help me blow a load, but if things don't turn out for them, then maybe I'll reconsider it.*

****

8:55 AM

Shane called from the bathroom when he heard the front door close. "Were you able to get me something to wear?"

Braden walked into the steamy bathroom as Shane was toweling himself off. "Yes, Shane, but I think you'll want to sit down." Braden handed Shane his sweats.

"What's wrong, Braden? You look like you saw a ghost or something."

"Baby. Can I call you, baby?"

"Yes, I love the sound of it coming from you."

"Ryan knows."

"What do you mean, 'Ryan knows'?"

"Ryan knows about us, about what we did last night."

"Shit! How? I don't understand."

"I forgot all about it. He came in here after you fell asleep, sometime after midnight. I think I had just fallen asleep myself. He was looking for you because you hadn't returned."

"And?"

"I'm sorry, Shane. I forgot."

"It's okay, Braden. Tell me what he said."

"He said he was looking for you to be sure

something hadn't happened to you. I told him you got drunk 'cause you were in so much pain, and that you'd passed out; and I knew I couldn't get you back to your quarters by myself and that I didn't think it was a good idea for your coworkers to see you like that, so I helped you to the other bed to let you sleep it off."

"That's a very reasonable explanation."

"He agreed. He also asked if I was able to help you."

"And what did you say?"

"I said I was able to help you some, but that you might need a few sessions before you were back to normal."

"That's true, too."

"Yeah, I know that, but just now, when I went to the security office to ask him for a change of clothes for you, I told him it was because you smelled like booze. Oh, God, he tried to give me an out for you, but I didn't take it."

"What do you mean, 'an out'?"

"He said everyone was either on patrol or eating breakfast and that you could sneak back in and that he wouldn't tell anyone."

"And?"

"I said you were in my shower. It's all my fault, Shane. I told you to take a shower here. I'm so sorry."

"Braden, baby, calm down. You've done nothing wrong. The only thing you've been is kind and loving. This is not on you at all. It's on me."

"Shane, when he came back with your sweats, he said that whatever was on you, meaning what you smelled like, was on me, too. He said I smelled 'ripe' and that I should take a shower before anyone smelled me, too. He said he could smell it when he was in here last night, that he '*smelled everything last night*'. He said, our secret is safe with him."

"Maybe he just meant that we got drunk, that he smelled the booze."

"No, Shane, he said he'd been thinking about *it* since last night, about how he felt about *it*. He said *it* didn't bother him. Then he said he realized he was happy for both of us, that he was happiest for you, but happy for both of us.

"Now, here's the clincher, he said you've been lonely for a long time, that he'd sensed it when he first met you and then he asked me to promise him that I wouldn't hurt you. He said that you don't look it, but that you're real sensitive and that you're a good guy. Then he said it again, not to hurt you."

Tears formed in Shane's eyes, and then he began to cry.

"It's okay, Shane. It's going to be okay. We're going to find a way out of this, I promise you. I'll take the blame for it. I'll say I took advantage of you. That I got you drunk. That you weren't a willing participant. That I put drugs into your drink. That when you passed out I tied you down and then I raped you."

Shane began to speak through his tears. "Oh, God! No, Braden, no, I could never let you do that. It would ruin you. You'd never be able to practice as a nurse or as a massage therapist ever again. You'd go to jail for it."

"Shane, you've got more to lose than me."

"Don't minimize yourself like that, Braden. Look, I love you for saying it all, but that's not why I'm crying."

"Then why?"

"Because someone knows. It's not a secret any more. It's like a huge weight has been lifted off my shoulders. I can breathe now. Whether Ryan ever says anything or not, he's accepted me for who I am. Oh, God, someone's accepted me for who I am!"

Section Three
Bringing in Reinforcements

Chapter Twenty-One
We Need to Talk

9:40 AM

Aaron glanced up from the dining room table where he sat looking over several typed-up pages. "Good morning, Braden, you're here rather late."

Braden's brow furrowed. "Good morning, Aaron."

"I missed you at breakfast. Is everything all right?"

"I'm fine. Is Jason around?"

"He will be. He's in the barn right now with the animals and Lars. It wouldn't surprise me if he's trying to eradicate all evidence that that bastard was here. He's still dealing with what he did to him."

"He will for a while. You, too, I think."

"Yeah, I lost it yesterday for a minute, but I'm better now. I'm trying to stay focused."

"That's good. It'll take time for you both, each in your own way. Jason doesn't impress me as someone who can sit still for too long."

"He better not let Conrad find him out there. He'll really catch it then. Jason knows he shouldn't be doing anything, but he's had Lars moving things around in there since yesterday. I didn't go with them this morning 'cause I wanted to go over yesterday's notes before we have another meeting. I'm trying to take up some of the load so that he doesn't have to try to do everything, not that I think it will make much of a difference. It wouldn't surprise me if he's out there right now, working beside Lars, 'cause I'm not there to stop him."

"From the little I know of Jason, I think you're right. He impresses me as someone who has always been very physically active."

"He is. It's probably healthy for him in a way. He needs to work through what happened to him, and if this is his way, I'm not going to be the one to stop him. I just wish he would pace himself."

"He'll find his balance. About Jason—"

"Oh, sorry, you said you were looking for him."

"Yes, I am."

"You look like you have something on your mind."

"I do. Would you and Jason have some time to talk sometime today?"

"Both of us need to talk to you, Mr. Aaron." Braden turned, and Aaron looked behind him to see Shane gingerly walk into the dining room, still favoring his left leg.

"Uh oh, did something happen?"

"We need to talk in private, Mr. Aaron."

"Okay, I'll find Jason, and then we can sit down."

"Please don't bother him, Mr. Aaron. Whenever you have time later on will be fine."

"Okay. Oh, by the way, we got a call from your father, Shane. He's not going to be back until Saturday at the earliest or Monday at the latest. Something to do with another client. He asked if you were available, but Jason told him he hadn't seen you yet."

"Thank you, Mr. Aaron. He left a message for me in the office. I've already spoken with him."

"Good morning, boys," Charity said as she walked in. "Are you hungry? You missed breakfast, but I can whip up something for you real quick. What would you like?"

"I don't want to be any bother, Miss Charity," Braden answered.

"I'll wait until lunch, Miss Charity," Shane added. "Thanks for offering though."

"It's no bother at all. You're growing boys, and you've got to eat. Now what would you like?"

"Thank you, Miss Charity," Braden answered. "If it really is no bother, whatever is easiest."

"That's very kind of you, Miss Charity," Shane said, "but I'll just have a bowl of cereal. I can get it myself."

"You'll do no such thing. A big man like you? That'll never fill you up. Now what will you have?"

"I'll have whatever Braden is having. Thank you, ma'am."

"Long time since someone's called me ma'am," Charity folded her arms in front of herself. Then a faraway look appeared on her face.

"I'm sorry, Miss Charity. I meant no disrespect."

"None taken. It's a sign of respect from where I come from. It's rather nice to hear it again," she said wistfully. "Now I'll be back before you can miss me."

After Charity walked out of the dining room, Aaron addressed them. "Can you guys give me a hint?"

"We should wait to talk to you both, Mr. Aaron." Shane pulled out a chair and sat down at the table. He didn't say another word.

****

"How's this, boys?" Charity carried in two heaping, steaming plates.

"It looks wonderful, Miss Charity," Shane answered.

"Thanks, Miss Charity," Braden added.

"Not at all, just leave your plates on the table when you're finished. Now I've got to get back to preparing lunch. We've got two newcomers arriving this morning. They should be here any time now, according to Mr. Rod."

****

10:55 AM

Jason walked out to the porch as the group approached the cabin. "Welcome, welcome, both of you."

"Boy, Jason, you weren't kidding." Claudia climbed the stairs and gave him a hug. "The place really has changed. How are you managing?"

"We're doing fine, Claudia. Winston, thank you for coming up, too."

"Are you kidding?" Winston shook Jason's hand and followed it with a hug. "I'm away from the office and out in nature for the first time in … in I don't know how long. I'd never miss a chance like this."

"I'll put your luggage in your cottages." Jack scooted around them and went in past Charity who stood holding the front door.

"Claudia, Winston, please meet Miss Charity Hopewell, our Chief of Household Operations," Jason said.

"And cook, Mr. Jason, and cook. Now all of you, come inside before you get yourselves a bad case of the frostbite." Charity beamed as she waved them in. "Please hang your coats on the hooks along the front wall. I think Mr. Jason wants everyone in the dining room, so have yourselves a seat. There's a pot of coffee and hot water for tea and some nibbles on a tray. Make yourselves comfortable. Lunch will be served promptly at noon. Hello, Mr. Rod. How was the flight?"

"It was good, Miss Charity, but I'll be glad to get inside where it's warm. Big Daddy has heat, but not enough this morning. I didn't let him get warmed up enough before we took off."

"Well, it's supposed to be a sunny day, and that will help to speed the work crews along. The weekend is supposed to be nice, too, or so I'm told."

"That's good. With the additional units to be added now, we'll need all the breaks we can get. I'm not sure whether Jack and I are going to be needed to stay the weekend. We didn't bring any luggage with us this trip, but we should still have at least a couple changes of clothes in our cottage."

"I can always wash and dry whatever you're not wearing in just a few hours. Don't you worry about a thing. as far as that's concerned."

Chapter Twenty-Two
Non-negotiable

1:15 PM
Jason and Aaron's office

"Well, this is certainly nice, Jason," Winston said. "From the outside I'd never expect to find an office this luxurious."

"I have to give all the credit to Rod. He's the mastermind behind all the additions, renovations, and construction, and with the crew he hired, they've all worked miracles. This unit wasn't even on the grounds two days ago. He's contracted with another air transport company to supplement his choppers and to handle all the heavy-duty construction materials, housing units sections, and supplies."

Aaron placed a tray with coffee cups on the table and then handed them out as he addressed them. "It's been nonstop around here from dusk to dawn with choppers coming and going, and the crews continue to work well into the night. From one hour to the next, you can visually track the changes that are taking place."

"Looks to me like you found yourself an operations manager," Claudia said.

"I wish, but no," Jason answered. "Rod's made it clear he doesn't want to give up his business. He's really doing us the biggest of favors right now."

"Do you have someone in mind? I can make inquiries if you like," Claudia said.

Aaron opened his portfolio. "Yes, as a matter of fact we do, but we'll have to move carefully. We owe her boss big time, and we don't want to upset the apple cart."

"Who is it?"

"You know her." Jason smirked. "It's Penelope Whitley."

"From Hinnen Valley Medical Center?" Claudia's jaw dropped. "*That* Penelope Whitley?"

"The one and only."

"That's quite a turnaround from two weeks ago, Jason, but I'll make some inquiries into her qualifications for you."

"You won't have to. We've invited both Penelope and Simone Jones up for the weekend. I'm going to be talking with Simone tomorrow to finalize their time schedule. I'll feel her out then. Now, about that other matter with Chief Steinecker."

"I've asked a friend of mine to get in touch with him. Joshua Bergmann is the best criminal attorney I know. I haven't heard back from him since we talked earlier this morning. He said he'd get right on it."

"A criminal attorney? Why?"

"Just in case. You didn't give me much to go on so I thought it best to arm for bear. If he doesn't think he'll be needed, he'll back out and refer your chief to someone more qualified to his needs."

"Very good. I'm going to turn this over to Aaron now. I've been threatened with mutiny by Conrad if I don't take it easy. Aaron?"

"Thanks, Jason. We had our brainstorming meeting yesterday, and the group has really come up with some great ideas and suggestions for Nathan's Promise. We're going to want to get moving on this ASAP. We'd like to get architectural and construction firms involved even before we have an idea of where we're going to build it. What have you learned about the land? Can it be done up here?"

Claudia scratched her nose, then let out a long breath. "Technically? Yes. There's nothing in the local laws to prevent it, but there's some hoops we'll have to jump through."

"But, you're sure we can do it?"

"Absolutely. We'll need to decide how we're going to structure the company. Whether it will be run by a board. Whether it'll be for, or not-for-profit, those kinds of things."

Jason sat up straight in his chair. He couldn't remain quiet. "I'll tell you right now, it's going to be Aaron's and mine. We're going to make all the big decisions."

"There's some tax breaks if you involve the public and public funding in it, Jason," Winston interjected.

"We can talk about how best to get the public involved, Winston, but Aaron and I are going to maintain control. That's non-negotiable!"

Claudia cleared her throat. "Just keep in mind, you're going to want to take insurance money, and that's probably going to involve government hands in the pot, that is unless you're planning to foot all the costs. You simply can't pay for it all yourselves, indefinitely. If you don't take insurance money, where's it going to come from? Are you going to expect the athletes to pay?"

"No, not at all. Aaron and I have thought about this a lot, and we can't help but believe the athletes will want to make donations voluntarily, at least some of them, but we would never expect it of them. What we've got to do is involve big money donors. There's got to be some super wealthy gay men and women out there, or at least wealthy, open minded, gay friendly people. I can't believe I'm the only one.

"Personally, I've lived off the grid for so long, that I wouldn't know where to start. That's one of the reasons we're bringing Simone and Penelope up here this weekend, to pick their brains and learn how they raise donations for the medical center."

"That's a good idea, Jason." Winston opened a binder. "Now, about your portfolio…"

"Yes. Lay it on us, Winston."

"You're doing quite well. You've made just over fifty million this past week, but I expect that number to double or triple for a few weeks, very soon. We've made some real lucrative investments. A lot of them are for the greater good, just as you directed. I also expect the big ones we've maintained in the tech market to really pay off over the next few months. The expenses you've incurred these past two weeks are negligible, well under half a day's income as far as you're concerned. They barely register on your spreadsheet."

"I'm glad to hear it. While we're on the subject, I want you both to come up with a plan to buy two large companies and one smaller one."

"What are they, Jason?" Claudia asked.

Aaron looked at Jason. "You never mentioned this to me."

"I know, Aaron, I'm sorry. I want us to buy the Nevada Bighorns, Channel 18 News, and I want our own security service for Nathan's Promise. I'd like to make an offer to buy Steinecker Security Systems before we look elsewhere."

"Really, Jason?" Aaron asked.

"Yes."

"Why?"

"If we can't buy the first two outright, then I want us to own a controlling share in the first two. There's some people I want to see fired from both of them. If we can't buy Steinecker then we'll start our own security service, but I think we should give them first crack at it."

"Jason, aren't you going a little overboard, I mean with the team and the TV station?" Aaron asked.

"No, Aaron, the Nevada Bighorns are trying to

shaft you. They fired you because you're gay, and that news station violated my privacy—our privacy. I want to make sure that both of them won't do the same to anyone else, ever again."

"Jason, I've gotten over it."

"I understand that, but you shouldn't have had to get over anything. The team did you wrong, and the news station did both of us wrong. I want to see to it that they both pay for it, dearly."

"What about the security company?" Claudia asked.

"However we negotiate Steinecker, if we can't buy it outright, I want us to hold a controlling share, just like the other two, but I want the chief to be able to hold onto a big chunk of it, that is, if he wants it. I also want him to run it for as long as he wants. Make him an offer he can't refuse."

"What's your limit?" Winston asked. "I only ask so I have an idea before we begin negotiations."

"Let's start with five million. That should give him a nice nest egg to retire on."

"I know better than to argue with you Jason, but that price is astronomical for such a small company, however, consider it done."

"Is there anything else?" Claudia asked.

"Yes, I'm now certain that both Aaron and I need a secretary or a personal assistant, or something along those lines, but we're going to try to find him or her through in-house references so you don't need to bother yourselves with that at the moment. If we can't, then we'll ask you to become involved. That's all I have, other than, how did you find your cottages?"

"They're like suites, like five-star hotel suites," Winston answered, "and they're wonderful."

****

2:15 PM

There was a knock outside the office door. "Come in," Aaron called out.

"Oh, Miss Charity, thank you for giving us a few minutes of your time. Please, make yourself comfortable." Jason waved her to the sofa. "We wanted to ask your advice about something."

"What's that, Mr. Jason?"

"We've realized we need some help with managing our day to day operations and our lives. We need a secretary or a personal assistant, or both. Obviously, whoever we hire will have to pass a background check. There's too much at risk for Aaron and myself. Recent events have made that more than clear. I think you know by now how we operate. Have you come across anyone in your travels who you might recommend?"

"I'm not sure it would be appropriate for me to recommend the people who come to mind."

"Why would that be?" Aaron asked.

"Because they're my children, Mr. Aaron."

"You have children? You never mentioned that."

"I try to keep my personal life separate from my work, Mr. Aaron."

Jason scooted forward in his chair. "How many children do you have?"

"Three, one son, Eugene, and two daughters, Fiona and Evelyn."

"Do any of them have the experience for what I mentioned?"

"I think all of them would, Mr. Jason, but it would be up to you, and I understand if you wouldn't want to bring families into your circle."

"We have no problem with family, Miss Charity. That's exactly what Aaron and I are trying to build up here. Everyone here will become part of our family, whether they're tied by blood or not. And while I'm at it, we'd like to know if you'd consider taking on an executive position with Nathan's Promise."

"An executive position? I don't know, Mr. Jason. It would depend. I'm not as young as I used to be, and I wouldn't want you to have to go looking for someone to replace me after just a few years. I would be happy just taking care of you and Mr. Aaron, and your home until I retire."

"When were you planning to retire, Miss Charity?" Aaron asked, "If you don't mind my asking."

"I haven't decided, Mr. Aaron, but I'm not a spring chicken any more. I figure I've got a good ten years left in me. Then I'll have to find a place to go, but I want to be near my children, wherever that may be, when the time comes."

Jason and Aaron exchanged glances. Aaron wrote a few words on a sticky note and passed it to Jason. Then Jason went on. "What we're looking for is someone to oversee the comfort needs of the patients and their families while they're with us. The position we'd like you to consider is Hospitality Director. It would involve overseeing everything the athletes and their families would need during their stays with us, outside of their actual therapy and medical care. The position would involve making major decisions about what we'll offer and how it will be offered, but there would be no backbreaking work involved at all."

"Can you give me a clearer idea of what you're talking about?"

"For example, choosing the china, linen, silver, and crystal patterns; selecting the curtains, upholstery, furniture, and linens; how the guests would be welcomed; designing stationery and informational pamphlets on the center and places in the area of interest for families to visit; how everyone will be settled in; parties and celebrations for when patients reach milestones in their recovery; or even birthdays and anniversaries, if those happen while they're with us. In essence, every creature comfort they could ever want or need."

"I'll think about it, Mr. Jason, but I can tell you now, both of my daughters could do that as well. All three of my children worked for the family I used to work for in various capacities."

"Do you have any more family who might fit in here for other jobs?" Aaron asked.

"Mr. Aaron, I love all my family, but there's some I wouldn't trust alone in my own home, if you know what I mean."

"I do, Miss Charity. Thank you for being so honest. As time goes on, we'll seek your advice on many different things, if that's okay with you."

"Any time, Mr. Aaron. Is there anything else?"

Jason looked at Aaron, then he looked back at Charity. "Yes, there is one thing."

"How can I help?"

"It's not more help that we need, Miss Charity. You won't ever need to find a place to go when you retire."

"What do you mean?"

Aaron stood up and walked to the sofa, taking a seat beside her. He rested his hand on her arm. "We'll take care of you, Miss Charity. We'll build a home for you, up here if you like. We've got 200 acres of pristine mountain land all around us. You can have your pick. Heck, we'll put on an addition for you right here in our home or build you something inside the stockade, if you'd like.

"If you wouldn't like something like that, we'll create a suite for you in or adjacent to the residential quarters of Nathan's Promise or build you a home on the grounds somewhere. If that's not to your liking, we'll build you a home wherever you want to live or pay for a home or apartment in a retirement community of your choosing."

Charity's eyes began to brim with tears. "Oh, Mr. Aaron. No. No. I could never accept something like that."

Jason smiled warmly. "Why not? It's one of the benefits everyone who works for us will receive."

"Oh, dear."

Charity stood up and hugged herself. "Oh, dear. Oh, dear. Oh, dear. I can't even imagine such a thing."

Aaron stood up and pulled her into his arms.

After a moment, Jason spoke. "You'll have plenty of time to begin thinking about it, Miss Charity. Thank you. That's all for now."

"No, thank you, Mr. Jason, Mr. Aaron. Oh, my, my own mountain home." Aaron patted her back and walked her to the door. "Oh, my. Oh, my. Oh my. Now how am I ever going to see about dinner? I can't think. I have the fullest house yet to feed tonight."

Chapter Twenty-Three
Blame It on the Whiskey

2:45 PM
Jason and Aaron's office

"Hello, Braden. Aaron said you wanted to talk to us?"

"It isn't just me, Jason. Didn't you tell him, Aaron?"

"Only that you asked to see us."

"You mean you didn't tell him that Shane wanted talk to you, too?"

"I wasn't sure what it was all about so I thought I'd let you tell us yourselves, either you, or Shane, or both of you."

"Excuse me. I'll be right back." Braden left the office and returned a moment later with Shane, who was still favoring his left leg. Jason and Aaron had moved from their shared executive desk to the two large chairs across the coffee table from the sofa.

"Have a seat, guys." Jason directed with a wave of his arm. "What's up?"

"Well, Jason. I'm not sure how to begin."

"Sometimes, just saying it is enough, Braden."

Tears welled up in Braden's eyes. Shane reached his arm around Braden's shoulders and hugged him.

"Mr. Jason, Mr. Aaron, something's happened that could create a huge problem," Shane began, "but you need to know about it, however this turns out."

"What on earth are you talking about?" Aaron asked. "Braden, why are you crying?"

"Aaron," Braden started, "I—I—I can't, Shane. I can't. Can you tell them?"

"Mr. Jason, Mr. Aaron…"

"Let's drop this mister stuff. It's Jason and Aaron

while we're here. Okay, Shane."

"Yes. Thanks, Jason. Okay, here goes. Jason … Aaron, we've done something that could have far reaching repercussions."

"Shane, have you killed someone?" Jason asked.

"God, no! Nothing like that!"

"Then what could be the problem?"

"Okay, I'm just going to say this, just like it happened. Last night, after dinner, I went to Braden's cottage because he was nice enough to try to help me out with my pulled groin muscle."

"We know that," Aaron said. "We suggested it."

"Yes, I know, but—well, Braden saw how much pain I was in, so he offered to let me soak in his whirlpool tub to help relax the muscles before he gave me the massage."

"Did you break the tub?" Aaron asked.

"No, sir, I mean, Aaron. No! No, we didn't break the tub. Anyway, okay, I have to be honest with you both. I sort of, well, I was distracted by Braden and well, I sort of took advantage of his good will, if you know what I mean."

"I have no idea, Shane," Aaron answered.

Jason's eyes began to sparkle as the briefest hint of a smile crossed his face.

"Well, I'd brought a bottle of whiskey with me as a gift to sort of thank Braden for offering to help me. Anyway, I was really in a whole lot of pain, so I drank some of it before I got there, even though it was supposed to be a gift. So, you see, it loosened me up in more ways than one.

"Anyway, and I can't say it wouldn't have happened, and I can't say that it would have, but the booze sure helped. So, you see, I couldn't get into the tub by myself 'cause I couldn't lift my leg over the side, and

I was completely naked, but I wore a jockstrap with the intention of keeping it on during the massage, but then Braden suggested the whirlpool, and I didn't want to get the jockstrap wet 'cause I didn't know how I'd explain it to the guys when I got back to my quarters, so I took it off and well, things started to happen. It has a mind of its own sometimes."

Jason covered his mouth with his hand to hide his growing smile.

Braden sniffled, then began to speak. "So Shane needed help to lift his leg over the side of the tub because of his pain. I had to take my shoes and pants off so they wouldn't get wet, because I'd already filled the tub. I climbed into it and steadied him while I lifted him up enough so I could swing his left leg into the tub. His penis rubbed up against my crotch, and it got even bigger. That was my fault. I should have thought of that. As I was lowering him—"

Shane interrupted. "As he was lowering me down into the water I made an inappropriate comment. Again, I don't think I'd have said it if I hadn't had the whiskey, but then I might have. I might have anyway. So when I said what I said he nearly dropped me, and he landed sort of in the water on top of me. It splashed up on his underwear, which made it see-through, and I saw his junk."

Braden cleared his throat. "Well, guys, you know what I've confided in you. I couldn't help it. Seeing Shane naked, I got all hot and bothered, too. I should have taken better precautions."

Jason tried to keep a straight face. "Guys, whatever it is, you're not in trouble,"

"Well, one thing led to another and … well … before we knew it, we started to have sex," Braden blurted out.

"I know it was wrong," Shane added. "I just hope you won't hold it against my father or his company."

"Whoa, Shane! That's it, you had sex?"

"Yes, sir."

"So, you didn't kill anyone, and you weren't on duty when it happened, right?" Aaron asked.

"Yes, sir. I mean no, sir. I mean, no, Mr. Aaron. I mean, no, I wasn't on duty, I mean."

Aaron expression was one of steel, but there was a twinkle in his eyes. "Please, Shane, no mister and no sir right now. Braden, were you raped?"

"No!"

"Shane, were you raped?"

"No, sir, I mean no."

"Were either of you coerced, threatened, or intimidated by the other?

"No!" they answered in unison.

Jason stood up. "Was a weapon involved?"

"No!" Again they answered together.

"Were either of you drugged by the other?"

"No!" they shouted.

"Did aliens take over you minds and perform sexual experiments on you?"

"No." Shane and Braden began to giggle.

"Good, so you see how silly this whole conversation is, right?"

"I guess so, Jason," Braden answered. "We were afraid for Shane's job and his father's contract with you. We didn't know whether it would change your opinion of them."

"Not in the least. You're both over eighteen. It was consensual, I'm assuming."

"Yes, it was," Shane answered, and Braden nodded.

"And you were off duty, right, Shane?"

"Yes, I'm on a medical leave sort of. I can't patrol the stockade with my groin pull. I'm off duty for a couple days."

"And you're both happy with the way it turned out?" Aaron asked.

"Yes, all three times," Braden added. "Oops, I didn't mean to say that, Shane. I'm sorry."

"It's okay, Braden," Shane smiled. "I think they're okay with it." Then, under his breath, "And it was four."

Jason took a few steps around the coffee table. "All I can say is I'm over the moon happy for Braden, and for you too, Shane, but Braden is very near and dear to our hearts. See, Braden, I told you that you were in a safe place, and now you've found Shane."

"We wanted to tell you first," Braden said. "One of the security guys, well, he figured it out, and we didn't want it to get distorted and then reported back to you."

Aaron stood up. "As far as I'm concerned, and I think I can speak for Jason on this, we're not going to say anything to anyone."

"Thanks, Aaron," Shane said. "I just have to figure out how and when I'm going to tell my father."

Jason clapped his hands together once, rubbed his hands together, and then folded his arms in front of himself. "As far as I'm concerned, Shane, it has no bearing on your employment here or our contract with your father's company. How and when and if you tell him is completely up to you. Speaking on a completely selfish basis, and I'm speaking on behalf of Braden here, I hope you both take advantage of his absence over the next several days and well, I think I've said enough."

"Can I say it, Shane?"

"Say what, Braden?" Braden whispered in Shane's ear.

"Yes, you can say it."

"Jason, Aaron, we're in love, and we have you two to thank for it."

"Us?" Aaron said.

"Yes." Shane put his arm around Braden's back. "If it hadn't been for you, I'd have never found the love of my life. I never knew it could be like this. I never thought I'd find someone so … so … so kind, so good with his hands. He's incredible. His hands, my God, his hands—"

"Um, Shane," Braden cut him off. "I think you've said more than enough."

Jason started to laugh. Then Aaron started, and then they all laughed together so hard, they were wiping tears from their eyes.

****

"So, Aaron, what did I tell you?"

Aaron smiled. "Yes, you called it, but did you think it would happen so soon? I mean, Braden seemed so shy."

"No, I really didn't, but the opportunity presented itself, and they grabbed for it. It was all I could do to keep a straight face though. Did you figure it out before they actually came out with it?"

"I had an idea, but I thought it best to let them talk."

"I'm happy for them, Aaron."

"Me, too."

"Did you notice, Shane seemed softer somehow just now?"

"He did. Maybe that's because he wasn't in uniform or carrying a loaded sidearm. I wonder what other romances might bloom up here?"

"Before you, Aaron, I lived up here all by myself for eleven years. It's interesting how opportunity can present itself. It may just come a knocking again, but for whom, I have no idea. While we're on the subject, I want you to know that I'm counting the days before I'm medically cleared for all activities. It's my turn next in the sling."

"I am, too, Jason. I am, too."

Chapter Twenty-Four
The Deflowering of Braden

7:00 PM

Braden heard voices coming from outside his door before there was a knock. He opened it. "Oh, hello. Come in, Shane, Natasha."

"Oh, sorry, no, Braden, I saw Shane on the porch here as I was coming back to the office to warm up for a bit. I'll be heading right back out on patrol in a few minutes."

"How are you feeling, Shane?"

"I'm a little better, Braden. Thanks."

"I'm glad to hear it. So what brings you here this evening?"

"I'm still sore, and I was wondering…"

"Do you need me to take a look at you again?"

"Yeah, Braden, I think it would help. If you don't mind, and if you have the time."

"Sure, I'd be happy to."

"I'll talk to you later, Natasha."

"Talk to you later, Shane. Hope you feel better soon. Bye, Braden."

"Bye."

Braden closed the door. He waited a moment and then locked it. "Boy, am I glad I heard another voice before I opened the door. She would have raised her eyebrows at what I had in my head to say to you."

"Come here, you." Shane pulled Braden to him and kissed him. "I've wanted to do that all day long."

"Me, too. How do you feel about another whirlpool?"

"I'd love it."

"Good, 'cause I've had a few ideas."

"Then lead the way."

Braden took Shane's hand and walked with him to the bathroom.

"So tell me about your ideas."

"I'd rather show you. Now you just stand there. I'm going to do everything."

Braden turned on the water heater and then began to fill the tub. As he walked back to Shane, he did a striptease as he pulled his clothes off and threw them into the corner. He ground his semi-erect cock into Shane's groin as he slid his hands under the front of his sweatshirt and ran his fingers up along his sides. Shane shivered when he ran them across his muscular pecs.

"Oh, baby, that so nice. You make me feel so good."

"That's not even the appetizer. Now kiss me again, but don't touch me."

As their lips locked, Braden slowly lifted Shane's shirt up to his neck. He broke the kiss and lifted it over his head and then his arms as Shane shrugged it off. He nuzzled Shane's armpits with his nose and inhaled deeply and then licked them and sucked the thick hair into his mouth.

"You taste so good, Shane. You smell so good."

"I didn't put on any deodorant after I showered. I wanted you to smell only me."

Braden lifted his mouth to Shane's again and then slid his hands down his back until he reached the waistband of his sweats. He worked his fingers under the elastic and ran his hands over the muscular globes of Shane's buttocks and then kneaded them and pulled the crack apart as he ground his fully erect cock against Shane's, again.

"Oh, baby, you're making my dick get hard."

"Really? Let's see just how hard."

Braden dropped to his knees and pulled Shane's

sweatpants down to his thighs. Then he leaned in and mouthed and sucked his bulging jockstrap, saturating it with his saliva. "Oops, your jock got wet. We'll have to take it off."

As Braden slid the jock down and then off, Shane's cock sprang out and struck his cheek as his swollen testicles dropped in their sack. Braden sucked one ball into his mouth, released it, then sucked in the other.

"Oh, God, Braden, God, your tongue, your tongue! Suck them." Shane groaned. "Suck them hard!"

"Mmmm, salty … so salty and so big."

"Yes, yes, lick them clean."

Braden moved his mouth to Shane's swelling cock. When it passed his lips, he raked his fingers along the back of Shane's scrotum, forcing his hips to lunge forward, driving his cock to the back of Braden's throat. Shane reached down and grasped the back of Braden's head and rocked it back and forth, sliding his cock in and out of Braden's mouth. Braden gagged, and his eyes began to water.

"Yes, baby, take all of me. Swallow my cock."

Braden pulled away. "I'm going to swallow your cock, Shane, but not with my mouth. Now let's get into the tub."

Shane put his hand on Braden's shoulder to steady himself and then gingerly stepped over the side. Braden followed and helped Shane down into the water and then kneeled down over his thighs so that Shane's cock pressed up against his own. "Shane, I want to take you inside me. I want you to make love to me, like love should be made."

"You've never had a cock inside you, Braden. Are you sure you're ready for this?"

"Yes, I cleaned myself out and washed my butt

real good. And anyway, what choice do I have? You're going to be my one and only, and your cock is going to be the only one my ass will ever know."

"Then I'm going to have to prepare you."

"I know. I've been reading about it, and I'm ready. However long it takes, whatever you have to do, I'm ready."

"I'll need you to turn around and lift your butt into the air so I can start to open you up."

Braden turned on the whirlpool jets and then climbed out of the water, placing his hands and knees outside of the tub's edge on the platform surrounding it and positioning his buttocks in front of Shane's face with his cock and balls dangling above the water.

"Lean back a little. It'll spread your cheeks apart. Yeah, that's perfect." Shane leaned forward and began to lick in circles around Braden's hole. When he hit the bullseye, Braden's anus contracted and his cock lurched upward.

"Holy crap! Oh, my God, that's amazing! Oh, Shane, eat my ass out. Eat my ass out!"

"Num, num, num, Braden, your virgin ass is so yummy. I'm aching just thinking about sliding into it."

"I can't wait, Shane. I can't wait for you to fill me with your spunk."

Shane wiggled his muscular tongue against the outer sphincter as he spread Braden's cheeks and pressed his face inward. "Relax for me, baby. It's real sensitive here, and a tongue feels wonderful inside. Let me make you squirm. Let me get you ready." He grasped Braden's ball sack and tugged downward, pulling his cock shaft along with it.

"Oh, oh! Oh my God! Yes! Yes, Shane, yes!"

"That's it. That's it, Braden, open up for me." Shane drove his tongue in further as he lapped and sucked against the tender, sensitive membranes. Braden began to shiver and moan.

Shane saturated his thumbs with saliva. He spread Braden's crack wide and slid them in and out next to his tongue, one at a time, as he loosened the muscles, opening Braden up further and further. "I can see the last barrier, Braden. It won't be long now." Braden's moans turned to groans.

Shane removed his thumbs and dipped two fingers into a jar of lube that Braden had put out and wiped them against the first two fingers from his other hand. He slid the middle finger from each hand in and plied Braden open some more. He leaned in and drove his tongue forcefully against the internal sphincter as he slurped and sucked, adding his index fingers to tease and pull Braden open, sliding them in and out until his hole was good and relaxed.

"You're ready, Braden. Turn around and face me."

Shane took Braden's cock into his mouth and slid two fingers back into his hole. Then he pulled them out, then he added a third and slid them in and out again and again, twisting them around in the process, until he reached Braden's quivering orb. As Shane pressed his fingers downward, Braden squealed when his anus clamped down and his hips thrust forward, driving Shane's head backwards. Shane was rewarded with a stream of clear, honeyed pre-cum that he sucked in greedily. Then he focused his lips over the corona of Braden's glans while he rapidly then slowly fingered his anus. Braden's body began to buck and gyrate as Shane continued for several minutes.

"You're going … you're going to … to make me come. I'm gonna come, Shane. I'm gonna come!"

"No, baby, not yet," he said after he pulled away

from Braden's cock. He slid in a fourth finger and slowly rotated them together, one way then the other, then pulled them out and pushed them back in, alternating the pace until Braden's anus finally relented and gaped open. He slathered a generous amount of lube around and into Braden's anus and down his own, turgid cock shaft. Then Shane grasped Braden's butt cheeks and lowered him down onto the swollen head of his throbbing, twitching cock.

As it disappeared into Braden's depths, Shane felt the warmth of Braden's rectum engulf it. When the head glanced Braden's prostate, Shane was only halfway in. Braden moaned and threw his head back and closed his eyes as he braced his shins against the tub's bottom.

"God, it hurts! It's so tight, but I can feel you inside me, Shane. You're inside me. God, you're really inside me." Braden began to slide up and down Shane's shaft, taking him in deeper, inch by inch until he was sitting on Shane's lap.

"Go slow, baby. I don't want you to hurt yourself. I know I'm really big."

"I can't help it. It hurts like hell, but it feels so good. I feel so full. It's stretching me so much, like I could tear open, but the pleasure sensations, oh, God, the pleasure is way more than the pain."

Shane's cock began to quiver as Braden rose and fell along the full length of his shaft. He watched Braden's face contort and relax, smile and grimace as he rose and fell. Shane contracted his PC muscles, driving more blood into his shaft, forcing it to engorge even more as pre-cum began to spill from the slit and lubricate Braden's insides.

"Shane, I feel so full, so full. It's wonderful, baby. It's wonderful. Fill me with your cum, Shane. Fill me up."

Shane grasped Braden's shaft and closed his hand around it, passively masturbating him as Braden lifted and lowered his pelvis, making his glans turn a deep purple. "You set the pace, Braden. You're in control. I'll hold off coming as long as I can, but know this, you're bringing me up beautifully. You're so tight, squeezing against my shaft."

"Shane, your cock is plowing my prostate. It feels incredible. It's wonderful. Wonderful!"

"Just ride me, baby, ride me into oblivion."

Braden slowed his pace, then sped up. "Shane, it's so warm. I'm so warm inside, and it's spreading out through my body."

"That means your climax is building, baby. It's going to grow and grow until you're at the threshold. You can make it last by slowing down until you find the pace that holds you where you want to be."

"How long does it last?"

"As long as you want, but at some point, you won't be able to stop yourself, and you'll push yourself over the edge."

"I want to stay right here, Shane … forever." Braden began to lick his lips as he rocked his head back and forth. "Oh, oh, oh, I'm so warm. I'm so warm. My face feels so hot."

Shane tightened his grip around Braden's shaft and began to pump it up and down. "Let me make you warmer, baby."

He began to lift his hips, meeting Braden as he came down, and then he began thrusting up forcefully, splashing water from the tub onto the floor. As their bodies slapped together, Braden's breath caught. He moaned, and his moan increased its pitch until it reached a steady wail.

"Stop now, baby," Shane said softly. "Let it calm

down so you can savor this moment. Make it last as long as you want it to."

"I don't want to stop, Shane. I don't want to."

"Trust me, baby. Trust me. It'll be so good for you. So good for you, baby."

"Okay." Braden leaned down and planted his mouth against Shane's. Shane released Braden's cock and wrapped his arms around his back pulling him down against his chest in a passionate embrace.

Breaking the kiss, Shane pulled Braden's head next to his and whispered in his ear, "I love you, Braden Darby, and I love you for allowing me to be your first. This is such a special moment for me."

Once again, Braden began to slowly lift and lower his pelvis, withdrawing and advancing Shane's shaft against his anus and caressing his prostate with Shane's engorged, mushroom head. Braden began to moan again as he drew in long, slow breaths.

"Shane, my anus is tingling. It's so sensitive. It's like I can feel each nerve ending as it fires."

"Enjoy it, Braden. Remember, you're in control. It's all you, baby. It's all you."

Shane used his right leg to raise and lower his hips, meeting Braden halfway. As their pace increased, Braden leaned back, changing the angle of Shane's cock so that it struck glancing blows against his tightening prostate, deep inside. As Braden continued to ride Shane's cock, Shane placed his hand around Braden's shaft and let it slide through his grasp on its own. The farther back Braden leaned, the more forceful the blows that Shane's glans delivered against his prostate became, making it contract and spasm with greater and greater force until it clamped down and held.

"Now! It's happening now, Shane. It's happening now!"

Braden's cock began to spasm in Shane's grip. Shane opened his mouth to the first stream of Braden's virginal orgasm. He clenched his PC muscles, and his prostate responded. Waves of cum flew past Braden's rectum into the depths of his colon.

Braden's spunk sprayed out, covering Shane's face as he lowered his mouth over the tip and directed the streams across his tongue. He sucked greedily, swallowing Braden's first fuck-stimulated cum down his throat.

When Braden finally stopped, he slumped forward against Shane's chest, breathing heavily. Shane caught him and embrace him as he nuzzled his neck. "Braden, you did it," he whispered. "You did it. You're not a virgin any more, Braden. You're a man. I love you, Braden Darby. I love you."

Shane began to lift Braden up, but Braden shook his head "*No*" as he buried his face into Shane's neck and wrapped his arms and legs around him.

Shane held Braden while he wept with Shane's cock still planted firmly inside him. Braden wouldn't let him go.

****

8:30 PM

While Shane lay naked, on his back, Braden pressed and kneaded his groin muscles between his muscular fingers. "I'm dreading the future, Shane."

"What do you mean?"

"This is all going to end too soon. What are we going to do?"

"We'll find a way, Braden. This morning I had the same feeling. That feeling turned into dreading my father's return, not that he'd be returning, no, I love him, but that we'd have to stop because he returned.

"I knew that I would tell him about us at some

point, but I didn't think that would happen any time soon. As the hours have ticked by though, I've realized that I'm too happy not to share my love for you with him. I just don't know what the best way will be to break it to him. I don't want to hurt him.

"He's hinted to me off and on about looking forward to becoming a grandfather and whether there are any prospective women on the horizon for me that he should take an interest in. The thing is, I haven't introduced him to any girls since I was in high school. Being away in the Marines took care of having to address that issue, and we've been so busy with his security business that it's been easy to avoid the subject, other than in passing. He has no idea what I really am."

"You shouldn't say it that way, Shane. It's not *what* you are, it's *who* you are. Calling being gay *a what* makes it sound like a thing to be shunned rather than a part of who you really are."

"I guess you're right, but it doesn't matter one way or the other. The first chance I find to have some quiet time with him, I'm going to tell him."

"It's your decision, Shane. Not to change the subject, but how's your groin? Is it easing up?"

"It feels great, Braden. It's not back to normal, but it feels great because the severe pain I had before is gone. It's more of an ache and sore now. You really know what you're doing."

"I'm glad. It makes me feel like I have something to contribute to this relationship, something that's of value to you."

"Whoa! You shouldn't put yourself down like that. You make it sound like your only value is in what you can do, not in who you are. You're an incredibly giving man, and you're kind. You radiate kindness, Braden. That's a quality that many people don't possess naturally or come by easily. I know it can be learned, but with you, it's innate. It's something to be cherished by those around you and acknowledged by yourself."

"That's not an easy thing for me to hear."

"Braden, I'm not saying you should wear it like a badge on your chest, just simply be aware that that's what you project.

"I'll try."

****

Over the course of the following day, Jason watched dramatic changes take place within the walls of the stockade. As pre-fab sections of cottages arrived, they were immediately lowered into place from hovering helicopters and attached to their foundations. While Rod and Jack worked tirelessly, running up and down the line to ensure each cottage met specifications, and meticulously oversaw the installment of their appliances and the delivery and assembly of their furniture, Jason ticked off checklist after checklist, ensuring nothing was missed. He watched the little group of cottages grow and grow, and he took pride in his idea to install a long, roofed, wooden sidewalk to run between the two rows, ensuring cover from the elements for his growing family.

He asked Lars to accompany him during several trips to the barn while he visited with the animals, knowing that Conrad would pay him a surprise visit to ensure that he was keeping to his word by not exerting himself. Jason smiled to himself when Conrad walked in and found him standing between his two beloved donkeys with his arms around their necks, and their heads draped over his back, nibbling his shirt while their tails swished back and forth.

He took great pleasure as Miss Charity beamed while she churned butter with his little machine and was beside herself with joy as she considered Aaron and

Jason's offer for a prominent position with Nathan's Promise. Even more, knowing that he and Aaron had the means to take care of her in her golden years and possibly even offer her three children places with them, too, gave him great peace.

Jason finally relented and accepted Aaron's demand to take some of the burden off him. He wouldn't see Aaron for hours at a time, while he busied himself in the office reviewing and revising notes and making phone calls to contractors and suppliers.

As Nathan's Promise drew closer and closer to becoming a reality, Aaron shared his memories of his former lover with Jason and the difference that Nathan had made in his life. He was determined to see that Nathan's name lived on, and Jason would do everything he could to help him realize that dream.

Whenever Jason wasn't in the barn, he was out in the yard with Rod and Jack or pestering Aaron trying to help, but Aaron just shooed him away. Several times, Conrad pulled him back inside and made him lie down for a nap, and he needed that.

He and Aaron gave Conrad an unlimited budget, allowing him to build his own little clinic, just the way he wanted it. He commented that Conrad was like a kid in a candy shop, spending hours scouring medical equipment and supplies websites on the internet, placing order after order. It was then when he recognized that Conrad could serve a significant role in the operation of Nathan's Promise by contributing his own expertise, direction, and advice as a valued member of the team. After discussing it with Aaron, they decided they would offer him a Directorship.

When Jason learned from Shane that he and Braden were spending all the time they could together in the hot tub, on the massage table, or in bed, finding comfort in each other's arms or sharing stories about their lives, he congratulated them both and encouraged them to take advantage of every minute they could find.

The following morning, as he watched everyone come together at the breakfast table, Jason looked towards the future with fresh eyes and new vision, for their lives were changing. They were growing together. They were becoming a family.

Chapter Twenty-Five
An Ill Wind

Friday, January 8, 2010, 9:30 AM

Jason picked up the phone in his new office. "Hello? Oh, good morning, Chief. I'm going to put you on speaker. Aaron's here, too."

"Hi, Chief," Aaron said. "How are things going?"

"There's been some further developments. It's not looking good. I'm not prepared to say any more over the phone."

"I'm sorry to hear that," Jason said. "Wasn't Joshua able to help?"

"Some, but it's more serious than I thought. I'll be flying back tomorrow."

"Tomorrow? So you're not going to stay until Monday?" Aaron asked.

"No, Mr. Aaron, and I'd like to meet with both of you when I get there, as soon as you can make time."

"Absolutely. Jason and I will be available to talk to you whenever you like."

"Listen, Chief," Jason said. "Whatever it is, it sounds serious. May I invite Claudia to the meeting? She's very good. Maybe she can offer you some advice."

"If you trust her, then yes. Will Rod be available on Saturday? Otherwise I'll have to hire a chopper."

"Yes, Chief," Jason answered. "Rod will be available to fly you up, but we have two other folks coming up tomorrow as well. I'd prefer coordinating you and them flying up together so Rod doesn't have to make two trips in the same day, if that's all right with you."

"That would be very helpful. Do you know what time they're planning to fly up?"

"No, I'm not sure of their schedule yet, but I'll be talking with them in about a half hour to firm up their arrival time. Can I let you know later this morning?"

"Yes, I'll wait for your call."

"Great, great. I'll call you back on your cell."

"Thank you, Mr. Jason. I'll talk to you then."

"Okay, Chief. I'll talk to you later this morning. Bye."

****

10:05 AM

"Good morning, Simone. How are things with you?"

"Doing well, Jason, but I'm more concerned with how you're doing. I hope you're not pushing yourself too hard. Are you okay?"

"Yes, thank you. I'm calling as promised to confirm that you and Penelope are still coming up for the weekend?"

"We're both looking forward to finally seeing this cabin in the woods of yours. How is Aaron doing?"

"Wonderful, he's wonderful. He's right here with me. I'll put this on speaker."

"What time were you planning to arrive at the airport?" Aaron asked.

"Hi, Aaron. Eight o'clock, unless that will be too early."

"Oh, that's very helpful," Jason said. "I was hoping to coordinate your arrival with my Chief of Security. He needs to fly back up tomorrow, too. I just talked to him a little while ago. He's waiting to hear back from me."

"That would be just fine, Jason. We look forward to meeting him."

"Eight o'clock it is then. That means you should arrive at around eight-thirty. Miss Charity will have breakfast waiting."

"Miss Charity? What a lovely name."

"Oh, yes, she's our Chief of Household Operations, and she'll give me what for if I don't say that she's also our cook. I think you'll love her."

"I'm sure we will."

"While I have you, do you have a moment?"

"Sure. Anything."

"Great. Aaron and I are looking forward to picking you brains about a few things. I was wondering if you could give some thought to them before you arrive."

"We'd be happy to. Any hints?"

"Wonderful. Yes. We need some advice on how to go about soliciting donations and establishing an advisory board and a volunteer auxiliary, or something along those lines. We're also looking for advice on soliciting bids from construction and architectural firms and how to navigate local bureaucracies to get the project approved. Finally, we're looking for an operations manager, you know, someone to run the entire operation on an administrative level. Aaron and I will make the big decisions, but we'll need someone who knows how to implement them."

"I'll draft a list of potential donors and companies along with their contacts and phone numbers. Regarding the last matter, someone comes to mind immediately."

"Really? Who?" Aaron asked.

"Penelope."

"Really?" Aaron said. "That's very interesting."

"Penelope advised me shortly after she returned, after her parents were killed, that she wanted to scale back and find a position that wasn't quite as demanding of her time. She agreed to stay on until I was able to find someone to replace her."

"She was?" Jason asked. "And you'd be okay with that?"

"Absolutely, we're friends before anything else. I only want what's best for her. I can't think of anyone who would be better for her than you and Aaron, and your mission for Nathan's Promise will give so much meaning to the position. I believe she'll be the perfect person for the job."

"Oh, Simone, I can't tell you how happy that makes us," Jason said.

"Wonderful!"

"One final thing. Do you think Hinnen Valley Medical Center might be interested in establishing a referral relationship with Nathan's Promise?"

"What would it entail?"

"Well, for example, if any of our patients would require medical care associated with their rehabilitation, beyond what we could provide here while they're with us, or if we had a medical emergency."

"Yes, absolutely. I was going to broach the subject of referring our athlete patients to you for rehabilitation once you're up and running. I have a good feeling about Nathan's Promise, Jason. I believe you're going to make a big difference in the lives of so many people."

"Great, Simone," Aaron said. "That's just great, and thank you for saying what you did about Nathan's Promise. That means a lot to me."

"It's the truth, Aaron."

"While we're discussing our mutual relationship," Jason added, "we wanted to broach the subject of our donation to the medical center. The one you were promised when Aaron was admitted."

"Yes? That was very generous of you."

"You deserve it, Simone," Aaron added. "Do you have any specific needs where we could direct the donation or are there any projects you've wanted to undertake that you haven't had the funds for?"

"There are so many areas where we could expand to help the community, Aaron. I can provide you with a list of projects along with their projected costs, or you can choose one of your own. Every penny is helpful."

"We were thinking along several lines," Aaron continued. "The day before we left you mentioned changes in the hospital's visiting policy and something related to families becoming involved in planning patients' care and participating in it."

"Yes, and it's going well."

"Can we help there?"

"Certainly, if that's what you want, Aaron."

"Also, we were both trauma patients. There's got to be a need for funds for the emergency and trauma center."

"More than you can imagine."

"Good. We'd want to be sure it's something that you really need. There's no sense just throwing money at something without having an idea beforehand as to how it will be used."

"I'll put together that list for you."

"Wonderful," Jason said. "Oh, and there's one more thing I forgot to ask. Do you or Penelope have any special dietary needs or is there anything you don't eat?"

"When I think of a cabin in the woods, I remember baked beans and hotdog casserole. I've eaten just about my fill of it over the years."

"Oh, that's funny."

"Jason, Aaron, I can't tell you how much I appreciate ... both Penelope and I appreciate being invited to visit with you. It's going to be a wonderful getaway and personally, I'm looking forward to roughing it a little."

"Wonderful, us too! Aaron and I look forward to hosting you both for the weekend, but I think we'll be able to do a little better than *roughing it* for you."

"Thank you, Jason."

"Okay, we'll see you then."

"Bye now."

"Bye."

****

Jason redialed the phone. "Hello there, Chief. How's eight o'clock for you?"

"I'm at your disposal. Eight is fine."

"Great, I'd be at the hangar at least fifteen minutes earlier."

"I'll see to it, and thank you, Mr. Jason."

"You're welcome. Aaron and I look forward to seeing you then." Jason hung up the phone.

"What do you think, Aaron?"

"I have no idea what to think, Jason."

"Maybe Shane will know."

"No, don't ask him, Jason. He shouldn't be put on the spot."

"You're right of course, but I have a feeling it's more than not good. We better advise Claudia and Winston to be ready for anything. There's an ill wind blowing."

Chapter Twenty-Six
Preparing a Feast

10:45 AM

When Jason and Aaron walked into the kitchen, Charity was preparing lunch. "Miss Charity, we're going to have three more mouths to feed this weekend, no, make that a firm five."

"Who's coming, Mr. Jason?"

"The chief will be back, along with the CEO and one of the administrators from Hinnen Valley Medical Center, Simone Jones and Penelope Whitley. They'll also be spending the weekend with us, and of course Jack and Rod will be staying, too."

"Is there anything special you would like me to prepare, Mr. Jason, or any extras for meetings and such?"

"Everything you prepare is special, Miss Charity," Aaron said.

"Well aren't you just the sweetest thing, Mr. Aaron."

"I asked Simone if she or Penelope had any special dietary requirements or things they didn't eat." Jason said. "I laughed when she told me that when she thinks of a cabin in the woods, she envisions baked beans and hotdog casserole."

"Oh, that is funny, Mr. Jason. I think we can do a little better than that. How many meetings will you be having?"

"I'm not certain. Saturday is going to be very busy. We're going to be having meetings all day long. You might as well think of it as one, very long meeting, and we may run over into Sunday."

"I'll take care of everything. Don't you give it another thought. While I have you, I did want to mention that I spoke with all three of my children, and they're all interested in positions up here. I told them to contact Mr. Rod to have him fly them up here tomorrow because you seemed eager to fill those positions. Should I cancel them?"

"Absolutely not, we've got plenty of room, don't you think?"

"Yes, Mr. Jason, and the work crews have all but finished. They just have a few minor things to complete. I've been told all external construction should be finished by the end of today."

"I'm so glad you told Rod to order those additional units," Aaron added.

"My girls can stay together with me in my cottage, and my son can bunk with the security folks, if that would be all right with the chief. It isn't necessary to open up two of the new cottages just for a day or two."

"We'll not hear of it," Aaron said. "Your son will have his own and your girls can, too. Even though they're your children, they're adults now. I don't think they'd really want to have to sleep with their mama at their ages. Let's think about this. Rod and Jack in one, Lars in one, Braden in one, Conrad in one, you in one, Claudia in one, Winston in one, the two separate bunk-quarters for security's men and women, plus the one for their R&R center, and the original one for the chief's office, your girls in one, your son in one, and Simone and Penelope can each have one or stay together. I guess we'll leave that decision up to them. So even with everyone, we still have extra space."

"Actually," Jason said. "You forgot Conrad's clinic. We have only one spare cottage, but it doesn't really make a difference and then there's the two double bedrooms in the back of the cabin."

"If you like, Mr. Jason, my son and daughters could stay in them. It's like I said, why mess up two cottages for just a day or two? No worries though, between all of us, we can figure it out. I was thinking that if any of my children are going to be employed as your personal assistant here, before Nathan's Promise has been completed, they might as well get used to rooming right here in the cabin in one of the spare bedrooms. It would make sense that they be close at hand for you, particularly while you and Mr. Arron are still recovering.

"And remember, you said there's going to be other folks staying from time to time. Architects, construction folks, surveyors, and the like. You and Mr. Aaron should not be disturbed unnecessarily by other visitors at night while you're still recovering from the hospital. Leave the extra suites for them."

"Really, Miss Charity, we're doing fine."

"Mr. Jason, it may not be my place, but I've watched you. You're still in pain from your surgery. Your face can't hide it. If it were up to me, you wouldn't be doing nearly as much as you've been pushing yourself to do. I've seen how you come in after you've been in the barn, and if Dr. Conrad catches you, I don't want to be anywhere nearby. I've heard him grumbling. Mr. Lars is supposed to be helping you. Why don't you let him?"

"He has been, Miss Charity, and Conrad was out there checking up on me. He saw how I was behaving."

"Really? Just how much? Are you doing any heavy work when he's not watching you?"

Jason didn't answer. A guilty expression spread across his face.

"As I suspected. It's enough you've been having all these meetings, Mr. Jason. That's stressful in and of itself. You're pushing yourself too darn hard, running around out in the yard. What were you thinking? Sorry, but that's just my opinion, if you don't mind my saying."

"I need to get myself back in shape to take care of

the animals, Miss Charity, so that Lars can go home to his wife and family, or at least get a break to go home on the weekends. I'm the only one who knows how to properly milk Heather. Aaron can't do it 'cause he's not allowed to bend over."

"Mr. Jason, the family my parents worked for had goats on their estate on St. Croix as well as back here in the States. I used to milk them. I'll take over with little Miss Heather anytime Mr. Lars needs to go home. Now you just put it out of your mind. And don't forget, there's plenty of fit young men and women around here, too. I sure any of them would be happy to pitch in out in the barn, if you asked that is."

"I can't ask you or anyone else to do that, Miss Charity."

"You didn't ask. I offered, and I think, if I may say so, the matter is now settled."

Jason smiled shyly. "Well, I guess you told me."

Aaron rested his hand on Jason's shoulder. "She's right you know, about everything, Jason."

"Yes, I know."

Charity smiled. "Is there anything else?"

"No. Thank you, Miss Charity."

Charity pulled Jason into her big bosom and held him tightly for the longest time before she released him. "There are so many people here who want to help you, Mr. Jason, who believe in the both of you." She reached out and patted Aaron's shoulder. "Who believe in what you're trying to build. Let them."

Aaron leaned down and kissed her on the cheek. "You're such a dear. Thank you."

"You're both welcome. Now that that's settled, I'm going to call in an order for a feast to remember. I'll have Mr. Rod bring it up tomorrow when he flies up the new guests. I'll make sure to have it delivered to his hangar first thing in the morning. What time is he planning to fly up?"

"Everyone is meeting at the hangar early enough to leave by eight," Jason said.

"Then I'll have the order delivered by seven-thirty, and I'll call my children and tell them to be there at the same time."

"Thank you, Miss Charity," Aaron said. "A feast you say. I'm looking forward to it."

"My pleasure, and I'll put my children to work the moment they unpack their luggage. I made sure they all learned their way around a kitchen when they worked for me at the hotel."

"I know better than to argue with you, Miss Charity. Is there anything else you need?" Jason asked.

"Yes, a favor."

"Anything."

"I've smelled your sourdough starter. It's excellent. How old is it?"

"Eleven years, why?"

"I know I asked you before, but I'd really like you teach me how to make your bread. It will make a wonderful addition to the feast I'm planning."

"I'm at your disposal. Let me know whenever is convenient for you, but I think you'll be disappointed."

"Why would you say that?"

"It's the absolute simplest bread recipe I've ever created."

"Don't fool yourself, Mr. Jason, that's the secret to wonderful bread."

****

1:15 PM
Jason and Aaron's office

"Claudia, Winston, there have been some developments with the chief. We don't know what's happened, but from his tone and what he did say, it sounds like trouble."

"You don't have any idea, Jason?" Claudia asked.

"No, none, but I wanted to prepare you. Something tells me he's going to need our help, so you should put together the proposal we talked about."

"We've already done that, Jason," Winston said. "It's all ready to go."

"I'd call Joshua, but he'd just quote attorney-client privilege," Claudia said. "On another matter, I've drawn up the final incorporation papers for the subsidiary companies you asked for. I'm going to need your signatures on a lot of papers, and we're going to need a notary."

"We can fly one up tomorrow with Rod," Jason said. "Do you know anyone who could come up on such short notice?"

"I'll find somebody."

"Thanks, Claudia. The chopper is leaving the hangar at eight. Let's plan to meet with the chief tomorrow around nine. He sounded like he wanted to meet the moment they land. Now, back to Joshua. How good is he really?"

"Jason, he's the best. He's cutthroat in the courtroom, and he's incredibly loyal. If he believes in you, he'll see to it you win. Believe me."

"Then put together an offer to hire him or put him on retainer, whatever is necessary. Something tells me the chief is going to need him. I just don't understand what could have gone wrong."

"I'll see to it, Jason."

Chapter Twenty-Seven
I Don't Know How to Help Him

7:15 PM

"Come in, it's open," Braden called to the knock at his door.

As the door opened, Shane appeared. "Hey there, baby. I'm glad to see you. I missed you at dinner. Did you want me to work on your groin again?"

Shane walked in and slowly closed the door. "Thanks, Braden. I'm sorry I wasn't there."

"Shane, what's wrong?"

"I can't tell you, Braden. I'm sorry. Can you just work on my groin again?"

"You can't tell me? Shane, you can tell me anything. Forget your groin for the moment."

"No, really, Braden. It has nothing to do with us. It's business."

"Shane, this doesn't seem like you."

"It's not, and believe me, I'd tell you, but I gave my word, and before you say it, yes, I trust you. I trust you completely, but I gave my word."

"Business? Does it have something to do with your father?"

Tears formed in the corners of Shane's eyes. "Braden, please, don't pursue this."

"Whatever it is, Shane, I'm here for you."

Shane leaned against Braden's chest and then wrapped his arms around him and began to cry. "He's hurting so bad. God, why did this have to happen now? He doesn't deserve this."

"Baby, no. Oh, Shane, it's going to be all right." Braden hugged Shane back and steadied him. "Whatever it is, it's going to be all right."

"You have no idea, Braden. You have no idea."

"Here, sit down."

After Shane sat on the sofa, Braden pulled him to himself and held him as he cried. He kissed his forehead and ran his fingers through his hair while he whispered, "Baby, oh, baby, it's going to be all right. Whatever it is, I'm here for you. I'm here for you both. I love you, Shane."

After several minutes, Shane leaned back. "Braden, I don't know how to help him. There's no way I can help him."

"Shane, I wish I could do something, but by respecting your wishes, I don't know what because I don't know what's happened. Is there anyone you know who could help?"

"Braden, you said something like Jason and Aaron are the kindest, most giving people you've ever met. Is that true?"

"Yes, Shane. I've never known anyone like them."

****

Braden stepped out onto the porch.

"What's up, Braden?"

"Thanks for coming, Jason, Aaron. Something's happened, and Shane couldn't think of anyone else to call. I don't know what it is, but he's really upset right now."

"Where is he?"

"On the sofa in the living room. Go on in."

****

"Hello, Shane. Is there anything Jason and I can do for you?"

"I don't know, Aaron, but I couldn't think of anybody else."

"Can you tell us what happened?"

"That's it, I can't. I gave my word."

"Shane, we'd like to help, whatever it is."

"Hi, Shane," Jason said. "Is it okay if Braden stays?"

"Yes, of course."

"Braden," Jason said, "I need your word that you will not repeat anything you hear while we talk with Shane."

"You have it, Jason."

"Shane, we spoke with your father earlier today. He's coming back tomorrow morning."

"I know. I've spoken with him, too."

"He didn't say much, but it seems something has happened with another one of his security contracts. He's asked to speak with us when he gets here."

"I know."

"And you can't tell us what happened?"

"No, I wish I could, but I gave him my word."

"Then we'll honor that. I can tell you that we referred a criminal attorney to him, but it didn't seem to work out."

"Yes, I know."

"He said there have been some developments."

"That's an understatement. Oh, Jason, Aaron, I shouldn't have said that."

"It's okay. Look it doesn't look like we're going to find out more until we've talked with your father, but I will tell you this, Shane." Shane looked down at his hands. "Shane, look at me."

He raised his head. "Yes?"

"Shane, Aaron and I have nearly unlimited resources at our disposal. We believe in your father. He's done everything possible to keep us safe. We're going to do everything we can to help him. Everything."

"Oh, Jason."

Shane began to weep uncontrollably. After a little

while, he dried his eyes and stood up and then hugged both of them. "I don't know what to say to you guys. Braden was right, you *are* the kindest most giving people anyone could ever meet. Thank you. Thank you for believing in him. Even if you can't help him, thank you."

****

After Jason and Aaron left, Braden led Shane to the bedroom and had him lie down. "Can I stay here tonight, Braden? I don't want to go back to the barracks."

"Yes, of course."

"Thank you. I feel so weak, like someone's let the air out of my tires."

"Your emotions were running pretty high, Shane. That can really wipe a person out. Here, I'll help you get undressed. What do you wear to bed?"

"What did I ever do to deserve you, Braden?"

"I could ask the same question. You loved me for me. That means the world to me. The world."

"Braden, I love you."

"I love you, too, Shane. Now what do you usually wear to bed?"

"In the bunk room, my underwear, but at home, I sleep naked."

"Naked it is then."

Braden helped Shane to sit up and pulled his sweatshirt over his head. The he removed his shoes and sweatpants. "Do you want the jockstrap off, too?"

"Yes, please."

Braden lay on the bed next to Shane and kissed his eyes, then his nose and mouth. "I love you, Shane." He moved down to his chest and kissed his nipples, then down further and kissed his abdomen and his hip bones. He slid his fingers under the band of the jockstrap and pulled it down.

He kissed the base of Shane's penis, then the

glans. He lifted it and kissed it where it met his scrotum. Then he moved to each of its globes and kissed them, too. He pulled the jock down his legs and kissed them as he moved from the thighs to the knees to his calves. He kissed his feet as the jockstrap fell to the floor and pulled the sheet up over them and then turned him to his side and wrapped his arms around him and held him.

"Thank you, Braden. Thank you for loving me."

"I do love you." Braden wrapped his legs around Shane's and pulled himself in tight and rocked him. As their cocks rubbed against each other, Shane began to softly moan.

"I love you, Braden. I love you so much." Shane's cock began to swell. He began to grind his hips into Braden's, their cocks rubbing together. Shane's cock grew and grew until it sprang up between them, and Braden's cock followed. Shane spit into his hand and reached down to grasp their cocks into his fist. He began to stroke them as he rolled Braden onto his back.

Braden reached for a jar of lube from the night table and held it up for him. Shane scooped out a handful and slathered it over their shafts as he quickened the pace of his strokes along them. He let go and reached down and moved a finger into Braden's anus. Braden relaxed his sphincter, and Shane slid his finger in to the hilt. Over the next few minutes, he added a second finger as Braden writhed in bliss, then a third.

"Make love to me, Shane."

Shane lifted Braden's legs until Braden grasped them with his arms. Shane slid his cock, unencumbered, into Braden's beckoning hole. "Yes, Shane, love me. Love me, baby."

Braden rested his legs over Shane's shoulders as Shane leaned in and lifted his butt off the bed. He thrust in slowly and stayed there, then pulled back and thrust in again. Braden's hole slurped and sucked as Shane's cock advanced and withdrew.

As the minutes passed, Braden whispered his love and acceptance of Shane's love in return.

"Oh, baby. Oh, Shane, it's wonderful."

Braden moaned. "Yes, baby, yes, that's it. That's the spot."

Shane lifted Braden into his arms and leaned back, shifting himself to the corner of the bed. He sat down and grasped Braden's thighs lifting and lowering him as his cock slid in and out of Braden's hole. Braden leaned in and kissed him, driving his tongue deep into his mouth. He wrapped his arms around Shane and rode the wave of Shane's passion.

Shane moved back and lay on the bed. Braden braced his knees and began to lift and lower himself as Shane slid his fingertips over Braden's cockhead and locked them beneath the corona, effectively forming a funnel with his hand. With each concussive blow of Braden's advances, the head of his cock plowed into Shane's palm, causing intense pleasure sensations to be driven deep into his core. When his sweet nectar began to dribble from the slit, Shane lifted his hand and allowed Braden to lick it clean. Braden quickened his pace.

"Shane, I'm getting warm. There's a glow spreading out from deep inside me. It's spreading through my body."

"Me too, Braden. It's so beautiful. You're so beautiful. I love you, Braden. I love you."

When Braden leaned down against Shane's chest, Shane wrapped his arms around him and rolled him onto his back as he began to thrust harder and deeper. Braden felt his prostate begin to quiver and spasm.

"It's building, Shane. It's beautiful."

"I feel it, too, Braden. It's happening to me, too."

When Shane kneeled and lifted Braden into his arms, Braden wrapped his legs around his waist. Shane began to thrust his hips wildly, slapping Braden's ass with his balls, and pummeling his prostate with his cockhead. Braden nodded his head, then began to rock it back and forth as he bounced up and down.

"Oh, baby, there's no turning back now. Love me, Shane. Love me!"

"Yes, Braden, I love you. I love you!"

Braden began to grunt with each of Shane's thrusts.

"Baby. Shane. Oh, baby."

"Braden! Oh, my God. It's building."

"Fuck me, Shane. Fuck me." Braden began to slam himself down against Shane's hips.

"Braden … Braden … oh, my Braden, my Braden. Baby, just like that. Ride my cock, just like that!

"Fuck me, Shane!"

Shane's prostate began to spasm. "It's building, Braden. Oh, my God, it's building."

"Fuck me, Shane!"

Shane began to whimper. "Braden. My Braden."

"Say it again, Shane."

Shane continued to whimper. "Braden, my Braden, my love."

"Yes, Shane! Yes!"

Braden's prostate clamped down. As cum began to fly from his cock and spray across Shane's chest, Shane thrust one last time.

"Braden, I'm coming. I'm coming!"

They came together, pumping out wave after wave of their musky spunk. Sticky globs of Braden's white cum clung to Shane's thick chest hairs. As Shane pumped his load deep into Braden's depths, Braden kissed him with more passion than he'd ever known.

They devoured each other's faces as their bodies gyrated in a synchronous rhythm of ecstasy.

When it was over, Shane leaned forward and gently laid Braden on his back. He held himself inside Braden until his cock slipped out on its own. A moment later, his load of cum gushed out of Braden and pooled onto the sheets. Braden turned to his side and offered his back to Shane, so he lay down behind him and wrapped him in his arms, and that was how they remained until the next morning.

Chapter Twenty-Eight
Where Do I Sign?

Saturday, January 9, 2010, 8:10 AM
When Shane and Braden walked into the dining room, Conrad and the security staff were already eating breakfast. Aaron and Jason were talking between themselves, having finished eating a good ten minutes earlier, and Claudia and Winston were going over papers together.

"Good morning, guys," Shane said to everyone. The staff nodded their heads, but didn't make eye contact with him. Conrad smiled, gently.

"Good morning, Shane, Braden," Conrad answered.

"Good morning, Mr. Jason. Good morning, Mr. Aaron."

"Good morning, Shane," Aaron said. "How are you this morning?"

"Much better, thank you."

"I'm glad to hear it."

"Thanks, Mr. Aaron."

"We're expecting your father at about eight-forty. Rod called to say they'd be a few minutes late taking off because there was so much luggage and supplies to load."

"Okay, thanks for letting me know, Mr. Aaron."

Jason cleared his throat and stood up. "If everyone could listen up for a moment. We're going to have a full house this weekend. We have five more guests arriving along with Rod and Jack. They're all very important to Aaron and me, so we'd appreciate it if everyone went out of their way to be helpful to them because they've never been here before. Also, for the security staff…" Jason waited until he had their attention.

"The chief asked me to let you know to keep yourselves available for a staff meeting around mid-morning. That's all I know." There were murmurs among them, but none of them asked any questions.

When Shane sat down several officers whispered questions to him. "Sorry, guys. I don't know anything about any staff meeting. I'll probably find out when you do."

****

8:50 AM

Jason, Aaron, and Charity waited on the front porch for the party of seven to arrive from the landing pad. While greetings began, a young man and two young women waited together in silence. Aaron spread his arms wide. "Welcome, Simone, welcome, Penelope. Welcome to our home."

"Aaron, this place is amazing. Jason, it's not at all what I expected."

"Oh, Simone, you don't know the half of it," Jason answered. "I didn't recognize the place myself when we got back here. There have been so many modifications, I don't think I've seen them all yet, but welcome, welcome nonetheless."

"Hello, Penelope. I'm so glad you were able to come up."

"Jason, Simone is right. This place is amazing!"

"Ladies, may I present Miss Charity Hopewell, our Chief of Household Operations and cook." Aaron placed his arm around Charity's back. "Miss Charity, this is Ms. Simone Jones, CEO of Hinnen Valley Medical Center, and Ms. Penelope Whitley, an administrator there."

"It's so nice to meet you both." Charity extended her hands. "Welcome. Your cottages are all ready for you."

"It's wonderful to meet you, Miss Charity." Simone's eyes beamed warmly. "I've heard a lot about you."

"How nice to meet you, Miss Charity." Penelope shook the offered hand.

"Cottages?" Simone asked. "Really, cottages?"

"That's what we've decided to call them." Aaron held the door open and waved them inside. "They really are rather nice."

"There's plenty of room," Jason added. "You can each have your own or you can room together. It's completely up to you."

Aaron began to address the three new faces. "Hello, and you must be—"

Charity interrupted. "Will everyone please come inside? It's too cold to be saying our hellos out here."

"Now that's better," she said once the door was closed. "Mr. Rod, how are you this morning?"

"I'm wonderful, Miss Charity, yourself?"

"I'm busy."

Charity signaled for her children to approach. "Mr. Jason, Mr. Aaron, may I introduce my children, Eugene, Fiona, and Evelyn."

"Welcome to all of you." Jason shook their hands.

"We're looking forward to talking with all of you later this morning," Aaron added. "Thank you for coming."

Charity extended her arms to Simone and Penelope. "Now if you ladies will follow me, I'll take you to your cottages. Where is your luggage?"

"Jack is unloading everything, Miss Charity," Rod answered. "I have to get back to him with the ATV. We'll be back shortly with everything, including your food supplies."

"Thank you, Mr. Rod. My children, please follow us as well."

"Hello, Chief," Jason said. "Would you like some breakfast before we meet? We have all day to talk."

"Thank you, Mr. Jason, but I picked up something on my way to the hangar. I'll make myself ready whenever it's convenient for you."

"Why don't you drop your things off at security and then meet us in our office?" Aaron suggested. "We've made some improvements for you and your staff during your absence.

"Thank you, Mr. Aaron. I'll be there in five minutes."

****

Jason and Aaron's office

"Have a seat, Chief." Aaron directed him to the sofa.

"Thank you for meeting with me, both of you."

"How can we help you, Chief?" Jason asked.

"I'm afraid I'm going to have to cancel my contract to provide your security services. I'm going to have to go out of business."

"What?" Jason and Aaron said together, shocked.

"Yes, I'm sorry, but it's out of my control. After the event that occurred earlier this week, I can no longer afford to stay in business. I'm going to have to liquidate the entire operation."

"Isn't there any way you can avoid this, Chief?"

"I'm afraid not, Mr. Jason. I just don't have the funds to continue operations. I never would have thought it would come to this, but unfortunately, it has."

"We'd like to help, Chief," Aaron said.

"I don't understand, are you offering me a loan?"

"Not quite, but we need to learn what has happened," Jason said. "May we bring in our attorney,

197

Claudia Duncan and our financial manager, Winston Tanner?"

"Yes, certainly."

After he dialed the phone, Jason spoke into the mouthpiece. "Claudia, would you and Winston please come to the office? Thank you."

A minute later the door opened, and Jason began, "Chief, this is Claudia Duncan, and this is Winston Tanner."

After they shook hands, everyone sat down around the coffee table. Jason picked up where he left off. "Chief, while we were still in the hospital, I began to think about security for Nathan's Promise. Aaron and I have talked about it several times since then, and we've decided that as much as we have been impressed with your operation here, we really want out own security force for the rehab center. Please do not think for one moment that this reflects negatively on you or your company in any way. It doesn't. It's purely a business decision. Aaron."

"Thank you, Jason. Chief, yours was the first company we thought about, and we planned to make an offer to you to either buy your company or invest in it as partners before we looked elsewhere. Regardless of whether you showed an interest, we had planned to retain your services for our personal security. Shall we go on?"

"Yes, please do."

Jason cleared his throat. "We're still interested, but we need to know the specifics of whatever this event was that occurred earlier this week in view of the fact that it has now forced you to consider closing up shop."

"Chief," Claudia began, "consider this as an exploratory meeting where investors learn about a company they're interested in. All information presented by both parties will remain in strict confidence. I have papers already drawn up to that effect if you would like to sign them for your own peace of mind. The only thing is, we weren't able to find a notary who could fly up here today."

"The papers aren't important, Claudia—may I call you Claudia?"

"Yes, of course."

"And a notary won't be a problem. One of my guards, Natasha, is one. As far as I know, she always has her seal and her log book with her."

"That's good to know, Chief."

The chief began, "Here's what happened. One of my guards shot and killed a man. It was a good shoot, but the deceased was an executive for the client company. He was assaulting a female employee, and when the guard tried to stop him, the man repeatedly came at the guard, threatening him with a knife. The guard shot him in self-defense after all other attempts to stop him had failed.

"When I spoke with you yesterday, my insurance carrier had already threatened to drop us the moment I notified them about the shooting. They claimed the incident was gross negligence and stated that our policy doesn't cover us for that kind of incident. Because the client is a major company they will do anything to prevent their reputation from being sullied by burying the truth about the incident. They have a huge legal division, and my carrier doesn't want to go up against them in court. The carrier informed me at the end of the day yesterday that they were dropping me.

"I appreciate you sending your friend, Joshua Bergmann, to me, Claudia, but with the carrier dropping us, I can't afford his fees. He's quite expensive. I'm going to have to liquidate the company to raise the cash I'll need to pay our legal fees with a less expensive legal firm."

"Joshua is worth every penny, Chief," Claudia said. "I can attest to that. He's one of the best criminal and civil attorneys I've ever worked with. I've never known of a case he believed in that he didn't win."

"So, the problem you're facing is because of the cost to defend your guard and your company?" Jason asked.

"Yes, I'm afraid so."

"And you know the guard to be honest and that it was a good shoot?"

"Yes, Mr. Jason, but what can I do?"

"That's where we can help you, Chief," Aaron said. "Chief, we'll hire Joshua to defend your company and the guard, and we'd like to buy your company for five million dollars."

"You what?"

"We'd like to buy your company," Jason said. "We would want you to run it as a hands-on CEO, but we want to own it. We envision expanding it regionally, then nationally, then internationally to include Canada, South America, and Europe. We're prepared to offer you a contract to that effect. All we need to know is how old you want to be when you retire."

"Mr. Jason, Mr. Aaron, my company isn't worth even a fifth of that, not even a tenth. All monies that come in have had to go right back out to pay salaries and expenses and for supplies like uniforms, communication equipment, and armament. That's way too much money."

"We're not just buying your assets, Chief," Jason went on, "we're buying your reputation and your knowhow. Don't sell yourself short."

"I don't know what to say."

Aaron leaned forward. "Say yes, Chief."

"I had always wanted to leave it to my children.

Could they have a part in it?"

"If that's what you want," Jason answered. "We're prepared to offer them positions and with you running it, you would have a say in who your successor would be. We're even prepared to buy, let's say, only sixty percent of it, but then our offering price would go down to three million."

Winston added, "After the restructuring, you could divide your forty percent between yourself and your children at ten percent each if that's what you want to do, and you'd all earn dividends on your shares. As the company makes money, so would you, in addition to your salaries. I can help you set that up if you like."

"Where do I sign?"

"I must advise you to use your own attorney to look over the contract, Chief," Claudia said.

"I'll take your advice, Claudia, but consider this a sealed deal. I'll give you my attorney's email address and fax number. You can send a copy of the contract to him by either method." Chief Steinecker offered his hand to Jason.

"Please don't shake his hand, Jason. If you do, it could be argued that you both have accepted the terms of the contract, and the chief's attorney hasn't read it yet."

"Then how about a hug?" the chief said. "It's not something I normally do, but it seems appropriate today."

After everyone hugged, the chief continued. "I have to tell you both that Shane spoke with me just before I came in here. He informed me that he had talked to you earlier because you'd learned that he was upset and that you surmised from our conversation that we were in trouble. He's a good boy, that one. You wouldn't know it to look at him, but he has a sensitive side. When he told me you wanted to help, never in my wildest dreams did I imagine that this is what you meant by *help*."

Chapter Twenty-Nine
Coming Out

10:15 AM

"How do you think the staff meeting went, Shane?"

"Fine, Dad, but can we go somewhere to talk privately? I need to talk to you about something very important, and I don't think the conversation should take place in the security office. People might overhear."

"I don't understand, but sure. Let me ask if we can use the new meeting room."

The chief picked up the phone and spoke briefly. "Mr. Jason says the room is ours."

****

"So let's start again, Shane. Tell me, how do you think the meeting went?"

"I think it came as a shock to everyone, including myself, but once it settles in, I don't think anyone will have a problem with it. How are you going to communicate the new order of things to the rest of the company?"

"If everything goes the way I hope, I'll call each of our operations and inform the person in charge. Then I'll send out letters to each employee to lay out the schedule for the transition, once it's been finalized. Just remember, the papers haven't been signed yet."

"Are you comfortable with your decision, Dad?"

"Surprisingly, yes. When I arrived here this morning, I was a broken man. I believed I had lost everything I've spent the last ten years building, but in a matter of just a few minutes, my life, all of our lives, yours, and your sister's and brother's, took a turn for the better. Those two men are unbelievable. I just can't understand why they did it."

"Dad, last night, Mr. Jason said to me, and I'm paraphrasing, 'They believe in you because you've done everything you can to keep them safe and that they were going to do everything they could to help you'."

"What I don't understand, Shane, and I'm not questioning why you did it, but why did you think to go the them?"

"I didn't, Dad. It was Braden."

"Braden? The nurse?"

"Yes, Dad, he's helped me more than you could know. He's a terrific guy. He told me that they were the kindest, most giving people anyone could ever meet and that he's never known anyone like them. Before I knew it, he had them come and talk to me.

"They were so kind and understanding. Even more, they were completely respectful when I told them that I couldn't tell them what had happened because I gave my word that I wouldn't. It was after that, even without knowing what was wrong or what had happened, when they said they were going to do everything they could to help you."

"Shane, I'm still not completely clear. How did Braden become involved?"

Shane became quiet. He lowered his head, and then his shoulders began to heave and shake. "Shane? Son? Are you crying? Tell me, what's happened?"

Shane spoke through his tears. "Can you just be Thaddeus Steinecker, my dad, right now and not the Chief of Security?"

"Oh, my God, Shane! Yes, of course. What's happened? Son, you can tell me, whatever it is."

"Dad, Braden has helped me so much. He's a lot like Jason and Aaron. He's so kind."

"I'm listening."

"Dad, I went to see Braden the evening that you

left so he could help me with my pulled groin muscle."

"Yes, I remember."

"He was so kind, and so gentle, and so understanding. We've become good friends in a just a few days. Dad, I haven't had a friend like that for a very long time."

"Oh, Shane, I'm sorry, I didn't know."

"I went to him last night for another massage, but I was too upset about what you told me on the phone, and I couldn't hide it. He immediately recognized that something was wrong. He tried to help, but like with Jason and Aaron, I couldn't tell him what was wrong, but that didn't matter to him. He listened, and he wanted to help, and the next thing I knew, they were there, at his cottage, offering to help you."

"That was very nice of him. At his cottage?"

"Yes, that's what they're calling the quarters for everyone but security. Dad, there's more, but before I tell you, I need your word that you'll listen to me before you say or do anything."

"Now I'm getting worried, Shane, but go on, I give you my word."

"Dad, I told you Braden is a lot like Jason and Aaron, that he's kind, but Dad, he's like them in another way."

"You mean…"

"Yes, Dad, Braden is gay."

"I would have never guessed. I'm glad to know that that's not preventing you from being friends with him. Your uncle Cornelius had a hard time keeping friends once they knew he was gay."

"Dad, that's not what I'm getting at. Yes, Braden is gay, just like Jason and Aaron, but Dad…"

"Shane?"

"So am I."

"Shane?" Thaddeus Steinecker's mind began to whirl.

"Yes, Dad, I'm gay."

The color drained from Thaddeus's face; then it flushed; then the veins on his neck and forehead stood out, and he turned purple.

"Please, Dad, you gave me your word. Please calm down."

Thaddeus's voice was strained. "Are you sure, Shane? Did he drug you? Did he do something to you? Did he take advantage of you?"

"No, Dad. Think about it. I've got at least seventy pounds on him, all muscle. Do you really think he could take advantage of me?"

"I don't know, Shane. It's possible."

"No, Dad, he didn't take advantage of me. He didn't do anything to me. It was more the other way around. I came on to him."

"Shane, I don't know what to say."

"Dad, please don't hate me."

"Hate you? I could never hate you. I love you, Shane. You're my son." Thaddeus Steinecker leaned over and kissed Shane of the forehead and hugged him.

"Oh, Dad."

"May I ask you something, Shane?"

"Yes, of course."

"How long have you known?"

"I really don't know when I first knew, but it's all I can remember, ever since I was a boy. I didn't know what it was, but I knew I was different, that I liked boys, not girls."

Thaddeus Steinecker became quiet. When Shane reached for him, he waved him away. "No, give me a minute." Then Thaddeus's pupils dilated. He raised his right hand from his lap and placed the back of it over his mouth for a moment. "Shane, I think I've always known. If I look deep down in my heart, and I'm honest with myself, I've always known."

"But, you've been asking me more and more about young ladies recently?"

"I guess it was because it was easier for me to avoid the truth, but I promise you, it wasn't a conscious thing. You made it so easy to do that, and I wanted grandchildren. I'm sorry, Shane."

"I had to hide it, Dad. I didn't have any choice, and what about Uncle Cornelius, Dad? He has children."

"Yes, he does, and I love them, but he had to adopt them. They're not his blood."

"Dad!"

"Oh, God! Forgive me. What am I saying? Shane, I'm sorry."

"It's okay, Dad. I can understand how a man can want his bloodline to go on, and it still can. There are women who become surrogate mothers for gay couples now, but that doesn't mean that a man can't open his heart up to a child who needs him."

"Oh, Shane, of course. You're such a good person, such a good man. I love you for saying that."

"I love you, too, Dad."

"Is he good to you, Shane, this Braden?"

"Dad, he's the most beautiful soul I've ever encountered. He makes me happy, and he loves me. And I love him. I know that may sound cliché and naïve, but it's the truth. I'm not going to go into the details of it, I don't think you want to hear all that, but I can tell you something clicked deep inside me, and I recognized it right away. It's never happened to me before. I knew instantly."

"I believe you, Shane. The same thing happened to me with your mother. I knew back then, too. I think she would be happy for you. She used to call you her *sweet boy*. So, when can I meet him? I mean, really meet him, formally."

"I don't know, but we'll make it happen. You should also know that Ryan knows. He figured it out, and I hope he'll honor his promise to not say anything about how he figured it out, but you should know that he knows."

"How do you want to handle this with everyone else?"

"I plan to live my life honestly … and openly. Now that *you* know, I don't have to hide it anymore."

"At some point, you'll have to tell your sister and brother, or do they already know?"

"They've known for a while, Dad. Please don't be mad at them for that."

"I'm not, Shane. I did the same thing for my brother. I understand. May I offer you one piece of advice?"

"Sure, Dad."

"Make an announcement to your coworkers soon. Just come out with it, and take advantage of the shakeup they're experiencing right now with the new company organization. Not that I think it would ever be a problem, but it will soften the blow for them and for you the sooner you do it."

"I'll talk to Braden soon. Maybe we can meet this evening in his cottage. It would be private there. Would that be okay with you?"

"That would be great. One thing though, I think you're taking a familiar tone with Mr. Jason and Mr. Aaron."

"Dad, they've asked me to call them by their names, no Mister or sir, but be assured, when I'm working, I'll be appropriate."

"Good, I'll plan on meeting Braden tonight, unless I hear otherwise."

****

10:45 AM

"Excuse me, Chief, Shane, I was just checking to see how long you'll need the meeting room. We have a list of interviews and meetings to get through today."

"Hey, Aaron," Shane answered. "Yes, we were just leaving."

"Thank you."

"Aaron, I've been talking with my Dad about Braden."

"Talking about Braden?"

"Yes, Aaron, I've told him."

"Oh good, I'm over the moon happy for you." Aaron hugged him. "I'll let Jason know."

"We're leaving right now. Thanks for the use of the room."

"You're welcome."

Chapter Thirty
Job Offers

11:00 AM
Jason and Aaron's office

Aaron greeted them on the porch, just outside the door. "Hello, Simone, Penelope. I can't tell you how much we've been looking forward to your visit."

"Yes," Jason added from the doorway, "we feel we owe you a debt of gratitude for the way you took care of us while we were in Hinnen Valley Medical Center."

"Jason, Aaron, you owe us nothing," Simone answered.

"Then, how should I put this? We're great admirers of yours. Sorry for the confusion, but we decided to meet in our office. It's more comfortable. Please, come inside."

After everyone was seated around the coffee table, Jason continued. "The way you conducted yourselves, your professionalism, and your genuine concern for our wellbeing has touched us deeply."

There was a knock at the door. "Excuse me." Evelyn pushed in a service cart. "I don't mean to disturb you, but Miss Charity asked me to bring these to you. She thought you might enjoy some refreshments."

"Oh!" Aaron stood up. "What did you bring us?"

"Tea, coffee, hot cocoa, and some *nibbles* as she calls them."

Aaron helped Evelyn move the trays to the conference table. "Miss Charity's nibbles are the best. Please thank your mother for us."

"I will, sir. Please call if you'd like anything else." Evelyn walked to the door and closed it behind her.

After everyone helped themselves to

refreshments, Aaron began. "Penelope, I don't know whether Simone has told you, but we're looking to forge a business relationship with the medical center once we begin operations at Nathan's Promise. We're hoping to use your facility for any medical needs our patients might have while they're with us or if emergencies arise where hospital care would be called for."

"She didn't go into detail, but, yes, she mentioned something along those lines."

"We're also looking to learn how you go about soliciting donors, how to navigate soliciting bids from construction and architectural firms, and how to deal with local bureaucracies to get the project started. Are there any companies you would recommend? We're really out of our league in these matters."

"We've drafted a list, based on who we would recommend. Simone has it."

Simone pulled several papers from her portfolio and handed them to Aaron as she began to speak. "I wasn't there when the medical center was built. There was a steering committee, and some of the key players are still on the board. There's some folks there who I think would be very beneficial to your mission."

"Thank you, but do you think they would be gay friendly? That will be at the heart of the rehab center."

"Absolutely, Aaron, many are philanthropists, and I believe there's some who would endorse and be very supportive of that kind of vision."

"Penelope," Jason added, "we've also realized that we might need to establish an advisory board and a volunteer auxiliary."

"I'm sure we can help with that, Jason. There's a list of names on one of the papers that Simone handed to Aaron."

"Simone, have you discussed the other matter

with Penelope?" Aaron asked.

"No, I haven't."

"Penelope," Jason said, "we're looking for an operations manager to run the entire facility on an administrative level. Aaron and I will guide the vision of the center and make the big decisions, but we'll need someone who knows how to put them into operation. We want to know if you might be interested in the position."

"Me?"

"Yes, you, Penelope."

"Penelope," Simone said, "when Jason and Aaron mentioned the position to me, you were the first person I thought of. I didn't tell him beforehand that you came to me looking to pull back on some of your responsibilities with us, and that you were going to look for another position elsewhere, but I think this might be the perfect fit for you. I know how the loss of your parents has affected your life. If you take the position, I would be genuinely happy for you."

"I don't know what to say, Simone." Penelope turned to Jason. "Jason, I'm very touched by the offer, especially in view of the way I treated you the first time we met. You truly are a kind and forgiving man."

"That's very kind of you to say, Penelope, but I have to ask you to never bring it up again. That's water under the bridge. We both made mistakes early in our relationship, and I'm not very happy with myself for the way I treated you either. So, please, let's never speak of it again."

"Very well." Penelope turned to Simone. "Simone, we've worked so hard together to make Hinnen Valley Regional the state-of-the-art medical center it is today. I've invested so much of myself in it, and you have, too. It's become my life's work, and I'll always be grateful for your guidance and your support."

Simone took her hands. "Penelope, I understand how difficult it can be to let go of something you've invested so much of yourself into, but you're my friend, and I want you to be happy in whatever you do."

"Jason, Aaron," Penelope said. "Can I think about it for a while? I don't know if I can even make a decision this weekend."

"Absolutely, Penelope," Jason answered. "We don't even have blueprints for the center yet, let alone an architect, but if you do decide to come on board, we'd want you get you involved whenever you would be ready to join us. Take all the time you need."

"Think about it," Aaron added, "that's all we ask."

"Okay, I will."

"Very good," Jason continued. "Now let's take a look at those lists you've prepared. We'll break for lunch, and then we can reconvene afterwards."

"Just a reminder, Jason," Aaron added. "We also have those four other interviews to conduct today."

"You're right. That completely slipped my mind. Thank you for reminding me. Now what's next on our agenda?"

"Lars."

"That's right. Let's do that before lunch. I'll give him a call right now."

****

11:35 AM

After they shook hands, Aaron waved Lars to the couch and then took a seat in the opposing chair not occupied by Jason. "Thanks for coming, Lars. Jason and I wanted to talk to you about something."

"Sure, guys. What's up?"

Jason began. "We want you to know how grateful we are to you for you coming up to help us out and for staying longer when I was ordered not to care for the animals."

"Well, I won't tell if you won't, but the good doctor was right. You should have been taking it way easier than you did."

"And I did, finally … after a fashion."

"Like I said, I won't tell."

"Truth is, it took all my willpower to not dig in and work right along beside you in the barn, but that's not what we wanted to talk to you about." Jason took a deep breath. "We're looking for someone to run a farm we want to establish that will provide all the produce, dairy, and much of the meat for Nathan's Promise, and we think you're the man for the job. We wanted to offer it to you first."

"Jason, as you know, I have my own farm to run at my home. It's not big, and I barely eke out a living, but it's mine."

"We understand that," Aaron said. "And you can still keep it if you want, but the position we're looking to fill comes with a lot of perks. I think it would be worth your while to consider it."

Jason leaned forward. "Can we at least present our case to you?"

"Sure. I'll listen, but I'm not making any promises."

Aaron reached to the table and picked up a typed-up piece of letterhead. "The managing director of the farm will have total control over its operation and will be responsible for designing it, overseeing its construction, outfitting it, and running it."

"I'm listening."

"The position comes with a home on the property, built to the director's specifications, and includes health, dental, disability, and life insurance, and an annual salary of three hundred thousand dollars to start."

Lars's jaw dropped. He was silent for a long time. Then he spoke. "Are you guys serious? Have you thought this out?"

Aaron smiled. "We're very serious."

"If I understand Nathan's Promise clearly, and what I assume will be the amount of food an operation that large will require, no one could make a farm of that size work on that much money and still pay their own bills. Not after buying seed, and livestock, and supplies and paying utilities, and staff, and such."

Jason interlocked his fingers in front of his knees as he scooted to the edge of his chair. "Those things wouldn't come out of the salary, Lars. That's what the job pays. All those other things would come out of the farm's operational budget."

"That's an insane amount of money!"

Aaron stood up. "We don't think so."

"Then I don't get it. You're going to pay someone that much just to run it? That's an astronomical figure. It won't even be able provide your produce over the winter. You'll have people knocking down your doors, clamoring for a job like that."

"We won't have to if you say yes," Aaron said. "And you've heard of greenhouses, right? They'd be used after the normal growing season, even during it, if that would work better."

"I don't know what to say."

"Say yes," Jason said.

"My impulse is to do just that, but I really need to think about it. I don't know how I'd manage two farms. I have a foreman and three other employees who are counting on me."

"You're welcome to hire them if you take the position, and you'd determine their salaries. In addition to all the insurances we already mentioned, housing would be included for them, too."

"I'll have to talk to my wife before I make any decisions."

Aaron looked at Jason. "What would you think of a joint venture?

"Good idea, Aaron, we never considered that."

Aaron sat down next to Lars on the couch. "If it's important to you, we'd be willing to front the money to get it started. You would earn a stake in it over time, if that would work for you. That way you wouldn't have to divide your attention between two separate farms. You could move all your animals to the new farm, even keep them separate if you want."

"Jason, Aaron, this is too, too much. I can't even wrap my mind around it. Things have been so tight for us. My farm is old. It needs a lot of work. So does my house. The money you've paid me to come up here is going to go towards making up the shortcomings for the past year. I don't know what I'd do with the kind of money you're offering."

Aaron laughed. "You'll spend it … on yourself … on your wife and kids. You'll take vacations with it and make a better life for you and your family. You'll move into a brand-new home with a new, modern farm, and state of the art buildings and equipment."

"Think about it," Jason said. "Call your wife and talk it over. Then come back to us with your answer."

"I will. I will. Thank you, both of you for thinking of me."

Jason stood up and held out his hand. "You're our first choice."

Lars stood up and shook both their hands one at a time, then awkwardly, hugged them.

When Lars turned to leave, Aaron patted him on

the shoulder. "Let us know as soon as you decide."

Chapter Thirty-One
Hires and Acquisitions

12:00 PM

As guests and staff gathered around the table for lunch, Aaron spoke with Charity in the kitchen while Jason entertained everyone else in conversation. "Miss Charity, Jason and I wanted to know about your children's needs for jobs. Are they all currently employed, or are they looking for something right away?"

"They all have jobs, Mr. Aaron. Why do you ask?"

"I've had a thought. You said you wanted to take some time to think about whether to accept our offer to become the Hospitality Director."

"Yes, Mr. Aaron, I'm still thinking about it."

"You also said that all of your children were qualified to be personal assistants or secretaries and then this morning you told us they all knew their way around a kitchen."

"That's true. What are you suggesting?"

"I'm suggesting that one of them could be your assistant, whatever that would entail. If you become the Hospitality Manager, they could step right into the position whenever you decide you want to retire. If you don't take the position, they can work here with you to learn the ropes of how we operate in our home. Nathan's Promise will operate much the same as we do here because it will reflect our values, just on a much grander scale."

"Mr. Aaron, I appreciate that, but I don't want any special favors. They have to make it on their own in the world. I've given them a good foundation to build from, but I'm not one for nepotism."

"Well then, let's just say that they're all qualified for all three positions. Who would you want as your assistant with the understanding that he or she would eventually move into the Hospitality Manager's position?"

"I'll give it some thought, Mr. Aaron."

"Wonderful."

****

4:00 PM
Jason and Aaron's office

Jason dialed the phone. "Miss Charity, I'm sorry to disturb you. I know you must be busy with dinner preparations, but would you have a moment to come to the office?"

"Yes, I can spare a few minutes. Would you like to see me now?"

"Yes? Thank you. We'll see you in a few minutes."

****

"Thank you for pulling yourself away from the kitchen, Miss Charity," Aaron said. "We've interviewed your three children, and we want to run a few ideas by you."

"Certainly, Mr. Aaron. How can I help?"

"Miss Charity," Jason began, "we've decided to hire Eugene as our personal assistant, but we can't decide which of your daughters would be best for the other two positions. We believe they're equally qualified. In speaking with them, however, we believe that Evelyn has a greater affinity for the hospitality end of things and Fiona seems to gravitate more towards the secretarial or office manager side of things. What are your thoughts?"

"Since Mr. Aaron spoke with me at lunch, I've given it some thought, and I have to agree with your assessment of all three of them."

Aaron added, "So to be clear, you would be

219

comfortable with us employing all three of your children in the capacities Jason has just laid out? If not, please say so now. We wouldn't want to create any problems for you. The reason I ask is that it's hard to read you on this issue. You've been very clear about nepotism and them having find their way in the world. We don't want to upset the applecart."

"Yes, Mr. Aaron, I'd be comfortable. I distanced myself from the matter because I've always wanted to be certain they could make their own way, and I didn't want my opinion to influence either of you. If you're really going to do this, it would make me very happy, but in a way, it's going to be harder for them, being employed here. No matter how I'll try not to be, I'll always be their mother, and their performance will be a reflection of what I've tried to teach them."

"We can live with that, Miss Charity, and a good reflection it is. Would you like to give them the good news, or shall we?" Jason asked.

"Mr. Jason, that's not my place. Now if you don't mind, I've got a crown roast in the oven that I have to get back to."

"Very good, we'll call them in one at a time and make our offers. Do you know where they are right now?"

"In the kitchen, with me."

"We promise we won't take more than five minutes with each of them."

****

Saturday, January 9, 2010, 4:25 PM

Claudia knocked and came into the office with Winston and Chief Steinecker. "Jason, Aaron, the Chief is ready to sign the contract. His attorney has approved it. I have Natasha waiting outside to notarize everything."

"Wonderful," Jason said.

"Where do we sign?" Aaron added.

"Chief," Claudia continued, "to be clear, it is Jaron Enterprises that is purchasing a controlling interest in your company, Steinecker Security Systems, not Jason and Aaron. Because you want to retain partial ownership, the purchase price for sixty percent of the company will be three million dollars. Jaron Enterprises, LLC is a private corporation. Jason and Aaron are the only shareholders. It was formed last week."

"I understand, Claudia. My attorney explained that to me. Just curious though, what does Jaron stand for?"

"It's a combination of Jason's and my first names," Aaron answered. "We're business partners now. We're depending on you to run the company so no more mister or sir. We're Jason and Aaron from this day forward."

"Understood." The chief shook their hands.

Winston walked to the door. "You can come in now, Natasha."

****

4:55 PM

There was a knock at the door.

"Come in," Aaron called.

"Hello, Aaron. Hello, Jason."

"Hello, Penelope," they said together.

"Do you have a moment?"

"Yes, of course." Aaron got up from his desk and waved her to the sofa. "Please have a seat."

Jason joined them.

"Thank you. After we met, I gave your offer a lot of thought, and I've decided to accept, if you're still interested in me."

"That's wonderful, Penelope!" Aaron stood up and shook her hand. "When can you start?"

"I have to give six weeks' notice, so immediately after that."

"That will be fine, Penelope," Jason said. "I must apologize, however. We failed to explain that you'd have to live up here for the interim since we're going to be running and coordinating everything from this base of operations. Would that be a problem?"

"I don't think so. I sort of assumed that, but there are a few details we'd have to work out. It would be a wonderful change of scenery, and I wouldn't have to live in my home. There are too many painful memories there that I need to distance myself from. You see, my parents lived with me. I think it would be good to be away for a while."

"Then I'm glad we can provide that for you. How do you find your cottage?" Aaron asked.

"It's really beyond words."

"Will it be big enough for you until Nathan's Promise becomes operational? We'll be building housing for the staff adjacent to the center, but that won't be ready until the center is up and running. Is there anything special you'd like to bring with you? Do you have any pets?"

"Yes, yes, and yes. I have a young cat, Sasha."

"Do you think there's enough room in your suite for whatever else you'll need to bring?"

"Yes, however, it's going to involve another mouth to feed, but that can come out of my salary."

"Can you be more specific?"

"It's my fiancé, Cody, Cody Shriver. We've been together for four years."

"That won't be a problem at all," Aaron said.

"The thing is, he's my administrative assistant at the medical center. I'd like to hire him, with your permission of course, to do the same here. Simone doesn't even know, about us."

"That sounds like a plan. Now we won't have to find someone for you," Jason said. "And don't worry, we won't tell if you won't. You see, we thought of you even before Simone recommended you."

"My lips are sealed, and I'm so glad you approve of Cody because I really wouldn't be able to take the position if we couldn't be together. If we were in the city, or I could drive home every night it would be okay, but I wouldn't think Nathan's Promise would be operational for at least a year, if not two. Being up here, where it's so remote, we'd have to be apart for too long. Don't worry though, I'll pay his salary out of mine."

"We wouldn't hear of it. We knew you'd need someone as your assistant," Jason added. "His salary will be paid by the company. Whatever you think is fair, but I hope it isn't more than what we've just offered for similar positions."

"He makes seventy-five thousand a year."

"Then you can up that by twenty-five thousand. He shouldn't make less than what we've offered to our other new employees."

"He'll be ecstatic with the news. He's also a writer."

"What has he written?" Aaron asked.

"He's done a lot of freelance work, but he's working on a novel right now. I think the scenery and seclusion will be wonderful for him."

"We can't wait to meet him," Aaron said.

"Thank you both so much. Now I have to go and tell Simone."

"There's just one other thing we haven't discussed yet," Jason said with a smile.

"I'm sorry," Penelope answered. "What have I forgotten?"

"Your salary. How does three hundred thousand a year sound? In addition, you will be provided with a new home, if you want it. Not like the cottage you're in now, but a real home with a driveway, and a garage, and a fireplace, and whatever else you want. A comprehensive healthcare package and disability and life insurance is also included."

"Jason, Aaron, I don't know what to say. That's over one hundred thousand more than I'm currently making, and yes, a new home would make all the difference in the world."

"You're worth it, Penelope," Aaron added, "every penny of it."

Section Four
Calm, Then Storm

Chapter Thirty-Two
A Feast in Celebration

6:00 PM

As people entered the dining room there were exclamations about the wonderful smells wafting from the kitchen. After everyone had taken their seats at the table, Charity and Eugene pushed in the serving cart featuring a large soup tureen on a matching platter, with matching bowls. While Fiona and Evelyn served, Charity and Eugene took a seat at the table.

"Miss Charity," Conrad said, "that soup smells incredible, and I've never seen a tureen that large before."

"Thank you, Doctor. There will be nineteen of us eating tonight, fifteen of us at the table now, and I've made special arrangements with the chief to have the security staff relieve the three who are on patrol right now, once they're finished eating, so that the others can come in and eat, too, while everything's still warm."

"Chief," Jason said, "while everyone's being served, I'd like to ask a special favor just this once."

"What's that, Jason?"

"Can we allow the guards who are on patrol to come in and join us? It's not fair that they should have to wait."

"You should know that goes against my better judgment, Jason, but in view of what's happened today, I'll allow it."

The chief spoke into his wrist. "They'll be here in a few minutes. They can watch the surveillance cameras from the monitor right there by the front door. That's my compromise."

As Fiona and Evelyn finished serving, Charity noticed the three additional security officers come in. "Oh good, here they come. Let's make places for them everyone. Then you three take a seat so I can say grace."

After the officers took off and hung up their coats and were seated, Fiona and Evelyn served them and then took their places at the table. Everyone bowed their heads.

"Dear wise and wonderful Creator of all that is, we thank you for this gathering, and we ask that you guide and look kindly upon all those present here today as they embark on the noblest of missions, to bring comfort, relieve the suffering, and restore the health of those who have been injured.

"We ask that you guide and look kindly upon those not here yet, but who will soon join our mission, and we ask that you guide and look kindly upon all who serve humanity and all the creatures who walk the lands, swim the seas, and fly the skies. Amen."

Everyone joined in. "Amen."

"Miss Charity, that was the most beautiful grace I've ever heard."

"Thank you, Miss Simone. It offends no one and includes everyone."

"That sounds like Nathan's Promise." Simone began to clap her hands. Then everyone joined in.

"To Nathan's Promise!" Simone exclaimed as she raised a glass.

"Hear, hear!" was exclaimed around the table as everyone raised their glasses to the future.

Conrad nearly danced in his chair. "Oh, my goodness, this is the best lobster bisque I've ever eaten!"

"This is out of the world!" Simone added.

"I've never tasted anything so good!" Aaron said

as he shimmied his shoulders.

"Miss Charity," Jason said. "You've really outdone yourself."

"Thank you all," Charity said. "I hope you enjoy the rest of the meal just as much."

****

After the soup was finished, Charity and her children cleared the table and returned to the kitchen.

A few minutes later, Charity and Eugene returned carrying an immense platter with a standing crown roast of beef, which they placed at the center of table in front of Charity's place. There were "oohs" and "ahs" all around. Behind her, Fiona and Evelyn carried in baskets of fresh baked bread.

"Miss Charity," Jason exclaimed as he and Aaron got up to help, "I know what I said before, but now you've really outdone yourself. This is incredible!"

"My goodness, I've eaten a few crown roasts in my life," Conrad added, "but this one takes the cake. I've never seen one this big before."

"Miss Charity," Simone asked, "how did you ever manage such a feast in a cabin in the forest? Linen, china, silver, and crystal on the table, an excellent Liebfraumilch with the bisque, and outstanding Cabernet Sauvignon now—good gracious, this rivals the most exquisite banquets I've ever attended, and I've eaten at the White House."

Charity glowed. "As you know, Miss Simone, this isn't just any old cabin in the forest, and that kitchen sure helps."

"Miss Charity is being modest, Simone," Jason said, "but I can answer your question. I did a little research. You're in the presence of the only chef to achieve three stars for ten years running in the state of South Carolina."

"Really, Miss Charity? That was you? I've eaten in that hotel!" Simone exclaimed.

"Yes, that was me, but that was in the past. The hotel has been gone for a few years now. This weekend was an opportunity for me to return to what I love, but I didn't do it alone. My three children worked right along beside me, and we're working in a state-of-the-art, restaurant-grade kitchen. Mr. Jason and Mr. Aaron made all this possible."

"Miss Charity," Chief Steinecker asked, "where did you get the recipe for these miniature loaves of sourdough bread? The aroma! They rival my mother's."

"Chief, that's Mr. Jason's recipe."

Jason beamed.

As Charity began to carve the roast, Eugene, Fiona, and Evelyn carried in more platters, bowls, and baskets. It was a great undertaking, but in just a few short minutes, and with Jason and Aaron carrying plates to everyone, they'd all been served and taken a seat at the table. Jason stood and held up his wineglass.

"A toast. To Miss Charity, Evelyn, Fiona, and Eugene, the preparers of this feast!"

"Hear, hear!"

"Another toast. To the love of my life, Aaron, from whom the vision for our mission grew, and to Nathan Taggart, in whose memory and name we journey forward."

"To Aaron! To Nathan!"

Aaron couldn't help himself. He stood up and kissed Jason in front of everyone. "I have a toast now, too. To Jason, my love and my life, my rescuer and my healer, without whom I would not be here today."

"To Jason!"

"Thank you, everyone," Jason said. "Aaron and I have a few announcements. First, and please hold your applause, Aaron and I are pleased to announce that three new employees will be joining us here, immediately. Eugene Hopewell has accepted the position as Aaron's and my personal assistant, Fiona Hopewell has accepted the position of Executive Secretary to Jaron Enterprises, and Evelyn Hopewell has accepted the position of Assistant Chief of Household Operations. Evelyn will move into the position of Hospitality Manager for Nathan's Promise sometime in the future.

"Dr. Conrad Tolbert has accepted the position as Medical Director for Nathan's Promise, and Braden Darby has accepted the position as Managing Director of Physical Therapy."

"Hear, hear! To Eugene! To Fiona! To Evelyn! To Conrad! To Braden!"

"Something new is the farm we're going to establish for Nathan's Promise. Lars Eriksen has accepted the position as its Managing Director."

"Way to go, Lars!" Rod shouted.

"To Lars!" the rest proclaimed.

"Another announcement, if I may, Chief?"

"Absolutely, Jason."

"Chief Steinecker, Aaron, and I are pleased to announce that as of four-thirty this afternoon, Steinecker Security Systems has joined the Jaron Enterprises family."

There was immediate applause from all the security staff.

"I have one final announcement. Aaron and I are also pleased to announce that Miss Penelope Whitley has agreed to join Nathan's Promise as Operations Administrator."

"To Penelope!"

"If I may?" Chief Steinecker ceremoniously pushed his chair back from the table and then stood, raising his glass. "To Jason and Aaron, the two most gentle, kind, and generous men I've ever met, and to Jaron Enterprises as we join their mission."

"To Jason and Aaron! To Jaron Enterprises!"

"Thank you, everyone," Jason said. "Now, please dig in."

As the meal progressed compliments, questions, and conversation abounded.

"This asparagus with Hollandaise is over the top."

"Braden, I'm so excited for you."

"Oh, this sauce, the Béarnaise, it's wonderful!"

"Did you see those adorable wood stoves in the cottages? Aren't they just the cutest things?"

"When will you begin, Penelope?"

"Are these carrots glazed with brown sugar *and* honey?"

"Oh, this meat, the marinade, the seasoning, Miss Charity, what's in this?"

"Is that a Glock? What kind of rounds do you carry on your belt?"

"Aaron, that was a lovely thing you said about Jason."

"Rod, I'm so impressed by the construction of the cottages, and to think, the heating and hot water are solar. Where did you ever come up with the idea for that?"

"Conrad, what has your practice entailed most recently?"

"I'd be interested to know your thoughts on exercise equipment."

"Fiona, you must be so excited. What did you do before?"

"Eugene, that's a lot of responsibility you're taking on."

"Miss Charity, may I have your Béarnaise

recipe?"

"That's a good idea, we could certainly install a fitness course. We definitely have the acreage for it."

"Can you believe these accommodations?"

"Have you soaked in your whirlpool tub yet? Mine is so relaxing, and the wall-mounted propane heater is so fast! Only sixty seconds and I had to start adding cold water."

"Oh, yes, I'll have more wine. I'm not driving anywhere tonight."

"These broasted potatoes are fabulous."

"Yes, we've all had a lot of experience in the hospitality field, but with what we're going to be doing with Nathan's Promise, it's going to be real special. We're so excited to be a part of it"

"Is your cottage satisfactory?"

As the meal wound down, Charity stood up to speak. "If I may, everyone, we're going to clear the table and bring out desserts. Why don't you all move into the living room while we make the change?"

The group's response happened organically. Instead of moving from the dining room, everyone began to carry their tableware into the kitchen. Conversations continued, and laughter abounded. Two assembly lines formed, one to scrape, wash, dry, and stack, and the other to wrap up and put away leftovers. All Charity had to do was supervise and point. In twenty minutes they were finished.

****

"Thank you, everyone," Charity said. "Never have I seen such camaraderie and cooperation at a dinner party."

"It just seemed like the natural thing to do, Miss Charity," the chief said.

"That meal was one for the record books,"

Simone added. "I'm so impressed."

"Miss Charity, this will be a night to remember," Conrad added.

"Miss Charity, do you contract out?" Braden asked. "I might have a need for your skills sometime in the future.

"Thank you, all. Thank you everyone. That means a lot to me, and to meet someone who ate in my restaurant years ago, Miss Simone, it warms my heart. Now I must insist, everyone leave my kitchen so we can prepare dessert."

****

While everyone waited for dessert. Jason served thirty-year port, Chambord, Limoncello, and a single malt scotch from behind a small bar that had been set up in a corner of the living room. The conversations that began at dinner, continued.

****

Charity stood at the doorway to the living room. "If everyone would please return to the dining room." Moments after everyone was seated the lights dimmed. A blue glow began to grow brighter and brighter, and then Charity entered carrying a tray of flaming baked Alaska.

After dessert had been cleared and the conversations dwindled, everyone said goodnight and returned to their suites.

When the dining room was clear, Jason whispered to Aaron, "Conrad has given me the green light to resume *all* activities, as long as I don't push myself too hard. Though he was pissed when he found out I had done some work in the barn, he realized I wasn't really pushing myself *too* hard. Lars chimed in to back me up. He told him he had taken over many times when I began to tire."

"That's good, baby," Aaron whispered back, "but

you're not the one who's going to be doing the pushing."

Chapter Thirty-Three
A Lay Down and a Sit Down

9:00 PM

Before retiring to the bedroom, Jason visited the animals with Lars and then closed them up for the night. He found Aaron waiting for him, spread-eagled on their bed, his semi-engorged penis lying across his left thigh.

"Oh, how I'm looking forward to this," Jason said as he leaned down and took it into his mouth. "I'm just a little jealous of my ass though."

"Why's that?"

"I'm not going to be able to taste your load."

"Then I'm going to have to be sure to make it extra special for you, my love."

"That's exactly what I want. I want you to make love to me, Aaron. I'm feeling really good about all we accomplished today, but we should still take it a little easy. I don't think I can tolerate too much aggression. Really, we're both still healing, so let's not get too wild."

"I promise, Jason, but know this, too, I can't wait either. The gas heater's on so there's lots of hot water if you want to shower first."

"I think that would be wonderful. Let's shower together, just like we did that first night."

"I was hoping you were going to say that, and the playroom is ready for us when we're finished. I've set everything up."

****

Aaron carried Jason from the bathroom into the playroom. "I've missed holding you like this, Jason. It was only that first day when I returned from physical rehab that I was able to cradle you in my arms, but I'm going to do it every day for the rest of our lives. Oh, Jason, I came so close to losing you." Aaron leaned his face down and kissed him.

Jason pulled away. "I've missed your embrace. Make love to me, my love. Make sweet love to me."

Aaron gently laid Jason down against the sling's soft leather and lifted his legs into the stirrups. "Yes, my love."

He moved to stand between Jason's legs and began to caress his chest and abdomen with his fingertips, raising goosebumps. Jason closed his eyes as his body began to tremble and his cock began to fill. When Aaron took it into his mouth, Jason gasped and began to rock his head from side to side.

"Oh, baby, yes!"

When Aaron began to caress Jason's sack, it drew up and tightened around the base of his shaft. Aaron moved his mouth to take in one ball, then the other and then rolled them around with his tongue until the sack had relaxed. As he lifted them with his fingers and gently massaged them in his palms, Jason sucked in his breath.

"Don't stop, Aaron, don't stop."

Aaron leaned down and parted Jason's crack as he drew his tongue across his anus, causing it to pucker. He began to lick in circles and then burrowed the tip of his tongue into the hole until it began to relax and open. He dipped into the jar of lube and inserted one finger, as he eased it in deeper and deeper until it was buried to the hilt.

Jason began to moan as Aaron added a second finger, working them in and out and around in circles, slowly opening Jason up further. When pre-cum began to drip from the tip of Jason's cock, Aaron covered the head with his lips and sucked the sweet nectar down. Jason clenched his anus as Aaron slid his mouth past his glans, forcing a small stream of the pre-cum up and out the shaft. Aaron drank from his offerings.

"Oh, Aaron, yes. Yes! Suck me, baby. Suck me!"

Aaron slid his fingers in deeper, until he grazed Jason's swelling prostate. He felt it began to spasm in fits.

Jason squealed. "Aaron! Oh, my God! That's the spot!"

Aaron added a third finger and continued. When the muscles, exhausted by their clenching, lost their tone, he added a fourth.

"Take me, Aaron. Please, make love to me."

Aaron's cock became so engorged with blood that pre-cum poured from the slit and formed a puddle on the hardwood floor below. "Yes, my love. I need you, too."

"Then fill me with your seed, Aaron. Fill me, please!"

Aaron slowly removed his fingers. He scooped up more lube and slid it up and down his throbbing shaft and then in one, graceful movement, slid himself inside until his balls slapped against Jason's butt cheeks.

"Yes, Aaron, yes!" Jason shouted. His cock began to twitch as his anus tried to clamp down against Aaron's shaft. As Aaron thrust, pre-cum was milked up and out the tip of his shaft, adding to the slickness of Jason hole as he pulled back. Jason's pre-cum flowed freely onto his abdomen as it pooled and then dripped down his sides. "Yes, Aaron, fuck me right there. Right There!"

Aaron pulled back then thrust forward slowly. "I love you so much, Jason. This is for you."

Aaron's pace gradually increased as his cockhead grazed the edge of Jason's prostate. Jason began to groan.

"It's building, Aaron ... Aaron, it's building. It's building!"

Aaron withdrew and slid in again. "Feel me love

you, Jason. Feel my love."

"I need you, Aaron! I need your love!"

"I'm here, my love." Aaron slid out just enough to pull past Jason's prostate. Then in short thrusts, he advanced and pulled back, in jackrabbit fashion, across the quivering orb. It swelled and swelled, growing firmer and firmer. "Feel my love, baby. Feel my love."

"Oh, my God, Aaron! Oh, my God! Please, Aaron. Please!"

"Soon, my love, soon."

****

"Welcome, Chief. Welcome to my home away from home," Braden said after he opened his door. "Come on in, both of you."

"Hello there, my boy," the chief said, extending his hand. "Thank you for having me here. Shane has been nothing but complimentary about you. I'm glad we can have this time to get to know each other."

"It's my pleasure, Chief."

"Please, call me Thad."

"Would you like something to drink, Dad?" Shane asked.

"I'll have a scotch, neat."

"Coming right up. Braden, something for you?"

"I'll have the same. Thanks. Please, Thad, have a seat."

"These really are amazing quarters, Jason and Aaron have provided for everyone. And have you seen what they did for my officers in just a few days? I can't imagine what all of this has cost them."

"I don't think that's even a consideration for them, Thad. They're generous to a fault, but it's like they're not even aware of it."

"I've gathered that. So, tell me a little about yourself, Braden."

"Let's see, I grew up all over the country. My father is an independent software developer, so we moved every few years when he took a contract with a new company. He's still working in the field. My mother is a librarian. I became a massage therapist five years ago, and while I worked doing that, I went to nursing school at an accelerated program and graduated with my Bachelor's Degree two years ago. I've been at Hinnen Valley Medical Center ever since."

"Here you go, Dad, Braden." Shane handed them each half-filled tumblers and then sat down next to Braden on the sofa.

Braden continued. "I was moving my way up to critical care when I first met Aaron as a patient. When he and Jason returned to the hospital, they asked for me. The rest is history."

"Well, it sounds like we're going to be working together and—"

A deep, rumble rattled the windows.

"That sounded ominous." Braden cocked his head to listen.

"There's a weather alert for the possibility of freezing rain tonight, but I don't remember anything about thunderstorms," the Chief answered. "What was I saying? Oh, yes, so we're going to be working together. With you managing physical therapy for Nathan's Promise, and us providing security, it looks like it's going to be a family affair."

"I'm looking forward to it, Thad."

****

Aaron began thrusting again. He lowered his hips, directing the head of his cock upward, striking Jason's prostate head on with each advance of his shaft.

"Oh, Aaron! Oh, my God! Yes, Aaron! Yes!"

Aaron encircled Jason's shaft with his meaty

hand and began to pump it up and down as he thrust his hips harder and harder.

"I'm ready, Aaron. I'm ready to come. I'm ready to come!"

Jason began to shudder and grunt with each of Aaron's advances. As Aaron drove his shaft in and out faster and faster, a deep rumble rose from Jason's chest, punctuated by the slap of Aaron's hips and balls against his ass.

"Please, Aaron, please," Jason pleaded. "I can't take it anymore. Make me come. Make me come!"

Chapter Thirty-Four
Strike One

The stockade lit up like daytime as a lightning bolt found its mark beyond the walls. Braden jumped.

"That was close." Shane put his arm around Braden's shoulders.

"I'm okay, Shane. It just startled me."

"Chief to patrol!" Thad spoke into his wrist. "Where was that strike?"

"*Outside the compound, Chief. Freezing drizzle has begun to fall,*" Alexandra replied. "*Patrick is checking it out.*"

"Let me know what he finds."

"*Will do, Chief.*"

"Sorry for the interruption, Braden, now that the two of you are in a relationship, have you thought about how you're going to conduct yourselves up here?"

"What do you mean, Dad?"

"Have you told your coworkers yet?"

"Yes, I told them before dinner. Everyone's cool with it. Even though I thought they would be, I was still a little nervous. You can never know for sure."

"They were very accepting of me, Thad," Braden added. "There was nothing but congratulations all around, and they welcomed me into the *family*."

"I'm glad to hear it, but what I was really getting at was, and I hope you don't mind me being direct, are you going to continue to be, and I can't think of a better word for it, *romantic, openly* with each other from this point on? I don't mean to be brash, but if you are, I'm going to have to consider how it will affect operations."

"Yes, Dad. I plan to move in here with Braden."

****

Jason's pleas became unintelligible. He began to

squeal again and again as his prostate clamped down. He found release as the room filled with blue-white light. Aaron could hold himself back no longer, and he let go as well.

Like a defensive guard on the line of scrimmage, Aaron thrust his hips forward as he drove himself in to the hilt, pushing Jason back and upwards as the sling's chains strained against the assault. Load after load of his semen pulsed from his loins and shot into Jason's depths.

As Jason's prostate clamped down in spasms, the first load of cum shot in an arc, up over his head. It left a trail from his hair, down his face and ended at his navel. Aaron leaned forward and took Jason's cock into his mouth. As Jason's cum shot from his shaft, he savored jet after jet of the musky, sweet nectar on his tongue, eventually swallowing a total of seven more streams.

****

"The thing is," Thad continued, "um, how should I put this? I'm concerned about what the other officers might want to do if they find they also want to take up with each other, or with someone else up here. Jason and Aaron seem to not only be okay with it, I think they're looking forward to it, and now that we're part of their company, I expect there'll be changes to that effect. The staff seems to be growing by the day, but I don't know how we could handle it.

"You're fortunate in that Braden already had his own place. I can't expect Jason and Aaron to provide separate quarters for the officers who become couples, and I'm afraid it could look like I'm showing favoritism towards my son if he isn't required to bunk in our barracks."

"On the other hand, Thad, it could create some issues if Shane spends time here in the evenings and then has to return later at night to sleep in the barracks. I'm thinking of the teasing and joking that may follow. If he stayed here, wouldn't it be more like *out of sight, out of mind*? What do you do at other facilities, where your officers aren't quartered on the premises? Do they go to their own homes when their shifts are over?"

"That's an intelligent assessment of the situation, Braden. I was thinking the same thing, but I was playing devil's advocate with you. You've obviously thought this through."

"And that's why I thought it would be all right to move in here, Dad," Shane said. "I was going to talk to you first, of course."

"I understand, son. The only problem is, we're out in the middle of nowhere. The others can't *go home*."

****

Aaron staggered backwards while his cock twitched inside Jason until Jason was lying flat on his back again.

Jason panted and gasped as he sucked air into his lungs. His arms and legs went limp, but his cock remained rock hard. Even after it had emptied, it continued to lift and fall erratically against his abdomen as his prostate was locked in a tetany-like spasm.

When Aaron pulled himself from Jason, cum oozed from his stretched hole onto the sling. Aaron leaned forward and lifted Jason into his arms. Jason wrapped his arms around Aaron's neck as he leaned his cheek against his chest.

"Oh, my love, my Jason. Thank you. Thank you for that. I was finally able to make love to you like love should be made. I feel like a man again."

"A man?" Jason groaned as he spoke. "Aaron, what do you mean?"

"All the times before, when I was injured with my broken leg and arm, I wasn't able to make love to you, not like it should be made. I just lay there. You had to do it all. Now, I can do it right. That lightning strike was exactly how I felt. I exploded."

"Aaron, my love, did you really think that what we had before was anything less than beautiful, less than perfect? And what about our last night in the hospital? What was that? You made love to me then. Oh, Aaron, no, no, I never thought it was less than anything. Please believe me."

"I do believe you, Jason, but I needed to be able to do it for myself. Yes, the hospital was wonderful, but we had to be so careful. I needed to do it just like this. Thank you for letting me."

Jason leaned back and looked up into Aaron's eyes. He caressed Aaron's face and kissed him deeply on the mouth. "I love you, Aaron."

****

From a helicopter in the sky

"Chuck, I don't know about this anymore," Frank said. "The weather's turning."

"Just get your camera ready. I know there's a story down there, and we're going to be the ones to break it."

Frank shook his head. "This hasn't been sanctioned by the station. How are you going to explain this?"

"Who says they have to know it was us who shot it?"

"Excuse me, gentlemen," the pilot said over their headpieces. "If this weather gets any worse, I'm going to have to return to base. We could start taking on ice, and the rotors don't like that."

"What does that mean?" Frank asked.

"It means we'd lose lift," the pilot answered.

"If you do bail," Chuck said, "you won't get

paid."

"Wanna bet?" The pilot rotated the yoke, jostling Chuck and Frank in their seats. "I'll sue your asses."

"Then take us down," Chuck shouted, "so we can get this over with! Let's get in and out."

****

9:50 PM

A rapid, deafening "whop-whop-whop" sound descended over the stockade. Bright light flooded the windows of Braden's living room and then traveled around the grounds.

"Down!" the chief yelled.

Shane wrapped Braden in his arms and dove for the floor as he rolled to his back to take the impact. He winced and grunted as he landed, then rolled again to cover Braden with his body.

****

As they stepped from the shower Aaron handed Jason a towel. He cocked his head, listening. "What the hell is that?

"That's a chopper, Aaron, a chopper!"

****

An alarm began to sound and a recording began to play around the stockade, throughout the main cabin. and in all the cottages.

"Take cover and hold in place. Take cover and hold in place. Response protocol alpha is now in effect. Take cover and hold in place. Take cover and hold in place. Response protocol alpha is now in effect."

"Shane, are you armed?" the chief shouted.

"No, Dad. I'm off duty tonight."

"Shane, are you okay?" Braden asked.

"I think I injured my groin again. Damn, it hurts."

"Security one to Chief," Patrick called in. *"We've got a situation. I'm still outside the wall. There's a*

chopper buzzing the compound, flooding the grounds and buildings with a spotlight."

"Take defensive positions. Institute response protocol delta. That's response protocol delta," the chief called into his wrist. "Shane, get to the armory. Braden, you stay here and take cover." The blinding light traveled past the window again.

"All civilians, take cover and hold in place. All civilians, take cover and hold in place. Response protocol delta is now in effect. All civilians, take cover and hold in place. All civilians, take cover and hold in place. Response protocol delta is now in effect."

As the chief ran to the security office, Shane skip-limped behind. Under the cover of the bridging roof, and carrying assault rifles, the security team emptied from the office, wearing bulletproof gear and helmets. As they descended the steps to the lawn, they began to slip and slide. The freezing drizzle that had begun to fall minutes before was now a thin sheet of ice. It covered everything.

****

Shane strapped on his sidearm while the chief put on his gear. Then the chief began to help Shane with his gear.

Shane pointed towards the door. "Go, Dad, go! I'll be right behind you!"

The chief armed himself with an assault rifle from the armory. As he headed out to join the team, he shouted to Natasha as he passed her at the electronics room. "Blind them."

From within the security office, Natasha directed four of the eight, high-powered, remote control spotlights, mounted around the top of the stockade's wall into the night sky, against the invading chopper by remote control.

"I've got them, Chief. They can't see a thing,"

she called over the radio. *"It looks like someone's hanging out the door with a camera on his shoulder. The aircraft doesn't have news markings, but I swear that's a news camera."*

"Make sure you're getting it all on the surveillance cameras," the chief answered back from under the bridging roof, "and that you're recording everything."

"I'm getting it all, Chief. I'm getting it all!"

****

The chopper's cabin was bathed in bright light, blinding everyone on board. The pilot recoiled as he covered his eyes and struggled to maintain control. "Shit, they're armed! I'm heading for higher ground."

"You stay right where you are," Chuck ordered. "If they start firing, I want to get it on video."

"You're crazy!" the pilot shouted as he pulled back on the yolk. "We're going up."

Chapter Thirty-Five
Strike Two

9:57 PM

The stockade exploded in blinding blue-white light, turning it brighter than daytime. A spotlight exploded as jagged, crackling electricity ran the length of the power cable down the post and out under the ground until it reached the surge suppressor at the generator. Frozen clumps of dirt, the size of tree stumps, flew into the air as the ground erupted from the electrical charge.

Lights throughout the compound dimmed, and the generator groaned. Body-armor-clad bodies froze in position and then fell to the ground, twitching. The lightning bolt reached into the sky, encompassing the chopper on its way to the clouds. Ozone permeated the air. The freezing drizzle became a steady, freezing rain.

****

Electricity danced across the chopper's control panel. It blinked off, then back on.

"That was close," the pilot said.

"Whoa, did you see that? Something exploded. Get that, Frank," Chuck ordered.

"Got it."

"Holy shit, bodies are dropping all over the place." Chuck bounced up and down in his seat. "Get that! Get that! This is going to be so great!"

"Getting it, Chuck."

"Drop down lower," Chuck ordered to the pilot. "Let's see if we can get their faces."

"Fucking asshole!" the pilot whispered to himself as he put the chopper back into a dive.

****

Natasha turned the cameras towards the interior of the stockade and zoomed in. She silenced the alarm and prerecorded message and spoke over the loudspeakers.

"Trauma emergency! Trauma emergency! All hands, report to the yard! Trauma emergency! Trauma emergency! All hands, report to the yard!"

Adrenaline coursed through Shane's body. His hands shook as he grabbed a rifle. As he headed out, his limping subsided.

****

As Braden opened his front door, he watched Simone and Penelope appear at their cabin doors in their pajamas and slippers. They began to run along the walkway towards him as he turned and headed for the yard. As they ran, Charity's cottage door flew open ahead of them. Closest to the stairs, she hurried down them in her curlers and robe, slipping along the way. A moment later, Fiona and Evelyn appeared in their nightgowns, too, just as Claudia's door flew open while she was pulling up a pair of sweatpants. She called out to him.

"Braden, what's happened?"

"I don't know yet," he yelled back over his shoulder as he almost ran into Winston, who had stopped on the little porch at the front of his cottage. Lars nearly knocked them both over as he came barreling out of *his* cottage, cocking a cartridge into the chamber of his multi-shot shotgun. Braden turned back and waved to the people behind him, then pointed out into the yard, just as Conrad appeared, still pulling on a pair of pants.

Braden shouted, "There's bodies down, everywhere!" just as Rod appeared sliding his thumbs under a pair of suspenders that held his pants up while Jack ducked under his arm as he tucked in a shirt. In a stampede, everyone rushed out to help.

****

As Eugene sprinted down the hall from his new bedroom at the back of the cabin, he called out, "Mr. Jason, Mr. Aaron, what's happened?"

"We don't know yet, Eugene," Jason shouted from his bedroom. When Eugene arrived at their door, they were half-naked, pulling on clothes.

****

"Okay, that's enough," Chuck said to the pilot. "Let's get out of here."

"The yoke is heavy," the pilot answered.

"What does that mean?" Frank asked.

"I can't get lift. We've taken on too much ice."

"Then pull up on it!" Chuck ordered.

****

"Eugene," Jason ordered, "go see what happened and report back to me right away. If you see Dr. Tolbert, tell him I'm bringing the trauma kits."

****

Inside the chopper, 100 feet off the ground

"It won't respond. I can't get it to climb." The pilot's voice was shaky.

A gust of wind struck the chopper. It began to list to the left.

****

As Braden descended the stairs, he found Shane cradling the chief in his arms. The chief's body was spasming. He was unconscious. "Is he breathing, Shane?"

"Braden, there's something wrong with him. I don't know what to do."

"Shane, is he breathing?"

"Braden, he won't answer me."

"Shane, move!" Braden pushed Shane back.

Braden felt the chief's neck. He leaned in and placed his ear over the chief's mouth and his open palm against his chest. The chief's chest rose and fell, slowly.

"Shane, he's got a pulse, and he's breathing. Carry him into the living room and get all this gear off him. Keep him warm."

"Braden, is he dead?"

"Shane, listen to me. He's alive, but he has to be kept warm. Carry him into the living room, get his gear off him, and keep him warm. There's blankets in the supply room. Now move!"

"Yes, Braden."

****

Chuck panicked. "Pull back on the stick!" He reached in front of the pilot and grabbed the yoke.

"No! You're gonna roll us!" the pilot yelled.

The chopper jerked backwards, then listed to the right. Chuck reached out to grab ahold of something as he fell to the side. His hand tightened around the yoke, pulling it with him. The chopper shuddered. It began to swing wildly in the sky. Then it fell like a stone.

****

As Braden ran out into the yard, he looked back to see Shane carrying his father up the steps.

Rod and Jack ran to the end of the bridging roof and looked into the night sky, just as the chopper began to roll onto its right side.

****

The chopper began to fall towards the ground. Frank struggled with the catch that hooked to the safety belt he wore around his waist with his left hand as he held onto the video camera with his right. As the chopper spun, the centrifugal force pulled the camera from his grasp. It disappeared into the darkness.

Plastered against the side windshield glass by the spinning chopper, Chuck screamed. "Help me, Frank! I can't move!"

Twenty feet from the ground, the catch released. Frank was thrown out the door, just as the chopper began to turn upright. He struck the ground and skidded away as the chopper hit.

As Chuck's body bounced from the impact, it was thrown through the cabin's shattered windshield. Driven against the rocky ground, the chopper's rotors fractured. Pieces flew out in all directions. Chuck's body was thrown into the path of one.

****

The chopper landed with a crash at the tree line, fifty feet beyond the wall. A deafening explosion sounded as a fireball rose into the sky, bathing the stockade in an orange-red light. Everyone within the stockade's walls ducked. Sleet began to fall.

As Shane reached the cabin, Eugene opened the door. "What happened?"

"There was lightning! There's something wrong with my dad!"

"Are there any others?"

"I didn't see. Braden told me to bring him inside."

Eugene hurried down the walkway and met Dr. Tolbert at the steps. "Sir, Mr. Jason says he's bringing trauma kits. What happened?"

"I don't know. Wait here." Conrad slipped down the stairs and landed on his ass. He pulled himself up and ran out into the yard. He found Braden performing CPR on a female guard. Another guard was performing CPR on a second guard. A third guard was on the ground, twitching. Charity was kneeling over him, cradling him in her arms while Simone checked for a pulse. Fiona, Evelyn, and Penelope each bent over a guard's face to block the frozen rain. Lars had his shotgun pointed towards the sky as he scanned it for more assailants.

Scattered all around them were large clods of frozen dirt along deep, jagged trenches cut into the earth. The exploded spotlight was smoking.

"Lightning strike," Conrad whispered.

****

When Conrad returned from the yard, Natasha met him just outside the office as Rod and Jack ran up at the same time and joined Eugene.

"What do you need, Doctor?" Natasha asked.

"What do you want us to do?" Rod asked.

Jack bounced in place. "Holy shit!" he exclaimed. "Holy shit!

"Tell Jason to set up for multiple casualties. My office isn't ready yet. Tell him to clear a triage area in the cabin. CPR's being performed on two security guards so far, and there's another one down. Electrocutions. It was a lightning strike. There's medical equipment and medications in my room. Tell Jason we're going to need all of it. I'm heading back out there now. One of you bring me my medical bag."

"Yes, sir!" they answered together.

****

Following the explosion, as the ball of fire illuminated the night sky, burning aviation fuel flew out in all directions. Frank came to a stop on his right side, thirty feet away, but he couldn't move. He couldn't move anything. As the fuel blanketed his body, Frank's skin and clothing burned. He screamed and screamed, drawing the flames into his mouth, the back of his throat, and down into his lungs.

A moment later, the remains of Chuck's head, arms, and most of his torso landed ten feet away. As Frank's voice box charred, his screams grew softer and softer until only the sound of rushing air escaped his mouth. The last thing Frank saw was Chuck's cold,

lifeless eyes staring back at him, watching him burn.
****

After finding Conrad's bag and carrying it out to him, Natasha joined Eugene in the dining room. They began to pull the chairs away from the table and set them against the cabin's front wall while Rod and Jack pulled the tables apart, making room for four bodies. Then they moved the room partitions against the cabin's side wall, opposite the kitchen.

After hearing Conrad's orders from Eugene, Aaron and Jason went to the supply room and carried in all the medical supplies and stacked it in on the chairs. Then Natasha and Eugene went with them to Conrad's suite and helped carry back a cardiac monitor, oxygen tanks, two bag valve masks, IV kits, and resuscitation medications and set it all up at the centers of the tables. Once the space was cleared, Jack and Rod went out to help carry the injured officers inside.

"I want each of them laid out so that their heads are at the table ends and their feet towards the center," Jason instructed. "That way we can manage their airways better."
****

10:15 PM

As the casualties began to arrive from the yard, Eugene directed them to the dining room. After Penelope put the officer she helped to carry onto the table, she got on her phone to arrange air transportation to the medical center.
****

Simone began cutting the uniform off one of the resuscitated officers. "Doctor, Jason, I'm a reserve trauma nurse with the Air Force. I can help. Miss Charity, get all the blankets and towels you can find and bring them in here, and turn up the heat. We have to keep these officers warm. Once you've done that, make coffee, lots of it. We're going to need it.

"You two girls, Fiona and Evelyn, start removing the other officers' clothes. Cut off what you can't pull off. There's more trauma scissors in this bag right here." She pointed. "We've got to get these cold, wet clothes off them and identify their entrance and exit wounds from the lightning strikes. When your mother gets back with the blankets, cover them up to keep them warm.

"Claudia and Winston, you inventory the clothing, and store it. Lars, you take charge of the firearms as they're removed from the officers and secure them until someone from security takes charge of them."

"Very good, Simone," Conrad began, "we can sure use you. We've only got one monitor, but plenty of electrode sets. Dry off their chests and apply a set to each of them. We'll rotate the monitor so I can get a look at their cardiac rhythms. Jason, Simone, Braden, start large bore lines in everyone, a 16 gauge if you can get it, and run in a liter of saline, wide open, then follow with a second, at least. Get a second trauma line in them if you can. They're going to have to be monitored for rhabdomyolysis, once they're in the hospital. Who's completely breathing on their own?"

"All but one, Conrad," Jason said. "It's Alexandra. She's making an effort, but she still needs help. I can't start lines as long as I'm bagging her."

"Then keep bagging her for now. Who can we teach to bag?"

"Eugene," Jason said, "there are small, white, Y-shaped splitters in baggies in both of my trauma bags. We've got only two oxygen regulators, but extra tanks. You're going to splice two lines into four. Shove one each into two oxygen tubes then connect the oxygen mask tubing into three of them. Put an oxygen mask on each officer. I'll use the fourth oxygen tube for the bag mask."

"Where's the chief?" Braden asked.

"He's in the living room with Shane," Penelope answered.

"Tell Shane to get the chief in here now," Braden said.

Jason added, "Put him down on the open spot on the table and then start taking his wet clothes off. Eugene, put a mask on him as soon as he's been moved in here."

"Penelope, what's the ETA on transport?" Simone asked.

"They can't fly until the sleet and freezing rain stops. We're on our own for a while, likely hours."

"Aaron, come here," Jason said. "You're going to learn how to use a bag valve mask. Penelope, you're going to help him."

Chapter Thirty-Six
Survivors

Sunday, January 10, 2010, 4:35 AM

Alexandra opened her eyes to see Jason looking back down at her "Hello, Alexandra, you've had quite a night."

"What happened? Where am I?"

"You're in the cabin. You were struck by lightning, but you're okay now. Dr. Tolbert is right here. We're going to fly you to the hospital very soon to get checked over."

"Where's the rest of my crew?"

Conrad leaned in. "They're all here, Alexandra."

"Are they okay?"

"Four of you were struck."

"Who, who was hit?"

Jason leaned back in. "Patrick, Natasha, and Shane are the only ones who came out unscathed. You seem to have been most affected by it, though, but Dr. Tolbert says you're going to be just fine."

"Where's the chief?"

"He was struck, too. Shane and Braden are with him. He's doing okay."

"My body feels like it's been run over by a train."

Conrad rested his hand on her shoulder. "That's from the muscle spasms, Alexandra, caused by the electricity from the lightning. It'll get better. You need to rest now."

****

Sunday, January 10, 2010, 5:50 AM

"Jason," Simone said. "Penelope just got an ETA for transport. We have to coordinate four medical helicopters, one for each electrocution victim. The chief will go last, his orders. He said he's not going anywhere until he knows all his officers have been airlifted.

"We have two helicopters, but I called in a favor. The National Guard is going to provide two more, and I've called in my entire flight staff. They're going to handle the medical end of things. The Guard will provide their own pilots and two flight medics to assist.

"I checked with Rod. He says they can't use the helipad because his helicopter is there. It can't be moved because it's still covered in ice, and it and the other pad are too far away anyway. Lars checked the yard. They can land one at a time inside the stockade because there's only one suitable spot.

"The first flight crew will be taking off in twenty minutes. The second will take off twenty minutes behind them and so on. That means we've got between ten and fifteen minutes to get each helicopter loaded and in the air."

"We can do that," Jason said.

"Excuse me, Jason," Claudia interrupted. "Miss Charity says she's worried about you. You need to get some rest."

"Thanks, Claudia. I'll sleep once everyone's been transported out of here."

Simone continued. "Penelope also notified the state police, and the FAA will be here to investigate after first light. Your friend, Inspector Addison, will be paying you a visit as well. Jack's gone outside to check on the crash site to make sure it's burned itself out. I'd have thought he'd be back by now."

"Thank you, Simone. You've been fantastic through this whole ordeal. I had no idea you were a nurse. If I may say so, you've got some damn fine skills."

"Thank you, Jason. Only a few people know it, but I pick up a few night shifts every month in our ED to keep my skills up. Now, Miss Charity is right. You need to rest. You should really consider getting yourself checked out. From what I've heard, you've been pushing yourself all week. If I remember correctly, Drs. Spencer and Baum reminded you to come back for a checkup next week. Remember, you're still recovering from surgery yourself."

"You're right, Simone. Aaron and I will both come in once everyone else has been taken care of. Rod will fly us down after the ice melts on Big Daddy. I promise."

"Good, we'll fly down together then. That way I can make sure you go. Oh, by the way, I've told Penelope she can start transitioning into her new position with you immediately. We discussed it, and she'll stay on at Hinnen Valley Regional for part of the time while she begins to take on her responsibilities for Nathan's Promise. As the time goes on, she'll work less and less with us and more with you."

"That would be great, Simone. If tonight's taught me one thing, it's that we can't build Nathan's Promise up here. Not unless we build a road to connect us to civilization. We can't afford to have another emergency arise and not be able to transport into the city immediately."

"I'm sure you'll figure it out, Jason. Penelope will be a resourceful asset for you."

"Oh, by the way, about our donation to Hinnen Valley Medical Center, I think you need at least a third medical chopper and another flight crew to staff it. That will be a good place for us to start."

"Jason! Jason! Oh, my God, Jason!" Everyone turned towards the shouting, coming from the front door.

"What is it, Jack? What's wrong? You're as white as a sheet!"

"Jason, we've got survivors! There's survivors at the crash site!

****

6:05 AM
The tree line, outside the stockade

"Doc, I've got one over here!" Rod yelled from just inside the tree line. "It's the pilot! He's busted up pretty bad, and he looks like he's in shock, but he's alive!" Rod opened a blanket and wrapped it around the man who was sitting on the ground with his back leaned up against a tree trunk.

"Doctor!" Simone called back as she and Jack kneeled down beside a charred body, twenty yards from the stockade wall. "This one's still breathing! Major burns! From the body shape I'd say it's male. He's really struggling. Eschar's constricting his airway and his chest and he's severely hypothermic. You're going to have to act fast if we're going to save him. There's also the upper half of another body over here, male as well."

"Simone," Jack gagged. "he looks like a mannequin that's been set on fire. He doesn't any clothes left."

"I know, Jack, but we're still going to try to help him."

"But his, his…" Jack pointed towards the burned man's groin.

"I know, Jack."

"They're gone, Simone. There's nothing there."

Conrad headed towards Simone's voice. "Hold on, Rod!" he called towards the tree line. "I've got to attend this one first, but put pressure on anything that's bleeding! Lars, pull the ATV up and shine the headlights on Simone and Jack so I can see what I'm doing."

As Simone moved to above the man's head and put on a pair of surgical gloves from her trauma kit,

Conrad kneeled down and opened his medical bag. When Simone placed her left hand along the left side of his face, the ash and charred remains of what had once been his ear crumbled beneath her fingers.

"Sir," Conrad said, "the swelling in your neck and chest are making it difficult for you to breathe. I'm going to relieve that."

After Lars positioned the ATV, Simone and Conrad, together with Lars and Jack's help, log-rolled the man onto his back with Simone supporting his neck.

"Lars," Conrad ordered, "go help Rod. Come back as soon as you can and report to me what you've found, but first, cover what's left of the other body."

"Yes, Doctor."

Jack unfolded a blanket and began to cover what remained of the man's charred body.

As Conrad pulled a scalpel from his bag, Simone noted, "He hasn't moved, Doctor. I think he's paralyzed."

"From his injuries, I'm not surprised. Burns like this would cause someone to run away. It appears he lay here and just burned until the fuel was consumed." Conrad removed the scalpel blade's cover. "Okay, here we go. Hold his head, Simone. I'm going to do a bilateral escharotomy parallel to his trachea and then down both sides of his chest. You might want to turn away, Jack. I don't think you'll want to watch this."

"But, Doc, he's gonna scream!"

"No, Jack, there's no nerves left with these burns."

Jack reached for the man's hand. "Squeeze my hand if it hurts," he said. When he lifted the man's hand, there were no fingers left. Jack turned his head away and vomited on the ground.

After Conrad drew the scalpel through the

charred tissue on each side of the windpipe and from the collarbones down to the top of the abdomen, the man's breathing grew less labored.

As the skin flayed open, and serum began to ooze from the surgical wounds, Jack retched again. "Oh, my God. It looks like medium-rare steak."

When Conrad began to apply sterile dressings over the incisions, the man tried to speak, but what remained of his tongue was barely moveable and what little was left of his lips were fused in place. In addition to his left ear, his eyelids and nose were gone, and his eyeballs were the consistency of hard-fried eggs.

As Conrad pulled a vial of morphine from his bag and drew up ten milligrams, Simone nodded towards the patient's right side. "Doctor, his right arm and leg have some second-degree burns. There might be IV access somewhere, but I can't let go of his head right now to help you. I don't know where you're going to give it. He's got third and fourth degree burns everywhere else."

"I'm going to insert a sixteen-gauge catheter directly into his internal jugular vein through the incision I just made and then suture it in place. Then I'll inject it directly into the catheter. He's got to be suffering from the second-degree burns. It's the humane thing to do."

"Yes, Doctor. I understand."

As Conrad drew the narcotic into the syringe, the patient's breathing became irregular, then came in starts and stops. After two, slow, agonal breaths, he exhaled. He failed to take another.

"Doctor." Lars appeared out of the dark. "Rod say's the pilot has a broken collar bone, some busted ribs, a deep head wound, and what looks like a broken right leg. That's what he's found so far. He's moving his arms and left leg, but Rod's afraid to move him around too much to check anywhere else. He says you should come quick."

"Tell him I'll be right there, Lars. I'm not needed here any longer." Conrad placed his right hand on the man's forehead and whispered, "Though I never learned your name, brother, be at peace." Then he pulled over his face the blanket that Jack had covered him with up. "Come on, Jack. I'm gonna need your help."

Simone pulled out her phone and called the medical center. After speaking with the ER doctor on duty to report an additional casualty, she called the coroner. Then she called into the cabin to inform Jason of what was going to happen. When she finished, she walked towards the lights that were set up around the pilot.

"Dr. Tolbert, the first helicopter will be arriving in about ten minutes. They'll land outside of the stockade and then transport this patient first since the four security personnel have been stable. Whatever we haven't completed, they'll take care of. I've asked that security rotate the spotlights on this side of the stockade to shine out here so my pilot can see where he's going to land. After that, the evacuation of the security staff should go as previously planned."

"Thanks, Simone, good thinking."

"I also spoke with the coroner's office. They're requesting that the other two bodies not be disturbed. I told them that there's wild animals out here and the remains could be carried off. They requested that we post an armed guard if at all possible until they arrive. I've discussed this with Jason, and he's going to have security stand guard."

"I can take care of that, Simone," Lars said. "I'll just need my shotgun. I left it in the cabin, along with all the security guards' weapons, but I think it was returned to my cottage. I also have a rifle in there."

Simone nodded. "I'll let you decide all that with Jason, Lars. By the time this patient is airlifted, we should have everything figured out."

****

When the medical flight crew arrived, Conrad gave them a report.

"He's hypothermic, and he's got a compound fracture of his right femur, several rib fractures along the mid, lateral right chest, a fractured left clavicle, and a fifteen-centimeter laceration across the top of his head, down to the skull. He caught it on windshield glass after he removed his helmet and dragged himself from the burning wreckage. He crawled all the way over here by himself.

"He also has some second- and first-degree burns on his hands, face and neck, but his flight suit saved the rest of him. We've stabilized his fractures, but his laceration needs suturing, and of course, he'll need his tetanus updated. We placed a 16-gauge line in his left antecubital. The bag that's hanging is his first. He's had 600 ccs of it so far. There's a second 16-gauge line in his right forearm. That line has 400 ccs in so far."

"Thank you, sir," the senior medic said. "We'll take it from here. Hello, Ms. Jones," he said, turning towards Simone. "I heard you were up here at the last minute. Weekend getaway?"

"Something like that," Simone answered with a crooked smile. "What's the ETA on the next crew?"

"We moved up the schedule for the second flight since this first flight was diverted to land outside the compound for this new patient. They should arrive any minute now. By the time they land, we should be ready to take off. We've added on an additional flight on at the end, but we'll follow the schedule as it was set up before."

Simone patted him on the shoulder. "Very good. Carry on."

****

Jason and Braden met everyone at the bottom of the stairs off the porch. As they climbed out, Charity whisked them into the living room, to in front of Jason's old wood stove and wrapped them in warm blankets, fresh from the dryer, while Eugene, Fiona, and Evelyn plied them with mugs of hot cocoa. They all opened their blankets towards the stove to allow the heat from the roaring flames warm them up.

****

While the other officers were being airlifted, the chief called Jason and Claudia over. "I've got to turn operations over to Shane. The good doctor says I'll be out of commission for a while 'cause of the burns and what that jolt did to my electrical system. Can I sign something to that effect before they fly me out of here?"

"I'll take care of it right now, Chief." Claudia went to her suite and returned with a lined legal pad. She wrote a few lines on it and had the chief, Jason, and Aaron sign it. She had Miss Charity, Simone, and Rod sign as witnesses, and then Natasha notarized it.

"That'll do it, Chief," Claudia said. "Now you rest and get better."

"I want to go with my Dad," Shane said.

Jason shook his head. "I'm sorry, Shane, you can't. There isn't any room in the chopper for you. You'll have to wait until the ice on Big Daddy melts and fly down with the rest of us. There's just no way around it."

"We'll take good care of him, Shane," Simone said, resting her hand on his shoulder. "I promise."

****

7:30 AM

Everyone gathered as the chief was carried down the stairs and out to the last chopper. As it lifted into the sky, Jason turned to Aaron and nearly collapsed into his arms. Tears streamed down his face. "Aaron, what is it? What have we done wrong? Why does this keep happening to us?"

"I don't know, my love, but just like everything else, we'll face it together."

Charity turned to them and pulled them into her motherly bosom, hugging them tightly. "Mr. Jason, Mr. Aaron, you are two of the finest men I've ever known. I can't say why all of this has come about, but I do know this. You've created a whole new family here, a family who are committed to see your dream come true. We're going to help you through this."

****

9:15 AM

Shane met with Patrick and Natasha. "You two are going to have to hold down the fort while I'm gone. Patrick, you've got seniority, so you'll be in charge. I've called in reinforcements from our staff at other sites. They'll be waiting for me at the hangar. Rod will fly them back up later today. I'll brief them, but you'll have to show them the ropes."

"We'll take care of everything, Shane," Patrick answered. "Don't worry about a thing."

"I'll be back as soon as I can. I just need to check on my dad and the others to be sure they're all right."

Chapter Thirty-Seven
Aftermath

Sunday, January 10, 2010, 3:30 PM
The cabin

Chief Inspector Cassandra Addison and Trooper Byron Stringer of the Idaho State Police stood on the front porch as the ATV pulled up to the steps.

"You know, Inspector," Jason said as he stepped onto the first step with his arm around Aaron's waist, "they're gonna start talking about the four of us," he waved his free arm between himself and Aaron and the inspector and Trooper Stringer, "if we keep meeting up like this." Rod, Jack, and Conrad walked up behind them.

Inspector Addison smirked. A perplexed expression crossed Trooper Stringer's face, then one of understanding, and he blushed.

"I'm sorry we're meeting again under such conditions," Inspector Addison said, "and so soon."

"And again, it isn't our fault," Aaron said. "Let's talk inside."

Charity held the storm door open as everyone paraded in. "There's hot coffee, tea, and coco set up in the dining room, Mr. Aaron, along with two trays of nibbles. Please let me know if there's anything else you need. Keep in mind, dinner will be served at six sharp unless you advise me otherwise. I'm making beef stew from last night's leftovers with biscuits and cornbread with honey, so save your appetites if you can."

"Thank you, Miss Charity."

"I'll be in the kitchen if you need me."

Conrad rested his hand on Jason's shoulder. "If you'll excuse me, Jason, Aaron, I'm going to go take as shower."

"I'm gonna do the same," Rod said.

"Me, too," Jack added.

"Sure thing, guys. We'll see you later."

When Jason and Aaron entered the dining room, there was no evidence of the temporary trauma center it had become just hours before. Everything had been returned to its proper place—the walls were back up and the table was covered with a cream-colored, linen table cloth. A man, whom Jason and Aaron did not know, sat next to Claudia and Winston. He rose from the table. Claudia and Winston followed suit.

Inspector Addison motioned with her arm. "Mr. Ackerman, Mr. Jaeger, this is Inspector Dick Freeman, from the FAA. He's just finished his inspection of the crash site. We were brought in because of the deaths. Our investigation is pretty much completed."

"Hello, gentlemen. Quite a place you've got here."

"Thank you, Inspector Freeman," Jason answered. "We've tried real hard to make it comfortable. Please, have a seat everyone. How can we help you?"

"It is my understanding, from my interviews, that you did not witness the crash."

Claudia nodded to Jason and Aaron.

Aaron nodded back. "That's correct, Inspector. We were in our bedroom at the time."

"And you didn't go to the crash site yourselves?"

Jason shook his head. "No, sir, we remained behind to attend the electrocution victims from the lightning strike."

"That's what I was told. Nor, did you examine or see any of the victims?"

"That is correct, sir."

"Inspector Addison and I have interviewed your man, a Mr. Lars Eriksen, who was guarding the site until we arrived, two security guards who were present, Miss

Charity and her children, and Ms. Duncan and Mr. Tanner here. We're going to need to interview the others—a Dr. Tolbert, a Simone Jones, a Rod Livingston, and a Jack Abraham, as well as security guard Shane Steinecker. When can they be available?"

"The three gentlemen are currently taking showers in their cottages. They should be available soon. We left Ms. Jones at the medical center. You can reach her there. Shane is still there at his father's bedside."

"Thank you. There's nothing left of the helicopter but a burned-out shell, except for a piece of the tail section that's still somewhat intact. We'll be removing all the debris we can find, but we ask that if you come across anything that we missed in the days and weeks to come, that you'll not touch it and notify us immediately."

"Jason nodded. "Of course."

"The remains of two individuals have already been transported to the coroner's office."

Jason nodded. "Thank you for letting us know."

"We've also recovered what appears to be the remains of a TV video camera. It will be turned over to the FAA forensics lab for analysis. From what we've gathered, particularly from the guard, Patrick, the helicopter made several strafing runs across your property while an individual made recordings as he hung out the door of the craft. Do you have any idea what they were doing up there?"

Jason shook his head. "None, sir. As Aaron has already told you, we were in our bedroom at the time. We never saw a thing, but please, you may have unrestricted access to everything both inside and outside of the stockade. If any of my staff can be of any assistance, please do not hesitate to ask."

Claudia smiled and nodded, encouragingly.

"I will. Thank you. Honestly, I don't think we're

going to learn much more up here. Any video we can recover might prove helpful, but I believe we'll learn the most from the pilot. I'm told he is expected to recover."

Aaron rested his hand on Jason's arm. "Neither Jason or I have had any contact with him. We made sure that the medical staff kept us steered clear of him when we were at the medical center. We can't even tell you what he looks like."

"I understand. We'll also interview the other security guards once they've recovered enough to be questioned."

"That may be a few days," Jason said. "They've all been admitted to intensive care."

"Is there somewhere we can meet with the doctor and the other two gentlemen?"

"Certainly, Inspector, you may use our meeting room. I'll give them a call and ask them to meet you there as soon as they're free."

"Thank you. You've had a quite a night. We'll try leave you in peace as soon as possible. If someone would direct us to the meeting room, we'll get out of your hair." He stood and motioned with his hand. "Inspector Addison, if you will?"

"I'll show you the way," Winston said as he stood from the table.

Inspectors Freeman and Addison and Trooper Stringer stood and followed him from the room.

"Good job, guys," Claudia said after they'd gone. I did prepare them ahead of time so they knew you really didn't know anything about it, but as the owners of the property they still had to interview you."

****

Monday, January 19, 2010, 10:30 AM
Jaron Enterprises, Corporate Headquarters
    "Jaron Enterprises, Fiona speaking. How may I

direct your call?"

"Hello, this is Inspector Addison from the state police. Is Mr. Ackerman or Jaeger there?"

"Yes, ma'am, they're both in. I'll put you right through to their office." Fiona put the call on hold. "Jason, Aaron," she said into the intercom, "I have Inspector Addison from the state police on line one."

"Thanks, Fiona," Aaron said into the intercom, "I'll take it."

****

"Hello, Inspector. This is Aaron, any news?"

"Hello, Mr. Jaeger, yes."

"I'll put it on speaker. Jason is right here."

"Hello, Inspector. What can you tell us?"

"Hello, Mr. Ackerman. The FAA recovered all of the footage that was shot by the cameraman, and it confirmed what we learned from the pilot. He was hired directly by a reporter, Chuck Jackson, to fly him and his cameraman, Frank Rice, up to your home as part of their investigation into your lives. The investigation was not sanctioned by the news station they worked for, nor did the station have any knowledge of it."

"I recognize that name—Jackson. He's the reporter who harassed the medical center when we were admitted two weeks ago."

"That's correct, Mr. Ackerman, and Rice was the cameraman who always worked with him."

"Inspector," Jason said, "we've had enough to deal with lately. We really don't want to know any of the gory details. Can you tell us what caused the crash without going too much into detail?"

"I understand, Mr. Ackerman. Certainly, it was icing, due to the weather, and a struggle that took place inside the cabin as the helicopter lost lift."

"And to think, two men lost their lives, another

was severely injured and will likely lose his pilot's license, four security guards were electrocuted, and for what? They didn't get anything."

"It's a sad world, Mr. Ackerman."

"Is there anything else, Inspector?"

"Unless you want to know more, no."

"This is Aaron. Thank you for calling, Inspector. We're going to go now."

"I understand, Mr. Jaeger. Good bye, then and good bye to you, Mr. Ackerman. I wish you both the best."

****

After Aaron disconnected the call, he rose from his spot at their large, shared, custom, executive double-desk and walked to behind where Jason sat in his chair. He leaned down and wrapped his arms around Jason and kissed the top of his head.

Jason tilted his head back and looked up into Aaron's eyes. "Don't say it, Aaron."

"I don't think that way anymore, Jason, not since that night. We've lived through enough catastrophes. No one deserves to die like those two men did. I feel sorry for them. That's all."

"Me, too, Aaron. Me, too."

Chapter Thirty-Eight
Moving Forward

Tuesday, February 9, 2010, 11:30 AM
"Welcome back, all of you," Jason said as he held the cabin's front door open and shook their hands.

"We're so glad to see you all," Aaron added, as he hugged them one at a time. "Miss Charity has lunch all ready. Just pile into the dining room after you've taken off your coats."

As the Chief, Ryan, Dustin, and Alexandra walked into the dining room, Charity pulled them to her chest, one at a time, and kissed them on the cheek. "We're blessed to have you back with us. Now take a seat with your fellow officers and relax. There's stew and biscuits waiting for you."

****

After lunch, Chief Steinecker met with all his staff in the large meeting room next to Jason and Aaron's office. "I'm very happy to see everyone back here and in one piece. I think that because we went through this catastrophe together, it's brought us all closer, or at least that's what I surmised from Alexandra, Dustin, and Ryan when they told me they were returning.

"I want to thank Freda, Reginald, Jasmine, and Xavier for stepping up to the plate and filling in for us while we were recovering, and I want to thank Shane for stepping in for me. Patrick and Natasha, I've been told that you two were amazing that night, and though I didn't witness your heroic efforts, it came as no surprise to me. Nevertheless, thank you from the bottom of my heart.

"In speaking with Mr. Jason and Mr. Aaron, things will be picking up here soon for Nathan's Promise with the arrival of representatives from the construction and architectural firms as well as local and state government. I'm not clear as to all the particulars, but from what I understand, they expect to break ground for construction at the site as soon as they can begin to dig.

"Security at all those locations will be the same as every other construction site we've patrolled. This will mean additional security staff to cover and manage two separate facilities. It will create some logistical hurdles for us, but I have no doubt that we can rise to the challenge.

"There's also plans for construction for a new corporate headquarters up here, adjacent to the stockade, and a farm and a retreat/spa are in the works. The farm will be located adjacent to Nathan's Promise, so construction for it will begin at the same time. Much of the dairy and eggs for the rehab center, as well as fresh produce and meat will come from there, once everything's up and running. There will also be several greenhouses to supply produce over the winter. The farm will also require a security staff so we'll be branching out in that direction once it's completed.

"The retreat/spa will be a separate facility. Its suites are for the family members of the LGBTQS athletes who are going through rehab or for any of the clients who want to take a brief respite. While they're all being built, the same goes for their security patrols."

"I've been told by Mr. Jason that a number of three-day, weekend retreats will be specifically blocked off for staff members, including security, on a first come, first serve basis, as long as they're not reserved by other guests. Those stays will be free of charge. Any questions?"

"Do you know the locations of the three sites yet, Chief?" Natasha asked.

"Jaron Enterprises has purchased another two hundred acres down the mountain in the valley with a tract of land that connects directly from here to there. They're going to build a road through that tract to connect the homestead with Nathan's Promise, so there's going to be new security measures instituted to limit access between them to keep this homestead and the corporate headquarters isolated and protected."

"Do you have any idea how many more security staff will be added, Chief?" Ryan asked.

"I'm not sure, Ryan, but by the time all is said and done, I'd expect somewhere between a five- and tenfold increase, if not more. We'll just have to wait and see."

"I heard they're going to be supplying housing for all the staff. Is that true, Chief? Does that include security?" Patrick looked briefly at Ryan after he spoke.

"Yes, Patrick. In addition to Nathan's Promise, the retreat/spa, and the farm, they'll also be building housing for each staff member. Before you ask, I don't know if that will be a large apartment building, or individual houses, or both. I haven't been included in those discussions, at least not as of yet."

"What about the staff's family members? Will they be allowed to live onsite, too?" Dustin asked.

"I don't know anything about that, Dustin, but if you want me to inquire, I will."

"Yes, Chief, please do."

"I will say this, if there's one thing I've learned about Mr. Jason and Mr. Aaron, it's to not be surprised by their generosity. Is there anything else?"

Everyone shook their heads no.

"Good, then let's get back to work. Freda, Reginald, Jasmine, and Xavier, I believe Mr. Rod will be flying you back at 3 PM. Please be sure you've collected all your personal belongings before you fly out, and again, thank you all for stepping up."

Chapter Thirty-Nine
In Memory of Gypsy

Saturday, March 20, 2010, 8:00 AM

Fresh from the shower, Jason finished buttoning his shirt. "Are you ready for this, Aaron?"

"I've got butterflies, baby. I can't believe the day has finally arrived."

Jason pulled on his pants. "I can't believe it all happened so quickly."

"I know. If it wasn't for the steering committee, and their connections to get things moving, we'd never have made it this far."

"I know, I know. We owe them so much."

"Rod said they'd be here at 8:30. I can't wait to see the new helicopter. In a way, though, I'm going to miss Big Daddy."

"I sympathize, he's done so much for us. Big Mama, too. But it'll be more comfortable to ride in a decked out, executive, passenger model. Don't you think?"

"Yeah, you're right, but our own eleven million-dollar helicopter? The reality of it is almost too much to comprehend. So much money has passed through my hands these past weeks, so many zeros. It boggles the mind."

"It's a business necessity, Aaron. We're going to need our own air transportation now that we're a corporation. We can't continue to ask Rod to accommodate us. He's got his own business to run and constantly tying up Big Daddy or Big Mama just for our purposes wouldn't be fair to him. There'll be so much more travel, particularly once we expand into other states, and once that begins, we're going to need our own jet."

"You're right, of course. Have you heard back yet about the installation of the new windmill and solar grids?"

"They're on the to-do list. It just didn't seem feasible any more to have to continue to depend on the diesel generator to run our home whenever the battery bank couldn't keep up. It was fine when it was just me up here, but with so many people up here now, those days are long gone.

"I thought about what Rod said, and he was right. Once we decided to expand on his idea and create our own power plant for Nathan's Promise, with all that power being generated by the new solar and wind systems and the solar panels on every building and cottage, including the new ones on the cabin and at the new headquarters, the entire complex will be self-sufficient. I think your idea to donate all the extra electricity to low income families through to the electric company's power grid was wonderful."

"Thanks, it just seemed it was the right thing to do. When the engineers told us how much power the system could generate and how much the complex would need on an average day, it was the first thing I thought of. Why not give back? I knew a lot of kids from school, growing up, whose parents couldn't make ends meet each month. It was so embarrassing for them, having to choose between food and utilities, and even rent."

"You're a good man, Aaron. And besides, if we had to buy that new tract of land for the road to connect us with the rest of humanity, we might as well take advantage of it to the fullest. With our winter weather, running underground power lines between the valley and up here just makes sense. If ever any one area requires more power than it's able to generate on its own, it can pull from anywhere in the system."

Aaron nodded. "And we still have our generator as a backup for up here, and there will be the generators in the headquarters building, Nathan's Promise and the spa, at the housing complex, and at Gypsy's Grove, just in case. It's a good thing Claudia and Winston are on board full-time now with the company. I'd have never thought to take those things as tax write-offs."

"Right. Even with Jaron Enterprises' corporate headquarters being built up here, none of them will be questioned, and we're going to have a lot more that will qualify."

"Did Miss Charity ever ask why we we're going to expand the stockade to six acres?"

Jason began to pull on his socks. "No, and I'm not going to say anything to her about it."

"Good. It only seems right, and with preparing to relocate most of the cottages to the valley, once things get going, the timing is right to do the expansion. There'll be plenty of room in here for her new home, once she's ready to retire, and in the meantime, our expanding, four-legged family can take advantage of the additional acreage."

Jason began to tie his tie. "I'm glad she said she'd like to retire up here, but I couldn't go along with her saying she didn't want to bother our lives, once she does. Her idea to live in one of the old cottages, outside the stockade, gave me the willies. There's still all the predators who come snooping around at night. I'd never sleep."

"We'll build her something beautiful, something with a white picket fence, and her own garden, and trellises with roses, and flowerbeds, and her duck pond, and…"

"And you'll design it with her, Aaron. I'm sure she'd love that."

Aaron smiled as he leaned down to kiss Jason. "Oh, while you were in the shower Penelope and Cody called to say they'd be ready by 8:15, and Eugene stuck his head in to say that he, Charity, Fiona, and Evelyn would be waiting for us in the dining room."

Jason reached for his work boots. "Great, it's a good thing we bought a 16-seat chopper. We're going to be full with Rod and Jack and Simone flying up."

The phone rang. Aaron answered it. "Hello?"

"Oh, hi, Braden."

"Yes, okay. We're just about ready ourselves. Jason's pulling his on boots right now. Are you wearing boots? It's going to be muddy down at the site."

"Good. Okay, see you in a few. Bye."

"That was Braden. He, Shane, Conrad, Thad, Claudia, and Winston are walking over. He also said that all of security is coming, too, to see the new helicopter."

****

8:29 AM

The muffled whop-whop-whop sound was nearly imperceptible inside the cabin, that is, to all but Shane. He cocked his head. "It's here."

"Really?" Braden asked.

"Yeah, don't you hear it?"

"No. You must still have that ingrained from when you were in the Marines."

"There." Shane pointed out the window. "Look there. It just cleared the top of the ridge."

"Wow!" Braden exclaimed. "It's magnificent!"

Everyone stood up from the dining room table and walked out onto the porch. "Oohs" and "ahs" abounded.

"Look at that!"

"You've really made it now, guys!"

"That'll sure make a statement!"

"I love the forest green on the white background, Jason. Was that your idea?"

"Thank you all," Jason said. "But credit goes to Ryan for the design."

"Really, Ryan?" Thad said. "I had no idea you were an artist."

"I was just doodling in the dining room one day when Mr. Aaron saw my pad. He told me about the new helicopter and asked if I'd make a few sketches in green for it and for the company logo. When I showed them to him and Mr. Jason, they liked what I'd drawn and asked to buy them."

"And the rest is history," Aaron said. "Ryan's going to be doing a lot of the graphics for the company. Once you find a talented artist, you don't ever want to let them go."

****

Jason had a faraway look on his face as he ran his hand over the name painted on the side of the new helicopter in small, lavishly ornamented, cursive letters.

"May I ask who Gypsy is, Mr. Jason?" Charity clasped her hands in front of her as she leaned her head against his right shoulder. As Jason spoke, she wrapped her left arm around his back and gently squeezed.

"She was my friend. She was Nellie's mother and Sarah's grandmother. A cougar climbed the stockade and tried to take Nellie. Gypsy was killed by him while she tried to defend her daughter. I still miss her. She's the reason that I topped the stockade with razor wire and had it electrified.

"Her name meant wanderer or traveler, Bohemian traveler, actually—a free spirited traveler who disregards established norms, beliefs, and customs. Her name serves as a reminder that I was a wanderer, even living here within the confines of stockade—that Aaron grounded me by giving my life purpose, that he freed my spirit and allowed me to dream again, and that together, we are disregarding the established norms, beliefs, and customs of society by building Nathan's Promise."

"That's deep, Jason," Conrad said.

"Jason's a deep kinda guy," Aaron said as he hugged Jason from behind.

Jack hopped down from Gypsy's belly, followed by Simone, who held a blue velvet sack with gold-braided tie cords.

"Okay, what's everybody doin' standin' around here?" Jack shouted. "We got work to do. All aboard! Ha, ha, I always wanted to say that."

Simone placed her hand on his shoulder from behind. "Just a moment, Jack. Jason, Aaron, this helicopter is magnificent. When Rod told me last week about the story behind naming her, I was so touched by it, and I thought on such a momentous occasion a little ceremony would be in order." She slipped a magnum of champagne from the sack while Rod reached into Gypsy's door and pulled out a shallow, wedge shaped piece of milled wood. One side was rounded and covered with felt. The opposite corner was covered with an ornate piece of cast metal that came to an abrupt point.

"For Gypsy's christening. I had it scored to ensure it would break properly." Then Simone slipped it back into the sack and tied it tight.

Rod fitted the wedge against the side of Gypsy's fuselage, just above her name. "It's padded, so it won't hurt her."

Jason started to cry as he pulled Simone into a hug. "She was so special to me. Thank you, Simone. Thank you for this kindness."

When Jason broke away, he reached for Aaron. "Let's do this together."

"No, baby, she was your friend. You should do it."

Jason grabbed the neck of the bottle within the sack and raised his arm up. "This is for you, baby girl." Then he swung.

With a crash, the glass shattered and champagne drained through the cloth.

"To Gypsy!" everyone cheered.

****

9:55 AM
The valley below

The photographer cleared his throat. "May I have your attention, ladies and gentlemen? We're going to do this in stages and several times if we have to, to ensure we get some good photos. While the TV crew is setting up, please allow me to review with you the instructions on how you're going to proceed. We're going to do this together, move by move. One, you're all going to place your spades against the ground along the trench. Two, you're going to put your right foot on the edge of the spade. Three, you're going to press down with your foot until the blade is halfway into the loosened dirt. Four, you're going to lift the shovel up with dirt on it. Five, you're going to toss the dirt forward, straight in front of you. Everyone got that?"

Epilogue

5:40 PM
Hinnen Valley, CHANNEL *18 evening news*
    "Coming up after the break, former Nevada Bighorns Quarterback, Aaron Jaeger, at the groundbreaking for a new physical rehabilitation center."
****

    "Ground was broken today in a low-lying region of the Bear River Mountain Range outside of Craggy Bend, Idaho, for a first-of-its-kind, state-of-the-art physical rehabilitation center.

    "Dedicated to the memory of Nathan Taggart, the Nevada Bighorns trainer who worked extensively with Aaron Jaeger, their former quarterback, Nathan's Promise will provide cutting-edge methodologies using the most advanced physical rehabilitation equipment available for today's LGBTQS professional and amateur athletes, as well as military and law enforcement personnel from around the world. As you may recall, Jaeger survived the plane crash in which Taggart was killed last September.

    "Included at the facility will be temporary housing in a cottage-style complex for the families of the athletes while they are receiving treatment, a housing complex for the center's staff, a solar and wind power plant, a new, organic farm named Gypsy's Grove, and a recreational retreat and spa. All structures within the complex will have solar panels on their roofs, with the intention of eliminating Jaron Enterprises' carbon footprint.

    "Through their altruistic philosophy and mission, Jaron Enterprises has chosen to donate any extra power they generate to low income families through the local electric company's power grid. In addition, no patient being treated at Nathan's Promise, or their families, will ever receive a bill for their stay or for their rehabilitation and care.

"Here we have video of the ceremony that included local dignitaries where some twenty shovels broke ground at the construction site for the center. Jaeger, seen in the center of the group, is now the president of Jaron Rehabilitative Services, a new healthcare company and subsidiary of Jaron Enterprises, based here in southern Idaho.

"After being released from his contract with the Bighorns, Jaeger became one of the cofounders of Jaron Enterprises. We must disclose that Jaron Communications, which now owns this station, is also a subsidiary of Jaron Enterprises.

"As we reported last month, The Bighorns were purchased by Jaron Entertainment, another subsidiary of Jaron Enterprises, following intensive negotiations, and after which the team's coach, Hank Thompson, and their general manager, John Forester, were released from their contracts.

"In a related story, the lawsuit filed against the Nevada Bighorns and Jaron Entertainment by Hank Thompson and John Forester was dismissed in court today. A countersuit was immediately filed by the Bighorns team and several of its current and former team members for defamation of character, discrimination, and breach of contract.

"In this video is Joshua Bergmann, the attorney for the plaintiffs of the countersuit, who met with reporters outside of the courthouse.

****

"Mr. Bergmann, why a countersuit?"

"Because an injustice has been committed. I am confident that we have more than sufficient evidence and witnesses to the effect to prove not only defamation of character and breach of contract by the defendants, but also a systematic policy of discrimination and intimidation, and wrongful termination of employment towards the plaintiffs who are no longer with the team. I look forward to meeting Mr. Thompson, and Mr. Forester on the stand."

****

"When Hank Thompson left the courthouse he spoke briefly with reporters before he was interrupted and pulled away by his co-defendant, John Forester."

****

"I swear by all that is holy, everything those people touch will turn to ash! I'll see to it! I swear!"

"Hank, shut up! Stop talking! Not now! Not now!"

****

"Representatives from Jaron Enterprises could not be reached for comment."

****

9:30 PM

"Mr. Aaron, Mr. Jason, will there be anything else this evening?"

"No, Miss Charity," Aaron answered. "We're just going to relax here in the living room for a time before we retire. It's been a long and eventful day. I think everyone else has turned in already. Thank you again for a wonderful meal, and thank you for participating in the groundbreaking ceremony today. It means a lot to Jason and me."

"The honor was mine, Mr. Aaron. It was a first for me and one I'll cherish for the rest of my days. Women like me just aren't included in such festivities."

"Well, they should be, Miss Charity," Jason said as he leaned forward. "You're an integral part of our family, and we can't imagine life without you."

"Thank you, Mr. Jason. I'll say good night then."

"Good night, Miss Charity," Aaron and Jason said together.

****

After they'd crawled into bed, following a relaxing soak in the whirlpool tub, Aaron pulled up the covers and wrapped himself around Jason.

"Our lives are changed forever now, Aaron."

"Do you have regrets?"

"Oh, no, I didn't mean it that way. I'm excited but also nervous."

"Nervous? About what, Jason?"

"About whether I'm up for the task. About whether I've … we've bitten off more than we can chew."

"We've surrounded ourselves with good people, Jason. They won't let us fail."

"I know that, but with our track record, I can't help but wonder what's going to go wrong."

"Jason, my love, we've weathered many storms together. I think fate owes us a bit of break, but even if it doesn't, we'll face whatever comes at us together, just like we always have."

"I hope you're right, about a break, I mean. We deserve one now."

"Good night, Jason, my love."

"Good night, Aaron. I love you."

****

The Vernal Equinox took place at 11:32 AM MST on March 20, 2010. As the daylight hours grew longer and the nighttime grew shorter, Jason and Aaron's new family grew and grew closer. New loves blossomed, established loves grew deeper, and the face of the mountain and valley below began to change as Nathan's

Promise progressed towards completion.

So filled with hope for the future, none of them were prepared for the challenges and disappointments, and ultimately, losses that would come, but in family there are numbers and there is strength in numbers, and their strength would see them through.

It would have to.

To be continued…

EVERNIGHT PUBLISHING ®

www.evernightpublishing.com